WADE ROWLAND
is a former CBC journalist who writes
and lectures extensively on the new media.
Among other books, he is the author of
Spirit of the Web, a popular history of
communications technologies that was
selected as Required Reading for 1997
by *The Globe and Mail*.
He lives with his family near Port Hope
and makes a living from a virtual corporation
on the Internet. He is presently working
on a new book about
the trial of Galileo.

Ockham's Razor

THE SEARCH FOR WONDER

IN AN AGE OF DOUBT

TRY to change perspective - put yourself in a diff. place

Wade Rowland

PATRICK CREAN EDITIONS

An Imprint of

KEY PORTER BOOKS

TO THE MEMORY OF MY FATHER

Canadian Cataloguing in Publication Data

Rowland, Wade, 1944-

Ockham's razor

ISBN 1-55263-031-5

1. Rowland, Wade, 1944-   – Journeys – France. 2. France – Description and travel.
3. Philosophy, Medieval. 4. Mind and body. I. Title.

DC29.3.R63 1999   914.404'839   C98-932997-6

THE CANADA COUNCIL | LE CONSEIL DES ARTS
FOR THE ARTS | DU CANADA
SINCE 1957 | DEPUIS 1957

The publisher gratefully acknowledges the support of the Canada Council for the Arts and
the Ontario Arts Council for its publishing program.

Canada

We acknowledge the financial support of the Government of Canada through the Book
Publishing Industry Development Program (BPIDP) for our publishing activities.

Key Porter Books Limited
70 The Esplanade
Toronto, Ontario
Canada M5E 1R2

www.keyporter.com
Design: Peter Maher
Typeset in Fairfield

99 00 01 02 03   5 4 3 2 1

CONTENTS

CHAPTER ONE
Toronto, Autumn 1997
9

CHAPTER TWO
Toronto to Paris
20

CHAPTER THREE
Paris: The Cult of Reason
29

CHAPTER FOUR
Paris: Magritte's Puzzle
47

CHAPTER FIVE
Seeing and Knowing
56

CHAPTER SIX
Chartres, Vouvray and Loches: The Maid of Orléans
62

CHAPTER SEVEN
Brantôme, Rocamadour and the Gîte
81

CHAPTER EIGHT
Carcassonne and the Cathars
86

CHAPTER NINE
Richard and Lily
95

CHAPTER TEN
Three Cathar Castles
101

CHAPTER ELEVEN
Montségur and Her Martyrs
118

CHAPTER TWELVE
Toulouse: Dominic and Aquinas
1 3 6

CHAPTER THIRTEEN
Toulouse: Aquinas and Galileo
146

CHAPTER FOURTEEN
Science and Reality
1 6 0

CHAPTER FIFTEEN
The Ant and the Grasshopper
1 7 0

CHAPTER SIXTEEN
Progress and Salvation: On to Avignon
1 8 0

CHAPTER SEVENTEEN
Culture and Cuisine: Georges Blanc
2 0 0

CHAPTER EIGHTEEN
Dijon to Paris
2 1 9

CHAPTER NINETEEN
Paris and Perpetual Motion
2 3 2

CHAPTER TWENTY
Paris to Toronto
2 3 9

CHAPTER TWENTY - ONE
Home Alone
2 5 3

Notes
2 6 2

ACKNOWLEDGMENTS

Being a writer has been defined in many ways. A definition I like is: "A writer is a person who conducts his education in public." While this book is ostensibly about teaching my teenaged children how to be civilized by taking them to France one summer not long ago, the educational pretext applied every bit as much to me as to them. Our collective intellectual journey provides a counterpoint to the travel narrative.

Children change and mature so rapidly it makes your head swim; Hilary and Simon are both different people now than they were then. They've grown up to become friends and colleagues of my wife Chris and I, and of each other. I am grateful to both of them for being patient foils in these pages. And I am eternally grateful to Chris for bringing them into the world and for being the glue that sticks us all together.

My publisher and editor Patrick Crean provided indispensable advice and enthusiasm throughout the long process of turning my scattered ideas into a book. My sincere thanks to him. And thanks as well to Bernice Eisenstein for her scrupulous copy editing.

I offer my gratitude, and that of my family, to Régis Bulot, International President of Relais and Châteaux, and to media relations officer Maryse Masse for their generous assistance with our travel arrangements. I also wish to acknowledge the kind assistance of the French Government Tourist office in Toronto, and in particular Séverine Tharreau.

Last, as promised, a warm "thank you" to Berkowitz, for services rendered.

WR
Hope Township, Ontario
November, 1998

⚹ ⚹ ⚹

*"You see, I keep thinking that we need a new language,
a language of the heart . . . some kind of language between people that is
a new kind of poetry, that is the poetry of the dancing bee,
that tells us where the honey is. And I think that in order to create
that language we're going to have to learn how you can go through a looking glass into another kind of perception, in which you have that sense of
being united to all things, and suddenly you understand everything."*

—André, in *My Dinner with André*[1]

A   NOTE   TO   THE   READER

The title of this book was inspired by William of Ockham, a medieval
scholar and theologian. Ockham's thought was central to the creation of
the great divide between science and religion—between fact and value—
that has come to define our own era. After Ockham, goodness and truth
were no longer two inseparable sides of the same coin, as they had been
throughout most of recorded history in the West. Truth became the
exclusive purview of science; and goodness, of religion. The effect would
be that while science prospered, religion withered—or, one might say,
while factual truth flourished, ethics and normative truth languished.

Ockham's strong belief in the power of mathematics and logic was
expressed in what came to be known as Ockham's Razor, a technique
of logic in which arguments must be stripped down to their barest
factual basis. Modern thinking is informed throughout by Ockham,
greatly to its detriment, since it has enormous difficulty incorporating
spiritual or metaphysical content.

Toronto, Autumn 1997

A Drive to the City ⚥ An Unfortunate
Student ⚥ The Puzzle of the Human
Resource ⚥ Economics Ascendant ⚥
A Submersion of Values ⚥ Lessons from
the Middle Ages ⚥ Planning Our Journey

The long drive into the city, into the molten sunset with Mahler's Fourth on the radio has left me feeling a little spacey, slightly disembodied. Or perhaps it is too much coffee. I turn south into the university campus and a parking spot appears as if by magic: I wheel the van in and turn off the ignition, thanking my lucky stars. As I step down onto the street, a breeze touches my cheek and a human shape flashes by in silence, torso straining forward, wheels on his feet—Rollerblades. Hermes, I think. Then a perfumed bicyclist, straddling her machine, legs pumping, taillight strobing, derailleur clicking softly. A centaur. Nothing seems quite what it is.

The clinging ivy has turned a vibrant magenta, softening the relentless geometry of the grey limestone walls and leaded windows of the student dormitories along St. George Street. Scarlet and gold leaves

⚥ ⚥ ⚥

drift to the ground from towering maples, gilding the lawns and side-walks and gutters. A hard, cold rain begins to fall; people scud through the shadows like tacking sailboats, leaning into the breeze, hoods pulled up like monks' cowls, books and papers hugged to their breasts. Umbrellas unfurl like spinnakers. Streetlights flicker and then ignite, one by one, like signal fires. For a few moments, I am living in a painting, or perhaps a poem. It seems to me that I am seeing things as they truly are—not as concrete, material objects, but as something less substantial and at the same time more real; as ideas and metaphors that have somehow jelled and taken on substance. The world is so much more beautiful like this! And then the crosswalk signal lights change and a driver taps a warning to me on his horn and I step back hastily to the curb and the feeling is gone.

The university campus gives my heart a lift; it strikes me as one of the few remaining places where you are welcome simply as a human being; where the facilities are designed to serve people, not as con-sumers or employees or executives or commuters or shoppers or tourists or entertainment-seekers or any other objectified, statistically quan-tifiable agglomeration—but simply as individuals. Of course, the blunt and insensible tools of instrumental reason, of the business ethic, of obsessive bottom line accounting are at work here as well, like some creeping fungus, but they have not yet managed to rot the fabric of so ancient and resilient an institution. There is room still for optimism.

I am late for my class, and as I run up the stairs of the Sidney Smith building, my shoes are flapping, the laces undone because they are the spindly, round kind that will not stay tied. They came with the shoes, which hurt my feet but which, on the shelf in the store, looked seductively comfortable in the suppleness of the leather and the sculpted design of the synthetic soles. Oxblood wing tips, they are track shoes for executives, for the executive I used to be, a holdover in my increasingly obsolescent wardrobe.

There are fifteen people waiting for me in the small seminar room where I am to teach an extension course on communications theory

꙰ ꙰ ꙰

and history. I write my name on the chalkboard and proceed with the formalities of an inaugural class. Fifteen people, ranging in age, I'd guess, from twenty-two to mid-forties. They are Chinese, Italian, Greek, Arabic, Anglo-Saxon, Jewish; a nice cross-section, and they come from all walks of life.

I am tying my shoelaces and organizing my papers while the students introduce themselves. Last to do so is the person on my immediate left, Berkowitz, who looks to be about forty-five, and describes himself wittily as an overeducated victim of downsizing.

"I was in hospital administration. I could say I'm a consultant now but I guess I'm actually unemployed," he concludes, laughing. "I'm a victim of your information age."

The forced humor, the bewilderment, the pain and vulnerability all wrapped up in his simple statement touches me. I have seen so many walking wounded just like him; I've created some, and been one of them in my own turn.

I don't know what to say and I feel my face flush. Finally: "Well, I hope I can offer some ideas that will help you to make some sense of the way the world works these days."

As a hospital administrator, Berkowitz had been part of a bureaucracy. Bureaucracies are all about control. Communication technology is also all about control: we communicate largely in order to exercise control. Machines communicate internally and among one another in order to control their internal processes. There are feedback loops everywhere in machinery, and in society as well, pumping information back through systems in order to control their operations. Because the roles of bureaucracies and communication technology are identical, they are largely interchangeable. One is expensive and messy, the other is cheap, easy to manage and getting less expensive every day. Which do you choose if the bottom line is your Holy Grail? Out the door go the managers who contribute nothing but information transfer and storage; in come the machines that can do it faster, cheaper, more efficiently, without complaint. Out the door goes Berkowitz. His department is reorganized into a self-managing work group, linked and supported by information technology. Next on the automation agenda—the work group itself, which can be replicated by nested algorithms: recipes within recipes.

I look at Berkowitz and I think he is like a mustard gas victim in the First World War, the war which was supposed to end wars; the war which was supposed to be over in a few weeks because, thanks to modern science, the impact of military technology was so terrible that it could not be withstood for more than a few days. It was technology not confined to machines and munitions, but which extended to techniques for managing the masses of ordinary men who made up the armies of democratic nations. Nobody stopped to wonder what might happen if both sides had access to this terrible, irresistible technology, which unfortunately was the case. What happens when an irresistible force meets an immovable object? Trench warfare, and carnage on an historically unprecedented scale.

In our shock and guilt we built magnificent cenotaphs, set aside a day and an hour and a minute each year to remember the sacrifices. Even now we hold poignant, straggling parades in which the survivors can shuffle along and be recognized.

But Berkowitz is not afforded even this much dignity. To be a sacrifice, you must have some intrinsic value, otherwise there is no sacrifice involved, just a shifting, a removal, a replacement. In the world in which terminology such as "downsizing" and "human resources" and "outplacement" is created and used without irony, values are banished. Not monetary values, of course, but human values, the kind that are not subject to quantification, the kind you can't measure. There is simply no place for them: how can you run a business, let alone an economy, if you're having to deal with "values" that are unquantifiable? Where in your Microsoft spreadsheet is the cell for loyalty or integrity, let alone something as ridiculously subjective as dignity?

✗ ✗ ✗

So Berkowitz, like the rest of us in the seminar room, like people everywhere, is now a human resource: subcategory "unemployed"; sub-subcategory "retrainable"; sub-sub-subcategory "poorly motivated" or perhaps "highly motivated," I don't know. The point is he is fixable. He can be motivated with the right psychological approach, the right incentives, the right threats; he can be retrained, by which is meant reprogrammed with skills more suitable to current market requirements; he can be reemployed, in theory, though in fact he looks a bit too old. Perhaps if he dyes his hair, dresses younger for interviews, uses eye drops, depilatories, moisturizer. Perhaps if he adjusts.

Erich Fromm wrote that the "adjusted" person in the work world "is one who has made himself into a commodity, with nothing stable or definitive except his need to please and his readiness to change roles."[2] To which French philosopher François Perroux added, "Slavery is determined neither by obedience nor the hardness of labor but by the status of being a mere instrument, and the reduction of man to the state of a thing."[3] A commodity; a tool. A slave, Aristotle said, is a living tool.

What I cannot comprehend is, how did we wind up accepting this notion of people as human resources? What in God's name is a human resource? An intelligent piece of meat? An automaton? Are we a kind of sentient cash crop, the way wildlife has become a "renewable resource" in the jargon of government "wildlife managers" and gun lobbyists, to be "harvested" during hunting season? Or, are we resources in the sense of land and minerals and oil deposits—raw materials for the production processes of the economy? The latter makes more sense; in fact, economists of every stripe, left and right, call labor a "factor of production." Human resources must be raw materials that are (incidentally) human. Berkowitz is raw material, waiting to be recycled. Maternity wards are filled with raw material, ready for processing and refining into entities that meet the needs of our economic engines. They will be recycled, in their time.

☇ ☇ ☇

And what purpose do human resources serve, exactly, in the contemporary economy? Why, they fill all the niches that are not yet filled by automated systems, by machines, by computers. Most of those positions are ones that it is not (yet) economic to automate; mostly jobs that involve creative thought, or dexterous physical activity like pruning a tree or flipping an over-easy egg or landing a disabled airplane or painting a still life or performing an appendectomy. Robots that can do these sorts of things are still terribly expensive, mainly because there is not a huge demand for them the way there is for, say, word processors or spreadsheets or the little black boxes that regulate most of the functions of an automobile nowadays, or for that matter the robots that assemble those automobiles.

humans do who robots can not.

Sometimes, in thinking all of this through, it is hard to avoid the conclusion that in winning the twentieth century's epic battles for freedom, we lost the war. That somehow, the measures we took to win—the Somme, Dresden, Hiroshima, the proxy wars, the nuclear arms race—debased our moral standards beyond recovery. The notion of "human resources" is at bottom a fascist idea, worthy of Stalin and Hitler and Pol Pot. And yet it has become one of the defining paradigms of late-twentieth century liberal-democratic culture.

we have

The great nineteenth century British economist Alfred Marshall said: "The economist, like everyone else, must concern himself with the ultimate aims of man." The *ultimate* aims. He must concern himself, in other words, with values. In Marshall's time, the discipline was called "political economy" and the reference to politics, which everybody knew could never become a science, is what kept economics human. Gradually, though, economics subsumed politics and today we hear a lot of loose talk about how government is largely unnecessary if we let the market have its way; how "big" government is inherently evil.

It sometimes seems as if we no longer have values at all, not in the sense of a body of shared, deeply held beliefs and standards. But, of course, we do: having values is a defining characteristic of being

✗ ✗ ✗

human, and no matter how hard we may try to be something other than human, we cannot succeed. We will always have values. What has happened is that our values have changed, and changed in a way that makes them fundamentally different from the values of any other age in recorded history. Our values, those we are willing to express publicly and transfer to our public institutions, are firmly scientific, implacably pragmatic and rational. It is inevitable that they should be so, since values reflect our view of the universe and our place in it, and that view, for us, has been shaped by the last four hundred years of science. (A philosopher would call us "rational empiricists," or perhaps "scientific naturalists" or "scientific materialists"; I will endeavor to stick to the first and last of these characterizations, occasionally substituting the word "materialist" for simplicity's sake.) Competing worldviews have been squeezed out of our frame of reference, relegated to the realm of superstition and cant. As a culture, our own highest value is productivity, which is not really a value at all but an engineering goal, a quality we attach to machinery. We seek to employ human resources productively and efficiently. Pity poor Berkowitz, who is too much a human being to be very efficient, and needs to be prodded into productivity. Our private values we keep to ourselves, like medieval Cathar heretics huddled in the high hilltop villages of Languedoc, living lives of feigned conformity to avoid the attention of the bloodthirsty crusaders and the Inquisition, with its exquisite instruments of psychological terror and its embryonic technologies of mass behavior modification.

The metaphor of medieval heretics and crusaders and inquisitors is not an accidental one. Two years of research into the history and philosophy of technology,[4] and an earlier holiday spent traveling in the south of France had combined to kindle in me an intense interest in the Middle Ages in that country. In our histories of human thought and achievement we tend to skip from Greece and Rome to the Renaissance, overlooking the thousand years which saw the development of many of our most enduringly useful technologies—the clock, the plow, the waterwheel, the windmill, the wheelbarrow, the draught horse harness, the stirrup, the printing press—not to mention a highly evolved system of thought and perception that was radically different from our own, and that permeated every level of human existence. The idea that worthwhile knowledge was to be gained by the accumulation of facts about the things in the world around us, indeed, that those things, ourselves included, had an existence independent of human consciousness and Divine will, was completely alien. The universe was filled with meaning, consciousness and intent, a vast and beautiful cathedral of interdependent hierarchies and we were at the centre of it, in both a physical and a metaphorical sense.

No country or region of Europe was more influential in the evolution of all of this than France. When, in the summer of 1997, I had the opportunity to return there for several weeks, I saw it as a chance to indulge my curiosity about a particularly fascinating episode in medieval history called the Albigensian Crusade, and the subsequent establishment of the infamous Inquisition. The story of the Albigenses—also called Cathars—and the terrible religious war against them, had haunted me since I'd discovered it on that first visit to the region known as Languedoc in the shadow of the Pyrenees, a half-dozen years earlier. It was a stirring tale of valiant lords and heroic knights resisting intolerance and oppression; of powerful, independent women who shaped both the civil and religious history of their times; of troubadours and the culture of romance; of impossibly virtuous men and women called the Perfect, and the iniquitous machinations of the Inquisition. I wondered if there might not be a metaphor here for our own time of moral and ethical struggle, one that I might perhaps develop in writing, as my own small contribution to our century's great, unresolved debate surrounding science, technology and spirituality.

The thirteenth-century Cathars, I was willing to believe from my initial contact, had been a beacon of joy and freedom and moral

✘ ✘ ✘

integrity dispelling the gloom of an otherwise corrupt, violent and repressive world. But as I went beyond the potted histories of guide books and travel literature and delved into the vast medieval history holdings of the university, and most of all as I walked the ramparts of the Cathar castles and the streets of medieval settlements and visited the cathedrals of the Catholic orthodoxy, I began to change my mind. I began to see, in fact, that the real meaning of the story was not only more complex than most standard treatments suggest, but that it was almost the reverse of what I had imagined it would be.

The Cathar heresy, I could now see, was in direct line of ancestry with the earliest European stirrings of modernism: that system of thought and imagination that strictly separates the spiritual from the material, and which in its fully evolved form has brought us to our present condition. That "condition" might be described as one in which scientific materialism, or a belief in the autonomous existence of objects in the world, has become more or less a state-sanctioned religion every bit as intolerant of heresy as was medieval Catholicism, and which successfully promotes the assumptions that what is old is bad, or at least inferior, and that intellectual progress (we do not dare speak of spiritual progress) consists in the endless accumulation of facts.

The Albigensian Crusade was just one small episode in a titanic struggle that engaged the Church throughout the first fifteen hundred years of its existence and beyond. Indeed, it lasted from the time of St. Augustine (AD 354–430) in the Dark Ages, up to the ultimate, decisive battle with the forces of materialism as championed by Galileo and the great Newton, who was born the year Galileo died in 1642. It was the epic struggle against the objectification of the material world, and the resultant alienation of man from God. It was a contest between two fundamentally different ways of understanding our place in the universe and it reached its climax in the slow transformation of the Age of Faith into the Age of Reason; indeed, it defined that transition.

ⵉ ⵉ ⵉ

During the autumn of 1996 and the winter and spring of 1997, as my wife Christine and I made plans for our visit to France, little of the broader significance lurking within the Albigensian episode was suspected by me. This was a trip we had been planning for years, a gift to our children, Hilary, then seventeen, and Simon, fifteen, and we were focused on the details of how to make it both enjoyable and valuable for them. For better or worse, given the modern dynamics of domestic life, it would probably be our last chance to travel together as a family. It was my good fortune that the history of the Cathars is best explored at the sites of the military outposts and fortified towns where they sought protection in their death struggle, and these are some of the most spectacular travel destinations in France. And then our prospects for making this a truly memorable journey were given an enormous additional boost by the splendid, unexpected offer of accommodation throughout France from the president of the Relais and Châteaux group of hotels, small country inns, for the most part, which house excellent restaurants serving authentic regional cuisine. These are successful holdovers from a time of more sedate and attentive—more civilized—travel. The trip suddenly took on an entirely new cultural dimension, not to mention a new range of sybaritic possibilities.

And so as Chris and I planned our itinerary we were full of high hopes, tinged only slightly by the resigned forebodings of parents faced with riding herd on a couple of independent-minded teenagers in a foreign country, and the knowledge that this would have to be a working holiday in the professional sense as well.

Rather than leave our home in the country east of Toronto unoccupied, and board the dog and two cats in expensive and uncomfortable accommodations at a kennel, we decided to look for a housesitter. My student Berkowitz had struck me as someone both trustworthy and in need of a change of scene: we invited him out to dinner and popped the question.

☓ ☓ ☓

He said, "I haven't spent more than two days outside the city since summer camp. My lungs could spontaneously combust in all that oxygen." He brightened up: "But I guess I could handle it. Anyway, 'caretaker' will look good on my résumé—Sharon, my outplacement consultant, says I have to be more flexible if I'm going to be 'marketable.'" He scratched the air with his index fingers to place quotes around the word.

We were set to go.

Toronto to Paris

PORTENTS ⚔ A NOSELESS MAN ⚔

DE MONTFORT'S VICTIMS ⚔ A LONG FLIGHT

⚔ OUR TRAVEL GOALS ⚔ REPRODUCTIONS

AND ORIGINALS

I am a believer in omens and portents. On a perilous motorcycle trip to Canada's subarctic years ago, I got in the habit of talking to ravens, which are a favorite disguise of Inuit shamans on the move. I try not to gloat over good fortune when it comes my way because I know that pride goeth before a fall. I seldom speak ill of the dead. I trust my instincts.

I say "believer," but I do not mean it in the way a devout Christian believes in transubstantiation or the Trinity, or a neophyte scientist believes in quarks and pi-mesons, all unprovable propositions necessary to the structural integrity of a particular worldview. I mean it rather in the sense in which the Greeks believed in their Olympic deities—that is, with a grain of salt, and because it makes life more interesting, more nourishing, more richly textured and full of possibilities and, in that sense, more real. And because I share the outlook of the elderly physicist who in a moment of whimsy said of the power of prayer that he did not believe in it, but found nevertheless that it seemed frequently to work. The world is what we make it.

⚔ ⚔ ⚔

We were busily stowing our cabin luggage on our flight to Paris when I saw that the old man three rows in front of us had no nose. This had to be an omen. It was disorienting to see his otherwise normal, weather-beaten face in profile as he stood there in the crowded aisle. My brain wanted there to be a nose where it ought to have been, but instead there was empty space through which I could look farther down the cabin towards the front of the plane. It was as though I had suddenly developed the comic book ability to peer through solid objects. I did a long double take and was able to see that in truth he had not the slightest remnant of a nose, and that there was opaque surgical tape over the resultant hole in his face. He seemed cheerful enough and in good fettle, and he was being helped with his bags by a stocky, rather fierce-looking old woman with a few wisps of close-cropped white hair and broad, thick-fingered hands, whom I took to be his wife. Despite her age and wrinkles, she had the tightly-coiled aggressiveness of a lioness.

Chris, I could see, had noticed as well; Hilary and Simon were already in their seats and preoccupied. Simon was studying the technical details of the aircraft in the seat-back literature and Hilary was organizing her space, finding spots for her camera case and shoulder bag and books and magazines.

I couldn't escape the feeling that I was being told something by the appearance of this noseless man in my life. I relished it. It helped me to see my world in a new way, to think about it from a different perspective. What made it a portent was that we were on our way to France, in part at least to explore the history and archaeology of the Albigensian Crusade, a feature of which had been the ruthless barbarism of Simon de Montfort, leader of the crusading armies from the north of France. In one campaign, he had captured a garrison of about two hundred men, sliced off their noses and put out their eyes as an object lesson in the folly of resistance. I had often wondered what became of those poor, disfigured men. Were they spurned and

ꓽ ꓽ ꓽ

21

abandoned, left to starve or die from infection, or to join the ragged mobs of itinerant beggars? Or would they have been rescued by their families and allowed to live out their lives in the deep shadows of the hearth? Their fate would say much about the world they lived in; more, it seemed to me, than the act of mutilation itself. Sadists have always been with us, but they do not define cultures: what does is how they are dealt with and how their victims are treated.

My noseless man, for his part, appeared to be comfortably well off, judging by his clothes and the fact that he could afford air fare to France, and people around him were politely averting their eyes so as to avoid making him uncomfortable. On the other hand I was pretty sure he'd never get work as a television news anchor or a greeter at Wal-Mart or a counter jockey at Burger King. His commodity profile was all wrong.

As the airplane climbed to cruising altitude and I slowly eased my grip on the armrests, Simon, in the window seat beside Chris, provided a running commentary on what was happening with the flaps and spoilers, and explained why the wings rose as we gained speed. I told him that I used to live in terror that the wings would rip right off in turbulent air, but that once someone had explained to me that it is not so much a question of the wings being fastened to the fuselage as the fuselage resting on the wing assembly, I had been able to relax. He found that hugely amusing, very quaint. He had recently been on a week-long high school enrichment program at Queen's University where he took a short course in aerodynamics, and as is his habit when he's interested, he'd pretty much memorized everything he heard and read. The right guy got the window seat, I thought, smiling to myself.

I was almost ready to forgive him for what he'd done in the airport. As we waited for our carry-on bags to go through the X-ray machines at the security barrier, he'd wisecracked about how it was a good thing he'd packed his Barretta in his checked luggage. I could not believe my ears! Every security guard within hearing range bristled

ⵝ ⵝ ⵝ

and stopped to stare at him: I'd had to give him a public dressing-down just to show he was with somebody responsible.

Hilary is leafing through the duty-free catalogue in the seat across the aisle from me. She is on a page advertising liquors.

"Have you ever had a chocolate martini?" she asks me with a sly grin.

"God, no!"

"They're delicious. The owner of *Ursus* gave me one."

My face registers the expected scowl of disapproval. *Ursus* is a popular dance club, part of Toronto's trendy Queen Street West scene. As a model, Hilary gets red carpet treatment, and loves it.

"Oooo, Johnny Walker!" She is trying to get a rise out of me. "It's delicious with Coke. Have you ever had it?"

"That's a hoser drink. They used to drink it in Winnipeg. Very unsophisticated."

This takes her off guard.

"Well, what's sophisticated?"

"Campari and soda for you. It's served in a tall glass, it tastes a little bitter so you're not tempted to chug-a-lug and one drink can last you all night. Nobody looks sophisticated when they've had too much to drink."

"Dad, spare me the lecture."

She has lost interest in the conversation and reaches into her bag to fish out *The Wild Girls Club*, which she has pilfered from Chris's studio at home. I suppose I should disapprove, but I am content to have injected another little shot of fatherly guidance through a chink in her teenage anti-parent armor. You have to take your victories where you can find them. One of the lesser reasons for bringing her and her brother along on this trip is to teach them something about drinking, and how to be civilized about it. The French will have no problem serving them an aperitif or wine with their meals, so that they can learn how it's done.

Our broader goal, though—in fact the primary reason for the

✗ ✗ ✗

trip—is to inoculate them against North American pop culture, to demonstrate for them that there are other modes of perception and other values abroad on the planet, that there is a world beyond what they see on Fox or at the Cineplex and read about in *Time*. We had a little less than a month—not a lot of time—but travel is a potent teacher. We all learn best and fastest when we're exposed to first-hand experience, to the real thing, because it is absorbed at so many different levels of sensory contact. We not only see it and hear it, we smell it and touch it and taste it and transport ourselves through it. Foreign travel, done well, provides lots of the real thing, and the real thing, in large doses, was just what the doctor ordered for a couple of teenaged North American kids.

One of the chief problems with the culture in which we'd been trying to raise our children is precisely that it fails to recognize the difference between the simulation or reproduction and the original. Rather than living lives, in the familiar phrase, we enjoy lifestyles. We see life, as it were, through a glass, darkly. The glass is made up of our many technologies of communication and tools for ameliorating the harshness of nature; nowadays, we see nature mainly through the lens of technology, and what we see is therefore an image, or a representation. It is a truism of postmodern philosophy that the process has gone so far that the images we now see are no longer even representations of "original" reality, but merely reproductions of other representations. This "hyperreality" is validated strictly on its own terms, without reference to the real world beyond representations. And so, Disneyland, for example, or Historic Williamsburg, exist to validate the memory of an America that never in fact existed except as a reproduction, an artist's rendering, an advertiser's pipe dream.

I had tried in the past to explain the concept to Hilary and Simon without, I feared, much success. The penny finally dropped for them at an exhibit of *The Scream* and other paintings by Edvard Munch.

The gallery's management having recently passed into the hands of marketing experts, the downtown had been papered with images of the famous painting in every conceivable form from lamppost banners to billboards to window displays featuring blow-up dolls to the inevitable T-shirts. It was clear even to them that the original, when they'd finally reached the head of the queue and looked at it for their allotted twenty or thirty seconds, had been somehow devalued by the existence of all the reproductions. It was as if the psychic juice had been sucked out of it. Paradoxically, however, its economic value had been enhanced by the many reproductions, so that thousands of people who would otherwise not have visited the gallery paid money to line up to see "the original" of the now-familiar reproductions. The value of the painting no longer resided in its being a unique embodiment of an artist's vision and skill, but in the fact of its being an original. And the monetary value of the latter is greater than the former, simply because the interested market is so much larger.

There is nothing particularly worrisome about this process so far as the world of art is concerned; one could even argue that our ability to communicate is enriched by having access to reproducible images which convey ideas that are difficult to frame in words. But what happens when these same processes of commodification are found to be at work in an image-rich medium as widespread and influential as television? Our view of the world is shaped to a very significant extent through television. However, what we see on the tube is a *reproduction* of reality. Furthermore, it is a reproduction of only a small segment of any given aspect of reality, that portion which the camera is capable of framing, or chooses to single out for close-up examination. And what is more, the so-called reality being reproduced is usually just another second-hand representation itself, a fictitious creation jointly fabricated by reporters, editors, producers, camera crews, scriptwriters, advertisers, spin doctors, owners and managers of media outlets, according to their own prejudices, who are in turn shaped by the "hyperreal" environment in which they live and work.

Television, and most of all, "reality-based" television programming, it seemed to me, had come to share in the chief vice of pornography, which, in presenting a reproduced image (in other words, by extracting or excising from its native context the rather narrow spectrum of information content which the medium is capable of reproducing), devalues the original act by making it, as it were, mechanical and strictly objective. Everything in the image, by the process of extracting it from the context on which it relies for its life, for its existence, is reduced to an object, and objects can interact in no other way than mechanically. Thus, all of television becomes rigidly formulaic and predictable. A political convention becomes, on television, a circus; a student revolt in Tiananmen Square becomes a morality play; a little girl trapped down a well, a fable; a presidential sex scandal, a soap opera. Television seemed to me a kind of continuous pollution, a corroder of reality as unrelenting as acid rain. (Others, I must acknowledge, find it merely amusing or comforting.)

On the interminable overnight flight to Paris we watched on the video screens before us two movies set in the United States, which was offhandedly portrayed as a sinkhole of violence and depravity, and a saccharine wildlife feature in which the badlands of southern Alberta were reproduced as a cinematic coffee-table book. We were also treated to several increasingly dated newscasts and, in between, many advertisements and a slowly scrolling map of the eastern seaboard of North America, the North Atlantic and Western Europe which purported to show our progress along the great circle route past the tip of Greenland, connecting us to our destination.

I wondered: Had we smuggled a medieval sailor aboard the plane, how long would it have taken him to believe that the surroundings he would see on arrival in France were actually, really and truly, Paris? How *could* he believe it, not having experienced the two months of

✗ ✗ ✗

2 6

ocean voyaging that he understood to be necessary to get from one continent to another? Perhaps he would rationalize his situation by convincing himself that the brief nap he had taken on the plane had actually been an extended coma, or an enchantment. I know that on my first flight to Europe, it took me several days to fully accept the idea that I had indeed arrived on a different continent, and several more weeks to begin to see my surroundings for what they were rather than "the original" of the many images I had absorbed over the years: in the intervening time I had simply suspended disbelief as I would in watching a play, so that I could continue to function. The process was a highly stressful one. Nowadays, it could be argued, most of us live most of our lives in such a state of suspended disbelief, operating almost entirely in an environment of second- and third-hand representations, in a world of hyperreality. No doubt this is stressful as well.

We arrived at Charles de Gaulle Airport, stiff, tired and out of sorts as one always is after a transatlantic flight. Waiting impatiently for our luggage to appear on a carousel, we found ourselves standing beside none other than the wife of the noseless man. She was older than I had first thought, perhaps seventy. But full of vitality. I had thought her face plain as an old garden hoe, but when she smiled at us it was positively beatific. Her hair was very thin, slicked straight back. Her extravagant bosom was cantilevered out over her stomach by some amazing piece of foundation wear, and I could see now that her dress was trimmed in the most delicate lace at the sleeves and neck. She wore tiny silver pendant earrings.

Chris, who has an easy way with people, struck up a conversation with the woman and soon learned through a *mélange* of French and English that her husband had gone in search of his brother, who was picking them up in his car. The couple came not from the depths of Cathar country in Languedoc, but from Sarnia, Ontario. They had emigrated years ago from Paris, and had raised a family in

❦ ❦ ❦

Canada. She and her husband had returned to France to attend her husband's older brother's wedding the following day in a small town between Paris and Dijon. She put her hand to her mouth, leaned towards Chris and giggled, "Of course he's far too old to be getting married," and there was a twinkle in her pale blue eyes.

It is amazing how direct experience of people can change your initial impression of them. When I think of her now, she is winsome, and I am sure she thinks her husband a handsome fellow. This, I am sure, is the reality. Maybe the victims of Simon de Montfort's blade fared better in their old age than I had feared.

CHAPTER 3

Paris: The Cult of Reason

ENCOUNTERING PARIS ❧ HILARY MAKES AN
IMPRESSION ❧ SUBJECTS AND OBJECTS ❧
THE HARD ROCK CAFÉ ❧ NOTRE-DAME DE
PARIS ❧ DESCARTES AND THE CULT OF REASON
❧ SIMON DISAGREES ❧ AUGUSTE COMTE ❧
THE ORANGERIE AND THE IMPRESSIONISTS

I n the concrete-and-steel convection oven of the airport taxi
ranks we stuffed half our luggage into the trunk of a pint-sized
cab and dragged the overflow behind us into the passenger
compartment for what I knew would be a terrifying ride into
downtown Paris. Our driver was a patient if stern Algerian who had
a lead foot and a *politesse* that extended to facing us directly in the
back seat to address us while rocketing through morning traffic and
simultaneously fielding calls on his digital radio keyboard. Our strangled cries of alarm were muffled by the roar of the open windows
and I tried to maintain my composure by focusing on how the kids
would react when we left the nondescript industrial environs of the
A-3 expressway and the semi-subterranean *autoroute périphérique*
to surface on Avenue Foch and the Champs-Elysées.

❧ ❧ ❧

I was not disappointed. We swept up an exit ramp to ground level and before we could relax our death grips on hand-holds and seat backs, the Arc de Triomphe filled the windshield, with the Champs-Elysées stretching beyond. Simon's jaw dropped and he craned forward. Hilary said, and I'll never forget it: "Oh, my God. That is *magnificent!*"

I thought, a little extravagantly, even if the trip is a washout from now on, it will have been worth it. It just got better as we drove along the Champs-Elysées and the kids' voluble amazement made even the cabbie smile.

In five minutes we were at our hotel on rue Balzac, the Vigny, where experience told Chris and me that we should sleep for a few hours, but it did not seem right to deprive Hilary and Simon of a little stroll first and so we performed our habitual jet-lag follies and walked until we were exhausted and, desperate for food, paid too much for lunch because we had no patience to search for a bargain, and returned to the hotel worn out and irritable. We slept until eight, showered, and feeling much refreshed, found a perfect terrace café on the Champs-Elysées and enjoyed a perfect supper of bistro food. Afterwards, we went for a long walk down one side of the famous boulevard and up the other, and Hilary's antennae immediately told her that she was attracting male attention. Drivers tootled their horns, bicyclists and rollerbladers did double takes, pedestrians swivelled their heads. She strode on ahead of us so as to give the impression that she was alone, and the effect was magnified. Even Simon, congenitally loath to admit special qualities in his older sibling, confessed he was impressed. She looked perfectly ordinary to us, and was wearing standard-issue khaki shorts, T-shirt and sandals—but she apparently seemed exotic to the local swains.

I was of two minds as to how to respond to this: on the one hand, it was nice to see her having fun and feeling so good about herself— it seemed to me that she had instinctively and immediately adopted the trademark insouciance of the native Parisienne, a cocky, hip-swinging confidence that I had always found attractive. She had picked up on, and adapted to the European male-female dynamic in which women are continually monitoring the image they are projecting, continually and self-consciously establishing a presence. They enjoyed being looked at and did not mind letting on. The men here appeared to understand the process as well, so that the whole web of relationships became an elaborate, sexually charged masquerade to which the rules were universally understood, and which gave pleasure to all the players, male and female. No one, it seemed to me, took it very seriously.

Now that I had a teenaged daughter, I saw the ritual from a new perspective. The whole process consisted in making objects of women, which can only be destructive to both men and women. Still, the leading argument in favor of scrapping the game—that women are not objects, but persons—was not as persuasive as it might be. Ask: "What is the difference between an object and a person?" and the only answer that is likely to be forthcoming in our scientific age is an emphatic expression of common sense understanding: "Why, a person is a *human being!*" which is not exactly the stuff on which to build a moral precept since it simply rephrases the question. And the fact was that not just women but men *and* women were being treated like objects in late twentieth-century society, and not just in relation to the mating game. Before we can deal with the problem in any of its aspects, it would appear to be necessary to provide a more compelling answer to the question: What distinguishes a person from an object, and why does one deserve different treatment from the other?

Hilary, with a year of professional modeling under her belt and a fat Ford portfolio containing dozens of images that I scarcely recognized as my daughter, had of course experienced the objectifying process in depth. No doubt that was why she was able to so quickly pick up on the game. It worried me, of course, as it worried Chris, who had been a model in her own time and had quit precisely because she could not stand being made first an object and then an

☿ ☿ ☿

icon. While we could see that the experience had given Hilary enormous self-confidence for a girl of her age, we could not help but wonder whether that confidence was really in her "self," or in the presence she projected for the camera, and to the world at large. Ernest Hemingway, of whom I was inordinately fond as a young newspaper reporter, said that it is okay for a serious writer to be a journalist for a while, but not too long, because journalistic style is inimical to the kind of good writing that gets at the truth. Newspaper journalism is in that sense a lot like print-making, as opposed to painting. I hoped, perhaps unfairly but in the same spirit, that Hilary's modeling career would be short and sweet.

The next day, a Saturday, we were up early and kept doggedly on the move on foot and by Metro, determined to see as much of the city as possible before our schedule insisted we leave for the south. The Orangerie gallery at Place de la Concorde, which had been under renovation the last time Chris and I were here, was tops on my list, and we eventually did get there after a subway ride to the Hard Rock Café for souvenir pins for Chris and Hilary. Hilary also bought a black baseball cap to keep the sun off her face. It had the Hard Rock Café slogan embroidered on the front: "Save the Planet."

Simon laughed when he saw it. Hilary bristled: "What's the big joke?"

"There's a newsgroup on the Net called 'alt.pave-the-planet.' I just realized where they got the name."

"Is that supposed to be funny?" Hilary snorted.

I thought it was hilarious. I wanted to be at the Orangerie. The Hard Rock Café, in fact, was about the last place in Paris I would have chosen to be. It was, like all the other Hard Rock Cafés everywhere from Acapulco to L.A. to Taipei, a "landmark" created wholly through cunning marketing. They made money solely via the creation and perpetuation of a brand name, which they then sold to the gullible in the form of (of course) T-shirts, and other trinkets: it was a business that

Ɏ Ɏ Ɏ

could only have existed in the Age of Information, but was, for me, a perversion of the spirit of the age because it embodied a lie. The food they serve represents the worst of American cuisine just as the places themselves, the very idea of them, represent the worst of American commercial culture abroad; the Disneyfying of the planet. They are a form of artificial reality, the mass reproduction of something for which there never was an original; dead, devoid of context, ultimately and definitively depressing. Save the planet, indeed. However, I knew that it would be tiresome and fruitless to put this forward as an argument against going there and so I kept my own counsel, contenting myself, while we were there, with being a surly and ill-tempered middle-aged man, a role I find I am able to slide into with increasing ease.

At a sunny terrace bar next door we ordered sandwiches and we told Hilary and Simon it would be okay to have a beer. Hilary, a young woman of some experience, immediately ordered up a Corona for each of them; I gave her a succinct lecture on the virtues of thrift and the folly of ordering Mexican beer in France, and explained to her the process of ordering *une pression*, a draft, at a quarter the price. It was a treat to watch Simon savor with studied insouciance his first drink in a public place; he seemed to morph back and forth between child and adult before our eyes.

We shot back to the Cité metro stop on Ile St. Louis, and emerged to find that Notre-Dame de Paris, home of the eponymous hunchback and much other myth and history, was for the first time in my experience free of repair scaffolding. What's more, the buff-colored stone had been cleaned from the top of the twin towers right down to the King's Gallery which stretches across the facade above the three entrance doors set in their Gothic arches. The pristine cleanliness of the stonework has revealed a surprising, almost Moorish delicacy that had been obscured beneath centuries of soot and grime. Taken as a whole, the structure is a virtually perfect work of art, an inspired statement in the humanizing of geometric forms, a masterpiece of

Y Y Y

thoughtful asymmetry in design and restrained exuberance of decoration. As we stood in the square before it and gaped, I read aloud from my trusty Michelin guide:

> Construction began in 1163, during the reign of Louis VII. . . . By about 1345 the building was complete—the original plans had not been modified in any way. With the Revolution, the Church of Our Lady was dedicated to the Cult of Reason and then of the Supreme Being.

"What the heck is the Cult of Reason?" Hilary wanted to know.

"It's a bit of a long story; do you remember Descartes?"

"'I think therefore I am.'"

"Right. The Church philosophers, the Scholastics, believed that there were different kinds of knowledge and different ways of knowing things, but Descartes said that knowing is always the same because the mind is what does the knowing and it is always the same, in all sane people. He said that all true knowledge is gained in just one way, by building on concrete, self-evident information, and that's why he went all the way back to what he considered to be the most fundamental piece of knowledge of all, 'I think,' and from that he deduced 'I am' (something had to be there to have the thought), and started building his philosophy from that foundation. Each new step had to pass the test of being as self-evidently right as that first step."

"So, what's that got to do with reason?"

"Reason, for Descartes, was what allowed him to say that a proposition is self-evidently 'true' or 'false.' He called it 'the light of reason' and said that all sane people have that ability built in from birth."

"Well, I mean, isn't all that kind of obvious?"

"Maybe it seems that way to modern people like us, but at the time a lot of people found the idea troubling because it seemed to them that Descartes' radically rational methods made the world into a machine. In fact, he explicitly said that not just the inanimate world but all animals except man *were* machines and operated strictly

ꓘ ꓘ ꓘ

according to the physical laws of nature. The trouble from the Church's point of view was that there didn't seem to be any place for God in all of this. Descartes used his methods to 'prove' the existence of God in several different ways, but in the end, there was nothing for God to actually *do* in a Cartesian world. Everything could run quite satisfactorily just by obeying the laws of physics."

"I still don't get it."

"It helps to know that he appeared on the scene when the mathematical ideas of the great medieval astronomers, Galileo, Kepler and Copernicus, were becoming very popular, in spite of the Church. More and more scholars and thinkers were beginning to accept the idea that there were scientific laws that governed the lives of the stars and planets, and of objects on earth as well. And those laws could be written down in terms of mathematics. Along came Descartes, and added to that the notion that mind and matter were entirely separate and distinct, and that the act of thinking was a process carried on 'in here' about things and events 'out there.' The implication was that the subject, the 'I,' was self-enclosed, and so everything else in creation became an autonomous object. In other words, a thing contained within itself everything it needed for its existence. The subject—us— could know these objects reliably only through inference from their mathematical properties. This was the only objective, and therefore the only reliable, information you could have about things external to yourself. It all added up to a new scientific view of nature as a vast machine run according to mathematical rules and relationships, independent of consciousness, independent of God."

"Ha! Exactly!" Simon interrupted. "You don't need to have some old greybeard sitting on a cloud somewhere and people falling down and worshipping him and all of that nonsense!"

"Not unless you stop to ask yourself where the so-called light of reason comes from. The Church had a two-thousand-year-old answer for that, but Descartes didn't, even though his entire philosophy depends on it."

⅄ ⅄ ⅄

"That's just because science wasn't advanced enough at the time. They didn't know anything about the brain, or about neurons and synapses and proteins folding and all that. You don't have to have some deity up in the sky somewhere to explain it."

"I think you're underestimating the sophistication of the Scholastics. But anyway, Hilary, the Cult of Reason got its start with Descartes' ideas, which grew out of inductive reasoning, where you start from a concrete fact and build on that, whereas the Church philosophers tended to use mainly deductive reason, where you take what seems self-evident in the world around you, or what the Scriptures tell you about the world, and work your way backward to understand individual phenomena. In other words, Descartes was arguing from the specific to the general and the Church tended to argue from the general to the specific."

"Inductive reasoning," Simon interjected, "is the scientific method. If we relied on deductive reason, we'd all still be living in caves and eating raw meat!"

"Oh, I wouldn't be so sure about that. Civilization had come a long way before science appeared on the scene, it seems to me. If you need evidence, just look at the building in front of you. Deductive reason meant the Church could take things that seemed to have a real existence, like love and joy and virtue and miracles and values, and have them at the center of its philosophy, but if you try to demonstrate their existence using Descartes' 'scientific' method, it's an almost impossible job because they're not measurable. You can't quantify them, so you can't prove they exist using science or mathematics. That really is the bottom line as far as anything being 'self-evident' in Cartesian terms. And so if you believe that Cartesian reality is the only reality, you're left with a world in which all these so-called spiritual things that seemed so real to the Church scholars, and in fact to most ordinary people, do not exist."

"Of course they exist," Hilary said.

Simon rolled his eyes and groaned: "Show me the empirical

evidence. You can explain every one of them in terms of advancing the cause of your genome. All they are is rationalizations to make people feel warm and fuzzy."

"What do you mean, 'Show me the evidence.'" She mimicked Simon's impatient tone of voice. "You can see it all around you unless you're totally blind and stupid."

I held up my hand to call for silence.

"Okay, okay, no need to be insulting. Anyway that's not the main point. The really subversive thing about Descartes was the emphasis he put on mind. To say, 'I think therefore I am,' is to give mind absolute precedence over matter, because the thought is the most basic thing of all: 'I think' comes before 'I am.' That was the basis of a tendency in philosophy called 'subjectivism.' It's also sometimes called 'rationalism' because it eventually led people to believe that it was possible to build an understanding of the universe through pure reason, without reference to the authority of the Scriptures or the Church. Who needs Revelation if you can figure everything out on your own? For that matter, who needs sensory perception? All the senses do is confuse the issue, because they are so easily tricked and misled. The thing is to start with a handful of basic certainties like 'I am,' and build step-by-step from there following the mathematically-sound rules of logical inference. That way, you'll end up with a bullet-proof picture of the world."

"I can never see why you have to have something thinking in order for there to be a thought," Hilary said, "I mean, why can't a thought just *be*?"

Simon laughed incredulously, and Chris shot him an impatient look.

"That is actually a very profound question," I said. "In fact it may be the toughest question you can ask of Descartes. I don't think he has an answer. It actually makes no logical sense for him to begin by saying 'I think,' because he hasn't yet established that there is an 'I.' He should really have said, 'There are thoughts.' But then, 'I am' no longer follows so easily, does it, Simon?

¥ ¥ ¥

37

"In any case you can imagine what a mind like Descartes' would come up with for a theory of nature and the relationships among things in the real world. He imagined a kind of vast machine, with everything connected by laws of cause-and-effect, just the way his theory of knowledge was so precise and rational and mathematical. Unfortunately, this undermined the idea of free will, because how can an individual change the course of his life if everything that happens is determined by the laws of nature? So the Church was very uneasy about Descartes. It wasn't that they disagreed with the idea of reason being important; the Church believed reason was God-given and could be used to understand and explain religious truths. What they were nervous about was the tendency to think that *everything* could be explained using reason, that there was no need for faith, and that everything that went on in the world was in a sense predetermined by mathematical rules, the way it is in a machine. Free will is bedrock dogma for the Church."

"Pah!" said Simon. "All they were really worried about was losing their power and authority over people. They wouldn't be able to control people any more by saying, 'You do this, or you'll fry in Hell,' because no reasoning person would believe that."

"Well, I think you're partly right about that. The Church had always believed strongly in social stability. Subjectivism implied, at worst, that everybody could write their own rules, because the individual was the only authentic source of knowledge. And that would mean anarchy. But you'd be wrong if you said that the Church always favored the established order. Because in the French Revolution, a majority of the Church representatives in the assembly of the estates sided with the third estate, the ordinary people, against the aristocrats. They could see a need for change, but they thought it should take place within the moral and ethical guidelines set out by the Church. In the end, of course, there was anarchy and it took Napoleon to stabilize the country again, and he went on to try to take over Europe and had to be defeated. Hundreds of thousands of people lost their lives. So you could say that Descartes' big idea caused a lot of strife. It's still with us, in my humble opinion."

"Well, in my humble opinion we wouldn't be standing here now if it weren't for him because without scientific thinking there would be no airplanes," Simon said somewhat acerbically.

We had made our way slowly around to the back of the cathedral and found a bench in the lovely little park at the very tip of the island. Half a dozen mothers with babies in prams and strollers were enjoying the sun. Before us was the intricately decorated chevet of the cathedral with its tall piers and flying buttresses, pinnacles and balustrades and gargoyles; and behind us, through a low hedge, was the fast-flowing Seine.

Hilary and Simon seemed to be in a mood for listening, so I continued.

"Around the time of the Revolution, this kind of thinking got mixed up with the anticlerical sentiments that went along with the hatred of the aristocracy and resentment over tithes and taxes and all the rest of it. And in a weird kind of inversion, reason was raised to the level of a religion at the same time as the whole tremendous wave of terror and vandalism was getting under way. All the bells in the tower here in the cathedral, for instance, were melted down, and the interior of the cathedral was used for storing hay and grain. A lot of churches were turned into stables. All those statues above the main doors running right across the front façade—there's twenty-eight of them—they were pulled down and smashed. It's called the King's Gallery and the Paris commune thought they were kings of France and that's why they destroyed them, but actually they represent the kings of Judea and Israel from the Old Testament. They were only replaced at the end of the last century."

"Oh my God," Hilary said. "That's the Cult of Reason for you." She shot a sidelong glance at Simon, who reacted with predictable vehemence.

"Reason has nothing to do with it," he fired back. "It's just plain

⋊ ⋉ ⋊

stupidity. What kind of cretins would do a thing like that to a building like this?"

"Rational ones," Hilary said, prodding him again.

Chris stood up: "I think we should go look inside, is what I think."

There is much to distract the mind and senses walking along the Seine on Isle de la Cité beside one of Europe's great architectural treasures, and we strolled in silence back around to the main cathedral square and the entrance doors. Once again Simon had managed to get under my skin by playing Mr. Spock. He'd been doing it for three or four years now, ever since he'd learned the rudiments of debating at school. Chris and I had often asked ourselves in exasperation which stage we preferred, the earlier one in which he'd simply said no to everything, or this one, where he debated you to death in a Chinese water torture of logic. Today I thought he was more Auguste Comte than Spock, though I was pretty sure he'd never heard of Comte.

Auguste Comte was born five years after the Paris commune ordered the destruction of the King's Gallery, and lived through the turbulent post-Revolution era of the Napoleonic Empire and the restoration of the monarchy. In his philosophy, called Positivism, he provided a coherent dogma for the Cult of Reason. Positivism was based on the idea that all knowledge of fact was derived from "positive" data gained from sensory experience, and that the relationships among facts could be known only through the pure sciences of logic and mathematics. The Positivist position was vehemently anti-metaphysical and anticlerical, and to the extent that it focused on moral issues it was utilitarian; that is, it described a "moral" outcome as being one which ensured the greatest happiness for the greatest number of people. Metaphysical thought was considered to be non-sense—"non-sense"—as was the theory of aesthetics. Comte himself nevertheless felt that people ought to be encouraged to practise ethical behavior and to that end he actually established a religion in which outstanding humanists were honored in elaborate ceremonies:

x x x

a biographer has described it as Catholicism without Christianity. It did not last. He is, however, regarded as the founder of the modern science of sociology which he himself saw as a scientific replacement for the outdated, nonsensical, non-mathematical teachings of the Church concerning human social behavior. Sociology, he believed, ought to be constructed upon observation and the formulation of general, scientifically valid laws in the same way as chemistry or physics. Psychology, he felt, should be a sub-discipline of biology and in this he anticipated our own century's Behaviorists.

Positivism's forerunners include Descartes, of course, and before him the medieval theologian William of Ockham, who has his own predecessors in Catholic philosophy and classical Greek thought, and who has contrived to surface more or less unannounced a number of times in the course of my writing this book. Ockham shares responsibility with other "progressive" theologians of the late Middle Ages for letting the genie of unfettered empiricism or materialism out of the bottle. Taking up the Positivist torch after Comte had died were the philosopher and economist John Stuart Mill and philosopher Herbert Spencer, as well as, I think it is fair to say, a majority of the inhabitants of industrialized nations, right down to our own period. We can safely assume that when it comes time to assign a suitable historical name reflective of the defining character of the era in which we currently live, it will be something like "the Age of Science" or perhaps "the Age of Fact," which would be a nice counterpoint to the Age of Faith, as we characterize the thousand years on the other side of the great watershed of the scientific, materialist revolution.

In the incense-scented coolness of the cathedral ambulatory, we had the great good fortune to be present for the last few minutes of a mass being performed before a small congregation seated in chairs before the magnificent gilded altar. A wonderful black contralto sang, her voice filling the vast space, magically warming and enriching it while the afternoon sunlight poured in through the vast stained-glass

¥ ¥ ¥

windows, painting the floor and columns of the nave in the subtlest of hues. How anyone, Parisian revolutionaries or anybody else, could sustain a strictly Positivist viewpoint in the face of such a sublime experience seemed a mystery to me as daunting as any in metaphysics.

We eventually found our way to the Orangerie and its splendid Impressionist collection, though we were too weary to do it justice. Simon was, as always, analytical in his interest, standing up close to the work, looking at brushstrokes and composition, seeking out allegorical messages. He seemed genuinely puzzled as to the popularity of some of the paintings on display, and his own reasons for liking them. He suspected there was a hidden meaning he could not see.

We were standing together in front of Claude Monet's *Argenteuil*, which depicts small sailboats moored in a little harbor under a dappled sky on a hot summer's day: "Does the fact that the two boats in the centre of the picture are red mean something?" he asked me.

"I think you're being too analytical. You should try just looking and being aware of the impressions it creates in you. A painting like this one is kind of like a joke; if you try too hard to analyze it, the meaning slips away from you."

"Well, you can certainly analyze a joke," he said. "What makes a joke funny is seeing somebody else in a difficult position. You laugh because you know you have a selective advantage over him and that makes you feel good because your genome is on top. Why else would people laugh at somebody slipping on a banana peel and falling down?"

I sighed.

He persisted:

"Why don't we get a big print of one of these Monets to go over the living-room sofa?"

We had had this discussion before. Back home, we had a big, blank wall which begged to be hung with art; from time to time we had rented large paintings from the Art Gallery of Ontario to fill the space. These were original works, costing far more to purchase than we could afford.

ϫ ϫ ϫ

"Why don't we, instead of renting second-rate originals, buy a print of a real masterpiece by a famous painter?"

"Simon, a print is a different thing altogether than an original. We don't particularly want to hang a print there. We'd rather leave it blank, or put up something original. One day your mother will paint something for that spot, if she can ever find the time."

"But that's ridiculous. Why should she spend all that time painting when she could be earning money with her business and then use that money to buy something by somebody who's a professional painter? It makes no sense."

I could see he was beginning to get hot under the collar.

"Look, Simon," I said, "you're just going to have to resign yourself to the fact that your parents are irrational beings. Its something all teenagers have to deal with. Meanwhile, look around you. You probably won't be back here for quite a while."

I walked into the next gallery, where I found Hilary staring out a window, looking impatient.

"Can we go?" she asked.

"What? You can't possibly have been through the whole building yet."

"Well, I have. I've seen all this stuff before, anyway. We took all of these guys in art history last year. Half of these paintings are in my text."

I was flabbergasted. "Yeah, but . . . these are the *originals!*" I heard myself say. The words sounded fatuous even as I uttered them.

"Dad, I already know what they look like. Can we go?"

"No, we can't." Now I was steamed. "You can wait for us in the gift shop if you want. And take your brother with you."

I strode through the last gallery on the main floor and found the staircase leading down to Monet's *Water Lilies* in the basement rotunda, where I found Chris standing in rapt admiration.

"This is wonderful," she said.

The paintings—really, cycloramas—had been done specifically

✗ ✗ ✗

for these two large, circular rooms in the basement of the gallery, and they were of the lilies covering the pond at the artist's famous garden in Giverny. The time of day changed as you turned and turned to look at the painting from one end to the other, and the light and color changed as well. We stood looking in silence for several minutes, first in one room, then in the other.

"Hilary wants to go," Chris said finally.

"I heard."

"Well, you can't really blame her. It's been a long day."

"But this is the bloody *Louvre*, for Christ's sake!"

"So? Unless you're here to study technique, it can be pretty boring if you already know the images. It's about as inspiring as a gene bank. They know this work, or at least they think they do. Isn't that what we encouraged them to take art for?"

"Well, are *you* enjoying it?" I asked, exasperated.

"Of course," she said, in a conditional way. "But when I look at some of these paintings what I think is, I could do this, if I only had the time. And I could, you know."

That last statement, made emphatically, was in response to a fleeting look of skepticism I'd been unable to suppress. She turned away from me and headed for the door.

This visit to the Orangerie was not turning out the way I'd hoped. By now I was completely confused and uncertain whether to be annoyed with myself or with everybody else. What I'd hoped to do was offer Hilary and Simon the same experience I'd had in discovering Impressionist painting almost thirty years earlier: first, Turner at the Tate in London, then the Jeu de Paume galleries at the Louvre and finally the museum of Spanish Impressionists in Barcelona. I had had no real opportunity to develop much of an interest in art until then, and the experience had been overwhelming for me: it changed my life. How? By helping me to understand that there are many possible ways of seeing the world. That in itself is a valuable lesson. But over the years I'd come to understand that at another level the

ɣ ɣ ɣ

Impressionists (and the Expressionists as well) had led me to the idea that reality is a dynamic creation jointly undertaken by our minds and our senses; that it is different for different people and it changes from moment to moment, from instant to instant. What I saw in Impressionist paintings was a snapshot not only of the scene being depicted, but of the interior of the mind of the painter in the exact moment of concretizing reality, and it was the latter aspect of the experience, I discovered, that so moved me. Impressionist painting comes closer to capturing the ephemeral, continuing process of making concrete reality of nature than any other painting ever has.

As an artist herself, I knew that Chris had a genuine appreciation of the work around us, but what about the kids? Had growing up in an image-saturated culture deadened their senses? Or was I wrong and Simon right? Maybe it was better, after all, to hang a print of a work by a great genius like Monet or Turner or van Gogh, than an original by a lesser talent. Maybe Hilary was right, that the essential value of the painting can be conveyed perfectly adequately by a reproduction in a text book. On the other hand, she sided with Chris and I and against Simon in the great Blank Space debate at home; she favored something original, even if it was 'merely' by her Mom. I suspected though, that this was because she, too, was an artist at heart, having inherited her mother's talent in that direction. What she'd really like to do is fill the space with her own work.

Be that as it may, the inescapable fact was that for all three of them, the "object value" of the works we'd seen did not impress. As I followed Chris up the marble stairs and back through the galleries to the front entrance of the gallery it hit me that this might be a good thing; that after all, maybe we had managed to raise a couple of kids who did not subscribe to consumer values, summed up so succinctly by Oscar Wilde as knowing "the price of everything and the value of nothing." Maybe they understood that the originals had been reproduced into virtual extinction. Maybe they'd avoided entrapment by the cult of object-worship. That perked me up.

¥ ¥ ¥

All I had to do now was figure a way to repair the damage I'd done in doubting Chris's ability to match Monet. Obviously she hadn't meant to be taken literally. All she'd done was express her frustration at never having time to paint. As we descended the broad stairway to Place de la Concorde I said, "When we get home I'll prime that big piece of Masonite in the basement and we'll figure a way to find you some time to paint. It's what you ought to be doing."

She offered me a conciliatory smile, half-ironic, half-defiant. "You'd better buy some lottery tickets, as well," she said.

Paris: Magritte's Puzzle

H O W   T O   T R A V E L   ✘   T H E   T R O U B L E

W I T H   L U X U R Y   ✘   H I L A R Y ' S   M I D N I G H T   W A L K   ✘

R E N É   M A G R I T T E   A N D   T H E   P A R A D O X E S   O F

P E R C E P T I O N   ✘   P L A T O   A N D   P R E - S C I E N T I F I C

R E A L I T Y   ✘   V I R T U A L   R E A L I T Y   A N D   T H E

M E D I E V A L S

From a pushcart vendor in Place de la Concorde, Chris bought a practical, wide-brimmed straw hat with an orange ribbon around the crown, which Simon and Hilary both found excruciatingly parental and dorky. But the price was fair and the quality was good, virtues we were to find in merchandise at major tourist sites throughout the country. I'm sure I embarrassed our kids in my own way, by wearing shorts and sandals, carrying a neon-blue nylon Eddie Bauer shoulder bag, and wearing my reading glasses on a tether around my neck so I could switch back and forth with my sunglasses; by constantly referring to my large-scale street map and Michelin Green Guide, and by pulling out my trusty, dog-eared copy of *The Taste of France* in every restaurant to decode

✘ ✘ ✘

the menu—though they did not explicitly say so. Perhaps they consider me beyond redemption.

I told them, "You have to understand, this is not the preferred way to travel. First of all, the minimum amount of time you should allow for a trip to Europe is not three weeks, but three months. It takes a full six weeks just to get acclimatized and begin to see things for what they are in themselves, rather than in contrast to what you're used to. That's when you begin to learn a thing or two."

"I could stay here for a *year*," said Hilary.

"Think of this as a survey course. When you come back on your own, find some place cheap to stay, find some inexpensive places to eat, or, better yet, shop in the markets and make your own meals, and stay a few weeks. Then you'll get to know the city properly. And you won't need a map and you won't have to lug around all this paraphernalia."

Never one to accept advice without an argument, Hilary responded, "Oh *sure*, Dad. Camp out in some fleabag and live on *gruel* for months. What*ever!* Give me the Hotel Vigny every time." My heart sank a little.

For as many years as we had been traveling together, there had been this identical tension between Chris and me, resolved in each case by my total capitulation. I had always felt uncomfortable travelling first class, but had never been able to explain why, hence my meek concession to her common sense approach: if it's offered, accept. It seemed to me that the least expensive modes of transport and accommodation provided the most authentic and therefore the most valuable experience of a place. Chris, on the other hand, reveled in luxury, provided only that everything was done with taste. I suspected that the sedan chair would have been her preferred method of locomotion, if it had been available to us; stout hiking boots or a bicycle were more in my line. It has always been like that with us, which is one of the reasons we make such good mates: together, we lick life's platter clean.

ɤ ɤ ɤ

Now seeing Hilary and, I suspected, Simon, picking up on Chris's position, I was forced to confront my own squeamishness afresh. It was a problem, of course, only because I had a choice: my publishing résumé and Chris's photography portfolio allowed us to make pretty well any arrangements for a trip we fancied. This journey was a case in point, though in truth the response I'd had from Relais and Châteaux hotels exceeded our wildest dreams. I'd suggested a night or two's accommodation at a reduced press rate; they had replied with the offer of meals and hotel rooms covering virtually the entire stay in France. These were the crème de la crème of the country's small hotels and restaurants. At first I shared Chris' astonished glee, but then the old question reared its head: Did I really deserve this? Worse, I now had to worry about my children: Was it good for Hilary and Simon to be exposed to this kind of luxury, and on their first trip to Europe? Did *they* deserve it? Would it warp them forever? I consoled myself with the thought that this would not be pointless opulence on the Las Vegas model. Relais and Châteaux existed now, as it had from its inception with the rise of automobile tourism in France, to provide solid comfort and good local food in authentic surroundings. Hence most of the hotels and restaurants were in converted mills, ancient hostelries, roadhouses, châteaux and other pre-existing buildings typical of their environs, and the menus were heavily weighted in favor of regional specialities. Maybe, I thought, the kids would even learn a thing or two about the meaning of quality from staying in these places.

Still, it bothered me that I could not fathom my discomfort. Chris put it down to Prairie puritanism which I'd brought with me, sewn into the lining of my coat, when I'd moved from Winnipeg to Toronto in my youth. It was a regional affliction which she liked to characterize, when in a provocative mood, as a noxious amalgam of seething envy and low self-esteem. But I was pretty sure it was not that. In any case I had decided long ago that if I could not understand, I would simply deal with it—hardly an unpleasant prospect—by enjoying myself as best I could. After all, I reasoned, what is provided at these places is a form of art—the art of hospitality and the art of cuisine—and art exists to be appreciated by those who are able. My solution, then, had been to study both cuisine and finer points of hospitality in the French tradition, so as to make of myself a worthy patron. I learned to cook from a Paul Bocuse cookbook, and read the critics: Brillat-Savarin and Curnonsky and Saulnier and Waverley Root and M. F. K. Fisher. I interviewed, with Chris, Paul Bocuse, Alain Chapel, Raymond Thulier, Claude Terrail and other leading lights of French cuisine, not to mention many fine hoteliers. It has not been an entirely satisfactory response, but it provides a *modus vivendi*, and I continue to hope that one day the scales will fall from my eyes and I will see that I am perfectly entitled to partake of the best this planet has to offer, simply by virtue of being a resident. In the meantime I suffer along. . . .

After the Orangerie, it was the Left Bank and the Marais and dinner alfresco and more walking and we dragged ourselves back to the hotel shortly before midnight, footsore and sunburned. Chris and I were getting ready for bed when Hilary knocked on our door. She was still dressed in her street clothes.

"I'm going for a walk on the Champs-Elysées," she said. I noticed she had refreshed her makeup.

I will spare my readers the dialogue that ensued (parents among you will be able to imagine it), except to report that at first we vetoed the idea, then insisted that Simon go along (she would not have it) and finally said, "Okay, but be back within the hour." This last demand she agreed to. Were we weak? Irresponsible? Both, it seemed to us during the subsequent hour of acute anxiety, during which I reassured Chris that she would be perfectly safe on a brightly lit, crowded thoroughfare, though neither of us believed it for a moment. Had we not seen the saturnine looks on those hirsute, earringed faces? We concluded this was exactly the wrong age to take kids abroad: they were too old to obey arbitrary rules but too young to understand the dangers the rules were designed to help them avoid.

⚥ ⚥ ⚥

Any younger, though, and they would not appreciate what they were seeing: it's a Catch 22, like most of life.

But Paris is not New York. Exactly on the hour there was a knock on the door and Hilary was there, safe and sound, eyes shining, bubbling over about how *magnificent* everything was and how she'd met four of the *nicest* guys who'd stopped her to ask for a light and how another pair had asked her to pose for a photograph with them (I had to admire their ingenuity) and how she'd talked to them for the *longest* time even though they had trouble with her French and how they'd invited her to a party in Versailles, but she'd said she had to get back to the hotel. "People here are *so nice*," she concluded with an ecstatic sigh. Chris and I rolled into bed, exhausted.

Hanging beside the bed in our room at the hotel on rue Balzac was a framed print of a famous painting by the French surrealist René Magritte. It is a meticulously realistic rendering of an ordinary briar pipe, underneath which is written in a precise, schoolroom hand, "*Ceci n'est pas une pipe*" (This is not a pipe). That was the last thing I saw before I switched off the lights, and the image floated before my closed eyes as I lay there, thinking back over the day. It dawned on me in those moments between wakefulness and sleep that there was a deep connection between the painting and that other work of art, Notre-Dame de Paris. And, yes, there was a connection between the painting and the man with no nose, as well! I thought of rolling over to let Chris in on my discovery. And then I was asleep.

Magritte created several versions of the pipe paradox, one as late as 1966. In this most recent one, the framed painting of the pipe with its underlining script is sitting on an easel, which is in turn standing on a rough wooden-plank floor. Behind this is a blank wall. Floating, suspended in space just behind and to the left of the framed painting is a very large version of the pipe in the framed painting on the easel. The work is called *Les Deux Mystères* (*The Two Mysteries*). Magritte thought of himself as much as a writer as a painter; a thinker who expressed himself on canvas. And in these pipe paintings, and many others, he addressed what may be the central philosophical problem of our millennium, the distinction between the subjective and the objective, and the tension that distinction creates. In another of his paintings, *Personnage marchant vers l'horizon*, a man in a fedora and overcoat is seen walking towards a dark, irregularly-shaped object on which is written the word *"horizon."* Over his head is another dark object bearing the word *"nuage"* (cloud) and near him on the ground are amorphous shapes marked *"fusil"* (gun), *"fauteuil"* (armchair) and *"cheval"* (horse).

Magritte is exploring in a characteristically playful way the profound question of the relationship between man and the material world, a puzzle that is as old as cave painting and as current as quantum physics. In *Ceci n'est pas une pipe*, he presents the modern position that words, which are the symbols we use to represent material things, have no real connection with the things themselves; that is, words are stand-alone entities, entirely separate from the things they name just as the painted pipe is distinct and separate from the real object it represents. The word "pipe" is not the thing itself, nor is the painted image the real object it represents. (Hence, "This is not a pipe.") In *Personnage marchant vers l'horizon*, he seems to be suggesting the opposite, that there is an identity between the word-symbols we use to identify objects and the objects themselves. Since the symbols are human constructs, there is suggested in the painting a linkage between our consciousness and the existence of objects in the material world. If the symbol and object are somehow dependent on one another for their existence, then the material world is in some way dependent for its existence on human consciousness.

The painting *Les Deux Mystères* appears to be taking yet another position on the issue, one expounded by Plato who believed that there is, on the "far side" of objects as we perceive them, an ideal form of those objects. True knowledge or wisdom is available only through an understanding of those ideal forms, and that understanding is available only to the intellect—in other words not via the

ﭼ ﭼ ﭼ

senses. Sensory information, in fact, was deemed by Plato to be mis-leading and distracting. He created a hierarchy of knowledge: the unreliable sort available to the senses; a slightly more respectable sort derived through the mathematical abstraction of the material world, as in geometry; and ultimate knowledge accessible directly by the intellect through contemplation. The big pipe in the background of *Les Deux Mystères* could be taken to be Plato's ideal form of "pipe," as it relates to the symbolic representation of the actual object in the framed painting.

As unlikely as it may seem, these three forms of knowledge, or ways of knowing the material world, have had a transcendent impor-tance in the history of Western civilization.

The thought of Plato was absorbed into the Christian theology and philosophy that dominated Western thought for the first fifteen hundred years anno Domini and profoundly affected the Church. But in one area there had always been fundamental agreement between the great Greek thinkers and the Church fathers, and that was the necessary involvement of human consciousness in the exis-tence of the material world. One way in which the idea expressed itself was that the world was made up of tiny, uniform, indestruc-tible particles—"atoms" they were called. The question was, how do these undifferentiated particles, which, as we now know, exist at vast distances from one another, come to represent a real object such as a chair or a book or a mountain? What is it that confers on them their familiar forms with their familiar solidity, shapes, tastes and smells? One could say that God is responsible for doing this, but that would be too easy an answer, and far from convincing.

The more satisfying answer worked out by the Greeks and accepted from that point onward as being essentially correct is that the material world exists, or rather comes into existence, through the interaction of our senses and minds—in a word, our conscious-ness—with the agglomerations of particles. There are many varia-tions and shades of interpretation of this basic theme, but in essence

ϒ ϒ ϒ

they suggest that people come to agree on the naming of what it is they perceive with their senses as interpreted by their minds, and in so doing they "create," or, better—actualize—the world around them, a world that in the absence of their consciousness exists only as masses of identical particles, swarming in a kind of limbo of potential, or *in potentia*. Once perceived, objects have a life or vitality that is derived from (or shared with) the perceiver who confers on them their "reality." This vital connection is absent to the modern eye but it was a matter of common sense to our ancestors, right up until the dawn of the scientific era in the sixteenth century, and in most segments of society, long beyond that. To pre-scientific minds, the literal and the physical were not what they are to us; instead, they carried with them the kind of multiple significance we find today only in symbols, in rituals and in surrealist paintings.

For the Neoplatonists, the Greek thinkers whose system of ideas contributed most directly to the foundation philosophy of Christianity, intellectual comprehension was a function of the soul and it was therefore important to regulate the kinds of things that occupied one's interest. Because the soul participated or, in a sense, mingled with the object being perceived, it was affected and shaped in the transaction. Hence, these pre-Christian philosophers warned against too much time spent indulging idle curiosity about the material world, lest the soul be separated irredeemably from its natural home in the world-soul or, in other words, in God. This theme would be carried over into the philosophy of medieval Catholicism, and expressed in a wariness (though never a prohibition) of science, as an unworthy, slightly sordid enterprise.

As a user and observer of modern communications technologies, I found it of no small interest to consider the fact that the medieval people who subscribed to this transactional view of reality would have had little trouble in dealing with the currently voguish issue of virtual reality in digital, multimedia environments. At what stage of sophistication, today's thinkers are asking, does a virtual environment in cyberspace become a "world" on its own? If I were able, at some time in the future, to take a trip to France entirely through virtual reality technologies, without having to leave my study, what would be the essential difference between that experience and real-life travel? What are we to think of digital avatars created by Internet users to represent themselves in virtual environments online? What is their essential connection with their creators? Virtual reality, the darling concept of late twentieth-century philosophers of science and technology and the subject of a growing library of books, papers, monographs and science fiction novels, would have held few mysteries for medieval thinkers, since all reality was understood by them to be "virtual," and they were able to draw on a thousand years and more of concentrated philosophical inquiry into exactly what that implied. They would have found laughable, attempts to demonstrate that digitally produced "virtual reality" was in some way a profound invention or experience. To the medieval thinker, today's virtual reality creations, however cunningly they mimic the processes of transactional reality in the real world, could be no more than toys and amusements, or at best tools, because they are entirely the creations of man. True reality, though "virtual" in the sense that it exists *in potentia* in the absence of consciousness, is a direct depiction of the mind of God. To have confused the virtual and the real would have been clear evidence of stupidity, or worse, blasphemy, which was treated as a kind of intellectual vandalism.

⅄ ⅄ ⅄

Seeing and Knowing

A PRAIRIE MIRAGE ❧ HOW PRIMITIVE PEOPLE

SEE ❧ WHAT THE ANCIENTS SAW ❧ THE

MEDIEVAL VISION ❧ TRANSACTIONAL REALITY

❧ REALITY AND INFORMATION

O n a country picnic one hot summer's day many years ago I saw the far-off city of Regina replicated in the shimmering prairie sky, so clearly that I could pick out individual buildings. It seemed palpably real but, as a mirage, it existed only so long as I or someone else looked at it: it required my eyes, working in concert with the interpretive faculties of my mind, to make it "the city of Regina" in phantasm. I didn't know it at the time, but for a thousand years, the acutest intellects on the planet had believed that an analogous process occurs in the perception of material objects of a more substantial kind. They subscribed to this participatory, "transactional" view of reality not as a theory or doctrine, but as an accurate and commonsensical description of how the material world worked. They took for granted an organic unity between man and nature, the one an integral aspect of the existence of the other; each, in a sense, a creation of the other.

❧ ❧ ❧

It seems a far-fetched notion today, but modern anthropology confirms that our ancestors saw the world and their place in it in essentially this active, participatory way. There had been a time when historians thought of early man as having had basically our own essential consciousness and mental makeup. That changed with the writings of Émile Durkheim and Lucien Lévy-Bruhl, who recognized that so-called primitives and, thus, presumably our own ancestors,

> see with eyes like ours, but they do not perceive with the same minds. . . . It is not correct to maintain, as is frequently done, that primitives associate occult powers, magic properties, a kind of soul or vital principle with all the objects which affect their senses or strike the imagination, and that their perceptions are surcharged with animistic beliefs. It is not a question of *association*. The mystic [or animate] properties with which things are imbued form an integral part of the idea to the primitive who views it as a synthetic whole. It is at a later stage of evolution that what we call a natural phenomenon tends to become the sole content of perception to the exclusion of other elements which then assume the aspect of beliefs, and finally appear [as] superstitions. But as long as this "dissociation" does not take place, perception remains an undifferentiated whole.[1]

The importance of the metaphysical implications of the transactional view of reality that served our ancestors for so long would be difficult to exaggerate. In the philosophy of the Catholic church as influenced by Plato, ideal forms on "the other side" of material reality were divine, were in some sense the mind or thought of God. And so, for the Church, the mind of both God and man played essential roles in the actualizing of reality out of potential. Material objects owed their character to both their ideal forms and to man's collective representations of them, his agreed-upon naming of them. St. Thomas Aquinas said in the thirteenth century, "Nothing is known

ℵ ℵ ℵ

except truth, which is the same as being." Nearly a thousand years earlier another churchman, John Scotus Erigena, had said the same thing in different words: "The knowledge of things that are, *is* the things." Knowledge, in other words, was a stage on the journey back to union with God. God's own knowledge was the cause of all things.

For medieval civilization, then, there was a continuum of inter-dependent existence from the world of material objects through man to God. In such a hierarchy the role of God was plain: God was the ultimate or final cause, the goal, the supreme good, the end to which all means were directed. It was also clear that man participated in the being of God, and it was that participation that gave him his own existence. Thus, in both metaphorical and very concrete senses, man was at the center of the universe.

For nearly two thousand years the Catholic church fought a deter-mined and at times bloody rearguard action aimed at preserving this basic metaphysical and epistemological schema—this description of the workings of the universe and of how we can know the things that are in it—a battle waged with differing degrees of success against a wide variety of heretical, alternative views. After our own millennium's midpoint (following Galileo and the scientific revolution), most of the crucial battles were lost. However in the twelfth and thirteenth centuries when great cathedrals like Notre-Dame de Paris were being built, this view of the world was still very much the dominant blueprint for reality throughout Europe. (A similar view prevailed throughout the East as well, and in North American Indian cultures, and in fact still does, but that is another story.) People, individuals, actively shared in the existence of the world around them: they were not entirely sep-arate and distinct from it—they participated in its existence at a very fundamental level, so fundamental in fact that they seldom gave it a second thought. But that participation gave them a sense of belong-ing and of security. And it conferred on them a certain creative power unknown in our day, since all that was required for a thing's existence was general agreement on the fact among sane and sober people.

ϗ ϗ ϗ

That, after all, was why chairs and trees and bees and horses existed, through collective representations. And so angels could have a real existence as well. It was a time of miracles.

It follows that for these medieval people the great cathedral of Notre-Dame de Paris was not what it is for us. It was not simply an object, a pile of stone and glass artfully arranged. It was that, and much more: it was an extension of their collective existence as humans, or, perhaps, a *projection* of their being; a reaching up to God by man and a simultaneous reaching down to man by God, as in Michelangelo's *Creation of Adam* in the Sistine Chapel. Men and women wore it, as they did all of the material world, like a cloak, like their very skin. Above all, they were a part of it and it exalted their existence, in ways most of us can no longer even imagine.

The transactional view of reality—reality as a kind of negotiation between consciousness and undifferentiated matter—was one that had a great deal of appeal for me, for a couple of reasons. First, because it seemed to confirm itself so frequently on trips like this one: the Paris I was seeing now was quite remarkably different from the Paris I had seen during previous visits. The very dimensions of the place had changed, as had its colors and textures and smells. Quite clearly, what had changed was not the city itself—the Eiffel Tower and Place de la Concorde and the Boulevard St. Germain were the same as they'd always been in terms of their physical characteristics— what had changed was my consciousness, the element I brought to the creation of reality. I was older, I had experienced many new things in the intervening years. Paris had changed for me in exactly the same way as everyone's childhood haunts will change, should they move away and then return. It is a fact that "you can't go home again," though home may still be there in some sense—still there *in potentia*—because consciousness changes and the reality it creates must change with it.

There was another, very different reason why the transactional view made sense to me. As someone who is interested in the theory and philosophy behind communications technologies, it seemed to me that there was a more modern but directly analogous way to express the basic idea Aquinas and John Scotus Erigena had had about reality: "Nothing is known except truth, which is the same as being," and "The knowledge of things that are, *is* the things." A modern communications theorist might say instead: *The reality of a thing is bound up in the information it contains.* This would amend Aquinas to: "Nothing is known except information, which is the same as being." Scotus Erigena would now read, "The information contained within things that are, *is* the things." Would either of these venerable thinkers object to this transliteration? I suspect not, given that throughout this century experimental physicists have been increasingly of the opinion that what they have traditionally called both "energy" and "matter" (which are of course interchangeable), and what is now understood by "information," are one and the same thing. A late twentieth-century physicist might well be heard to say, for example, that information is what it takes to eliminate entropy.

To my ear, that last sentence has an evocative ring because information, according to the famous theorem of Claude Shannon, founder of the science of information theory, is "the elimination of uncertainty." The best way to explain that basic idea is with a well-known word game, in which missing letters in words and phrases must be guessed. If I tell you that the missing letter in "une_plained" is x, then I probably haven't given you any information because you already knew that. However, if I tell you that the missing letters in "af_ _ _ _ _on" are f-l-i-c-t-i, then I will have given you information because I have, with each newly revealed letter, progressively eliminated your uncertainty as to the hidden meaning. Probably, the information content of the last one or two letters will be close to zero in this case as well.

Shannon's theorem places information in a solidly human context, for only intelligence can recognize whether or not uncertainty has been eliminated, and uncertainty is a thoroughly intellectual concept.

¥ ¥ ¥

If, then, the reality of a thing *is* its information content, that reality depends on the presence of intelligence. In fact, just as the ancients suspected, reality is a transactional affair involving both the raw data of our natural surroundings and the consciousness we bring to bear upon it. Or, put it another way: reality cannot be contained entirely in the objective world of "things." It can exist only in the presence of consciousness. There is no such thing as purely "objective" reality.

Admit that, and the rest of the medieval worldview, the hierarchy involving God and man, begins to make some sense in a modern context. Information, of course, remains every bit as ineffable an entity as grace or love or *ch'i*, but for science it is apparently a more culturally acceptable mystery. So be it.

CHAPTER 6

Chartres, Vouvray and Loches: The Maid of Orléans

VERSAILLES ⚸ THE LESSONS OF CHARTRES ⚸
THE ICONOCLASTIC CONTROVERSY ⚸
AN EMERGENCY AND ITS LESSON ⚸ A NIGHT
IN A CAVE ⚸ LOCHES ⚸ BARBARISM IN AN AGE
OF FAITH ⚸ ST. JOAN'S STORY ⚸ AN ALLEGORY
FOR CHANGE ⚸ REALITY AND HISTORY ⚸ THE
MYSTERY OF PREHISTORY ⚸ THE TURING TEST

S unday morning Hilary and I were up early in the buttercup
sunshine while our roommates slept, to walk along the
scrubbed and all-but-deserted Champs-Elysées, around the
Arc de Triomphe and up Avenue de la Grande Armée into
the wonderfully humane and elegant residential quarter of putty-
colored stone apartment buildings and tree-lined streets where our

⚸ ⚸ ⚸

rental car was waiting. Along the way she skipped a few steps, hugged herself, hugged me and said, "Oh, I have *sooo* always wanted to go to Paris!" I had the strong impression that her happiness was enriching my life not just in the present moment, but retroactively as well. In her joy was reward for the pains and anxieties of seventeen years of parenthood, and justification as well.

By mid-morning, having figured out, at the expense of no small effort on our part, and with copious advice from several of the Hôtel de Vigny staff how to respond to the car's extended repertoire of digital voice prompts (all in mellifluous female French), we were rolling through the wheat fields west of Paris en route to Chartres, having made a short stop at Versailles, which we knew would be clogged with visitors at this time of the year but was nonetheless impossible to pass up. As it turned out it was worse than we had anticipated, with hour-long lineups to get inside the palace (we demurred), crowd-control barriers fencing off the topiary gardens and an appalling odor of rotting algae wafting from the spectacular fountains and reflecting pools. You could have fried eggs on the cobbles in the vast court-yard. Simon and Hilary were duly impressed, most of all by the thought that the cost of its construction had impoverished all of France and helped to foment the Revolution: for myself, its unrelenting opulence had always seemed depressing and ultimately banal. The stench in our nostrils might have been the stink of totalitarianism. There is nothing here to fire the spirit; it was designed merely to overwhelm. The trenchant Blue Guide to France, always delightfully frank, quotes Richard Ford: "Nothing is more tiresome than a palace, a house of velvet, tapestry, gold and bore. . . ."

But Chartres . . . Chartres is another story.

We began catching tantalizing glimpses of the cathedral spires across a featureless sea of golden grain half an hour before we arrived at the town that nestles in the valley of the languid Eure at a spot considered sacred by the Romans, and the Druids before them. We parked the car in the shade of a plane tree on the riverbank below the

ꭗ ꭗ ꭗ

escarpment and crossed an old wooden footbridge to where the long, long winding series of stone ramps and staircases leads to the cathedral square. In the river, hardly more than a stream here tamed by cut-stone embankments, there was a fleet of whimsical floating sculptures made of brightly-painted Styrofoam packing material.

"There's art everywhere in this country," Simon exclaimed, "even in the creeks!" Hilary snapped a picture.

In the eleventh century, 1,587 churches were built in France in an outburst of millennial enthusiasm. A hundred years later, when Chartres was begun, the pace of construction had slowed—500 great French churches were built between 1170 and 1270—but the style of architecture had evolved from the down-to-earth solidity of the Romanesque to the breathtaking scale and eggshell fragility of the Gothic. The pointed Gothic arch, derided at first as barbaric (hence, "of the Goths"), by its inherent mechanical strength allowed architects to express their vision on an ever more striking scale. Flying buttresses supported impossibly high ceilings, and walls, freed of their roles as supports, could be devoted almost entirely to windows of stained glass, multistoried murals in light. None are more wonderful than those of Notre-Dame de Chartres, and of these, 176 in all, the three circular rose windows are the very finest of all, and the most exquisite of these is the thirty-three-foot diameter Rose of France high up in the west façade. Chartres is an irreplaceable treasure enclosing even richer jewels.

It would take days to even begin to fully appreciate Chartres. Like most visitors, we spent an hour gazing at the exterior from various angles, admiring the profusion of sculpture spanning the styles from early to late Gothic. By then Hilary and Simon were unable to restrain their curiosity about what they would find inside, and neither were Chris and I; the only other time we'd been here it had been raining and the windows were not at their best.

We entered through the west doors to find ourselves in a cool, serene and graceful space like none other on the planet, 470 feet from end to end, the ribbed vaults of the stone ceilings 123 feet high, a row of massive, fluted stone pillars along either aisle to support the roof, and the most amazing light playing on the grey stone, flooding in through acres of stained glass under the early afternoon August sun. In its engineering sophistication, its transcendent artistry, its restraint and exuberance, it seemed to me a distillation of the human spirit at its most exalted. We walked part way up the aisle and turned to see the Rose of France in its full glory, delicate as a snowflake. Chartres is justly famous for its glass, most of which is original; the blues of the Rose of France and other windows are so extraordinary that they have come to identify an artist's color called "Chartres blue." Looking at those windows in the slowly changing light of an afternoon, you realize that stained glass artists are really painters— painters in light. As the sun moves across the sky, as it is obscured by cloud, or turns red at sunset, the windows change, and the way they paint the stone of the cathedral interior changes as well, from warm and brilliant to cool and somber, with an infinite variety of tonalities between. The effect achieved by a "painting" in stained glass— you could almost say, the painting itself—is created by a transaction between the sun and the glass, and is in this way a collaborative creation of the artist and nature. It would be difficult to imagine a more appropriate art form for a society which viewed all reality as a similar collaboration, between matter and consciousness, between spirit and nature, between the minds of men and the mind of God.

We drifted apart to wander, running into one another every few minutes to exchange notes. Simon sat quietly in a pew looking up to where a tiny lens in one of the windows high above was focusing a laser-like beam of pure, white light the size of a saucer on the polished stone floor. I found Chris looking at a display of photographs showing how the windows had been painstakingly removed for safekeeping during World War One. I put a coin in a box and lit a taper in one of the side chapels, hedging my bets. I found Hilary photographing the crowd of sculptures depicting biblical stories, around the Renaissance choir screen.

✗ ✗ ✗

"Look at all the statues!" she whispered. "There must be hundreds of them. There is so much art in here. When I think of Grandma and Grandpa's church in North Carolina . . . it's just a bare room with pews in it. I mean, they go out of their way to avoid decorating it."

"That's a very old argument in the Church," I replied, *sotto voce*, "whether art that depicts religious themes and especially people is a good thing or not. It's called the iconoclasm controversy. For a while, during the late Roman Empire, all religious art was made illegal and people called iconoclasts went around smashing religious objects. The fear was that a statue of a saint, for example, might be worshiped as a holy object in itself, rather than as a representation of the actual saint, and that would amount to idol worship, or the worship of icons, which is forbidden in the Bible."

"They would worship the statue or whatever as a kind of god?"

"That was the concern. In the end, the Church decided that on balance it was better to have the art than not, because of its educational and inspirational value. And there was another, less obvious benefit as well: all of these statues, all of this art, helps to reinforce the principle that the divine is not remote from this world, but is part of everyday life. That was one of the important ideas that made Christianity different from earlier, pagan religions that involved secret knowledge and rituals and gods that were indifferent to humans and their problems."

"It's good that the iconoclasts lost," she said.

"I agree."

"Because, just think of it, even without the sculpture and the paintings of saints and everything, this building itself would still be an incredible work of religious art. Wouldn't they have objected to that as well? They'd probably have torn it down."

"I imagine they would have. Fortunately the construction of cathedrals didn't get under way on a large scale until well after the controversy had been resolved."

⅄ ⅄ ⅄

We parted company and continued to wander on our own. This was a place that invited solitary contemplation.

The abbot of St. Denis, in what is now a Paris suburb, wrote a detailed account of how the abbey church was restored in the revolutionary Gothic style only a decade before Chartres was begun. His description of his feelings on entering the newly consecrated building in 1137 ring true down through the ages:

> I seemed to find myself, as it were, in some strange part of the universe which was neither wholly of the baseness of the earth, nor wholly of the serenity of heaven, but by the grace of God I seemed lifted in a mystic manner from this lower towards that upper sphere.

As amazing as the building is, Chartres struck me as even more moving in what it said about the society that had built it. For one thing, none of the thousands of sculptures that grace its exterior and interior is signed, nor are the windows. We do not even know the name of the architect. Notre-Dame de Chartres was built before the notion of authorship had put down roots in Europe, something that would come only much later with the enthusiastic embracing of individualism in the Renaissance. And so this most magnificent of structures was raised up in just twenty-five years to the glory of God by people who attached none of their individual ego to it, who had no apparent wish to take credit. Remarkable, as well, is the fact that the project was undertaken by a town of just ten thousand souls, barely big enough today to support a shopping mall. The sense of community in those days must have been extraordinary. The bishop of Rouen wrote of the construction of Chartres in a letter to the bishop of Amiens:

> The inhabitants of Chartres have combined to aid in the construction of their church by transporting the materials . . . the faithful of our diocese and of other neighboring regions have formed associations for the same object; they admit no one into their company unless

he has been to confession, has renounced enmities and revenges, and has reconciled himself with his enemies. That done, they elect a chief, under whose direction they conduct their wagons in silence and with humility.

It would be a mistake to think of the fruits of their labor as being enjoyed only at Sunday mass in awed silence: Chartres and the other great cathedrals of the era were community meeting places as well as places of worship. Merchants set up stalls in the church precincts, travelers were allowed to sleep there overnight and the locals strolled up and down the side aisles engaged in small talk with their friends and neighbors. Often they would have their dogs with them. On the steps and in the square, morality plays were acted and town assemblies were held. The cathedral was, for the men and women who built it, not an object, a thing separate from themselves to be looked upon and admired, but rather a part of themselves, and it was the most natural thing in the world for them to feel at home in it.

We had lunch in a crêperie across the square and down a crooked alleyway from the cathedral and were soon on our way again, driving south towards Tours where we planned to spend the night, and soon Hilary was complaining of an upset stomach, and then complaining more. It was urgent that we find a place to stop; we were on the outskirts of Tours by now, and finally I spotted a McDonald's and wheeled into the sun-baked parking lot with squealing tires. Hilary and her mom were out the door before I could turn off the ignition. They knew where to find the washrooms because the building was exactly the same as a McDonald's anywhere in North America. Then Simon suddenly bolted for the building, leaving me alone to wait and play with the car's digital radio, whose LED screen, I discovered, told me not only the station frequency, but also its name and the kind of programming it carried. In time, the three of them returned looking much relieved. Simon reported he had been "in agony" since leaving Chartres an hour and a half earlier, just like Hilary.

ꙮ ꙮ ꙮ

"Then why on earth didn't you say something?" I asked.

Chris turned around to look at him: "Well?"

"Well, because there was nothing that could be done about it and so it would have been just whining."

I felt a sudden, helpless irritation. Where do kids get these ideas? Am I such an ogre? I cheered up, though, as we drove out of the parking lot and the golden arches shrank in my rearview mirror, and I realized that we had put the place to the only use it's fit for. We all had a laugh over that.

"Can you imagine," Hilary said, "building a McDonald's in France, of all places!" She was getting the idea.

Her mother, ever practical, observed, "It's a good thing somebody did."

Near Tours, in the village of Vouvray, we stayed the night in a hotel whose rooms and façade are carved out of the limestone banks of the River Loire, as are many fine homes in this region. As we prepared for bed I was tempted to ask Chris whether she'd ever (before she met me, of course) had the pleasure of spending the night in a cave with a naked man, but experience made me think better of it. I just counted myself lucky that I was the man spending this particular night in a cave with her.

The following day we continued south through the Loire château region towards the Dordogne. We were now just a few miles from the tiny village of Descartes, which I had hoped to at least drive through, but there was no time if we were to have a good look at the castle of Loches, which was next on our agenda: such is the life of the author as family man. We were in Joan of Arc country and I wanted Hilary and Simon to see at least one place where the Maid of Orléans had lived and acted out her destiny, and in that way resurrect her for them. As for Descartes, I suspected that it might figure in what I would have to say about this trip, but was uncertain enough to let myself be persuaded by majority vote to roll on south. It is named for its most famous citizen, René Descartes (1596–1650) whom we

ᛉ ᛉ ᛉ

have already encountered, and who was born there, and baptized in the town church. The Blue Guide calls the church "interesting"—a rave from that parsimonious book.

Descartes, the village, thus avoided, we had a long lunchtime stopover in the walled town of Loches, an important strategic settlement in the Hundred Years War that laid waste to so much of this region of France. The fortress that dominates the town was captured in a lightning attack by Richard the Lion Heart in 1194, shortly after he was ransomed; it later became an infamous prison in which enemies of Louis XI were entombed like rats in suspended cages of wood and wrought iron, just six feet high and wide. Cardinal Jean Balue, who is said to have been the inventor of the cages, found himself occupying one for eleven years after his plottings against the king were uncovered: a replica is on display outside the castle.

It was a puzzle to Hilary and Simon how the well-known cruelties of medieval times squared with the other striking aspect of this Age of Faith, its ubiquitous and ever-present Christian spirituality.

"You mean they actually put people in this? How could they do that?" Hilary said.

Simon was ready at the draw: "What do you mean, 'How could they?' Religion has been responsible for more wars and killings than anything else in history. Just look at the Crusades!"

"Hold on a minute," I interrupted. "First of all it wasn't the Church putting people in these cages, it was the local lord, the civilian authority. I grant you that the Church did even worse in the Inquisition, but that's a special case. It's not their natural instinct by any means. And to say that religion causes wars and to then use that as an argument against religion makes about as much sense as saying that politics is responsible for wars and so politics should be abolished as well. Religion was at the very center of peoples' lives all through the Middle Ages, so of course it was mixed up in their wars and squabbles. It was a part of everything else they did, as well."

"We don't want to throw out the baby with the bathwater, do we, Simon?" said Chris.

Still, the barbarisms of the era puzzled me as well. Historians past, though few of our own pragmatic time, have called the eleventh and twelfth centuries in Europe the highest summit to which Western civilization has yet succeeded. Will Durant, writing in the post-traumatic years following the Second World War, said that in order to understand the Middle Ages we must

> enter sympathetically into the world of men disillusioned . . . finding all dreams of utopia shattered by war and poverty and barbarism, seeking consolation in the hope of happiness beyond the grave, inspired and comforted by the story and figure of Christ, throwing themselves upon the mercy and goodness of God, and living in the thought of His eternal presence, His inescapable judgment and the atoning death of His son. . . . They had had Stoics long enough; they had seen the masculine virtues incarnadine [redden] half the world. They longed for gentler, quieter ways, by which men might be persuaded to live in stability and peace. For the first time in European history the teachers of mankind preached an ethic of kindness, obedience, humility, patience, mercy, purity, chastity and tenderness.

In a passage that movingly reflects the contemporary despondency at the recent carnage in Europe, the Holocaust, the atomic bombing of Hiroshima and Nagasaki, he continued:

> Not till wealth and pride should return in the Renaissance would reason reject faith, and abandon heaven for utopia. But if, thereafter, reason should fail, and science should find no answers, but should multiply knowledge and power without improving conscience or purpose; if all utopias should brutally collapse in the changeless abuse of the weak by the strong: then men would understand why once their

ϗ ϗ ϗ

ancestors, in the barbarism of those early Christian centuries, turned from science, knowledge, power and pride, and took refuge for a thousand years in humble faith, hope and charity.[1]

All of this is true in its way, and no one who studies the period can fail to be impressed by the strength and universality of the commitment to the values of the Catholic church throughout Christendom. And yet, we have the cages of Loches, the rack and the stake and a hundred other monstrosities. Nor was their use confined to the laity; the Church from the mid-thirteenth century onward employed torture under papal sanction, though not without serious misgivings and only in the pursuit of heretics, who were considered to be the agents of the Devil. How did this fit with an ethic of kindliness, mercy and charity? It is a question vast armies of scholarly adversaries and apologists have tried to answer on behalf of the Church; my own rather prosaic suspicion was that the answer lay in justification of means by their ends, which is the seductive, and fatal, rationale of the fanatic, and at the same time a defining feature of modernism in its embrace of instrumental reason. But I am getting ahead of my story.

At Loches, I was anxious for Hilary and Simon to see, especially, the great tapestry-hung hall and the adjoining royal chambers where in 1429, following her famous victory over the English at Orléans, Joan of Arc met with the timid crown prince Charles and urged him to continue the fight to expel the English from France. There is in this broad stone room with its dark-timbered ceiling a copy of the great transcription of Joan's trial at the hands of the bishop of Beauvais acting at the behest of the English. Few tales from history are more baffling to a modern reader, nor at the same time more expressive of medieval thought and values, from the simple piety of Joan to the convoluted and ultimately corrupt sophistry of her inquisitors and executioners. Perhaps most inexplicable of all to the modern reader is the plain fact that almost no one doubted her supernatural inspiration: the English believed she was a witch; the French believed

ꙏ ꙏ ꙏ

her to be a saint. Only the learned doctors of the Church, who tried her, were skeptical.

Her whole life, it seems, was miraculous, from the voices of saints she heard as a young village girl spinning wool at her mother's side and throughout the rest of her brief life, to her ability to convince the crown prince and his many advisers to accept her divine mission and place her at the head of an army. The simple facts of her life—her unshakable belief in her mission, her amazing courage and even more surprising competence in battle, her prophetic visions, her unswerving loyalty to the crown prince, her compassion, her eloquence in inspiring the French to action and later in defending herself before the power of the Church's inquisitors, are almost impossible to countenance. And yet, they are amply supported by the exceptionally detailed historical record. Her crucial role in stiffening the backbone of Charles VII (as the crown prince became) and the peoples of English-occupied territories in France is unquestioned: her lifting of the siege of Orléans is widely accepted as the turning point of the Hundred Years War. Those parts of her story that have been disputed relate to the motives of the English and those around her in the French court: her own reputation is unsullied and, indeed, she was canonized in 1920 by a repentant Church.

To a modern mind, the story of Joan of Arc is so full of events and circumstances which defy plausibility but are nonetheless objectively true, that it creates an unsettling disjunction between two apparently separate and distinct worlds of reality, that of St. Joan's lifetime in the fifteenth century and that of our own fact-obsessed era. Hers is a history that the doctrines of coincidence and statistical probability cannot support at any stretch. Those who are most disturbed by this dismiss her as a simple-minded, hysterical neurotic subject to hallucinations and cleverly manipulated by the clergy. This view, though, cannot be supported by the historical record. In a more measured skeptic's accounting, Anatole France, the man of letters much admired in the early decades of our century, struggled with

✗ ✗ ✗

her story and was able only to conclude: "The thought came to her to restore the Dauphin to his heritage. For this she gave her life. Thus it was that she survived her cause and that her devotion remains an everlasting example. Here was martyrdom without which men have established nothing great or useful in the world . . ." It seems a sadly pallid and inadequate explanation for so extraordinary a career.

On her arrival in the village of Loches with the royal entourage, she had been mobbed by hundreds of the villagers whom she had so inspired and who had already recognized in her a saint. They had kissed her hands and feet, even the feet of her horse. It was adoration she neither sought nor rejected, and she had been warned by Pierre de Versailles:

> "You do ill to allow these things. This is not due to you. Defend yourself from them or you will lead men into idolatry."

To which Joan replied,

> "In truth, I do not know how to guard myself from it, if God does not guard me."

On the worn and polished stone slabs on which we stood, Joan had knelt before the future king and pleaded with him to advance with his armies to Rheims and be crowned:

> The king was in his private room—what we call in French his "retreat"—and with him were my lord Christophe de Harcourt, and the Bishop of Castles, then the king's confessor, and my lord of Tréves, who had formerly been Chancellor of France. Before entering this room, the Maid knocked on the door, and the moment she was inside fell on her knees and embraced the king's feet, pronouncing these words or others like them: "Noble dauphin, do not take such long and copious counsel, but come as quickly as you can to receive a worthy coronation."[2]

Ɏ Ɏ Ɏ

As on so many other occasions, her unshakable belief in her convictions swayed him and his cautious advisers, and spurred them to action. She seemed to have the ability through sheer force of will to conjure into existence highly improbable realities. A month later, against all expectations, Charles was anointed with holy oil at a solemn coronation ceremony in the great cathedral at Rheims and became the Sovereign of France. Throughout the ceremony, we are told, Joan stood at his side, in full armor and with her famous battle pennant.

Her death was no less extraordinary than her life. She was burned at the stake on the morning of May 30, 1431, in the Place du Vieux-Marché in Rouen, in a spectacle designed to put a public and ignominious end to the supposed miracle worker who had caused such damage—fatal damage, had they but known—to English interests and prestige. Ten thousand people were to see the ceremony and the English authorities, determined to end her existence, both mortal and symbolic, let the flames lap at her body until her cries stopped and then raked back the fire to expose her corpse to the crowd. A contemporary account continues, "When they had stared long enough at her dead body bound to the stake, the executioner got a big fire going about her carcass, which was soon burned up."

Some of her judges, though, were crying. One said, as Joan died, "Please God that my soul be in the place where I believe this woman to be." The executioner, who had been employed in his trade for twenty years and more, sought out a pair of monks, to whom he confessed, "I greatly fear that I am damned, for I have burned a holy woman." And before long the rumor sprang up that Joan had somehow escaped the flames and was yet alive. At least one impostor appeared, claiming to be her, and was "honorably received" by the people of Orléans. A contemporary English chronicler was sufficiently skeptical to write of her execution: "Finally, they burned her publicly, or another woman like her: concerning which many people were and still are of different opinions."

I posed Hilary in the great hall for a photograph which I hoped might have meaning for her at some stage in her life. At the moment she was only mildly interested in the Maid of Orléans, having heard nothing at all of her throughout her school career, and only dimly remembering her from childhood books, but she indulged me nonetheless. Breathes there a father who does not think there is a little of Joan in his daughter?

The story of Joan of Arc might be taken as an allegory for the transition from the consciousness of the early Middle Ages, early Christian and pre-Christian times, to the modern consciousness we know today. Joan, an exemplar of the medieval worldview in the very essence of her fabulous life, died at the hands of Church scholars of the University of Paris, under whose authority her inquisition was conducted. The university was at that time under the influence of the thought of none other than William of Ockham, that early advocate of what we would now call positivism, the view that material reality exists autonomously. Already in the fifteenth century, the Church was increasingly in the thrall of Reason in its modern guise, and had begun to doubt the existence of the supernatural beyond what had been recorded in Scripture.

To my mind the story of St. Joan is, as well, the clearest possible example of how perilous it can be in examining history, to project, not just our modern biases and values, but our own "reality," back across the great divide of the scientific revolution of the seventeenth century, into a time of what I have been calling transactional reality. A current biographer of Joan has assembled a modern, psychoanalytical (that is, scientific and therefore "rational") explanation for her role as savior of France. In summary, it amounts to this: Joan, a humble village girl like thousands of others in her region, pious and obedient, felt that her parents were overly protective of her and that she was unduly constrained in her life. Her father had had a dream in which Joan had left home to follow one of the many armed bands criss-crossing their part of France as the Hundred Years War ebbed

꙳ ꙳ ꙳

and flowed, and it had alarmed him to the extent that he had remarked he would rather see her drowned than succumb to the sorry fate of a camp-follower. This dream may be interpreted as an incestuous rape fantasy. Moreover, Joan's career tells us that she probably shared the fantasy: how else to explain her desire to leave home as a teenager, if not to avoid violent sexual contact with her father? The repression of her sexual feelings towards her father led to her experiencing the voices of the saints, which, though actually projections of her own wishes, gave her the strength of conviction to confront the future king and eventually to lead victorious armies against the English. Further evidence of her sexual turmoil is to be found in the fact that she dressed in men's clothing while travelling through dangerous country and when engaged in battle: this the author describes as her "transvestitism," a sign of uncertain sexual identity. Joan was able to relate to Charles VII because of a "double displacement" phenomenon in which her incestuous feelings for her father were transferred to her older brother Pierre (whom she recruited into her retinue) and from there to the future king. The king was for her both a father figure, since he was royal, and a substitute for her brother, since he, too, required sisterly support in his times of need.[3]

That this explanation (I have reproduced it here, I believe fairly) did not collapse prior to publication under the weight of its own fatuousness can only be attributed to the fact that alternative explanations—for instance, that Joan actually was under divine guidance—have been ruled out in advance as "supernatural" and therefore impossible. But the idea of "supernatural" is here misunderstood. It is easier to understand why the misunderstanding occurs, if we realize that by "supernatural" we mean super-real, that is, beyond our conception of reality. The important point is that what is "real" and what is "natural" are *functions of the prevailing state of human perceptions*. Reality is what we jointly perceive it to be—nothing more and nothing less. What Joan and Charles VII and the king of England and the people of Orléans and the learned doctors of the University of Paris perceived in 1430, we cannot. Our current reality is built up of what we call "facts," in other words, phenomena, which gain that designation by virtue of being quantifiable, or at least reducible to quantifiable elements. We forget, however, that our entire system of quantification and analysis is a human intellectual construct of relatively recent origin, and that its sole recommendation is that it "works" in the sense that it explains in a satisfactory way those aspects of life which we currently care most about, that is, the material aspects. But the reality of 1430 also worked.

The more radical adherents of that branch of philosophy known as phenomenology argue that history, the past, does not really exist, since it is not being actively created by human consciousness. We may accept historical records as having been made by individuals who were involved in the creation of contemporary reality. But it is important to bear in mind that the consciousness that created them will have been different from our own, sometimes radically so, and to try to interpret the records in that light. It is an error, for example, to look upon medieval alchemy as early gropings towards a science of chemistry: it was in fact something altogether different, based on an utterly foreign consciousness of the material world and man's place in nature. It is only by projecting our own consciousness back onto the past that we can arrive at the conceit of alchemy being the precursor to chemistry.

And prehistory, the happenings on earth before Homo sapiens had made an appearance, cannot be known at all, since, in the absence of any form of consciousness, it did not "exist," and something that does not exist cannot be known. Therefore descriptions of the pre-human evolution of the planet are merely imaginings. The fossil record and the evidence of geology are of course real, but our interpretation of them is artificial and fanciful in the sense that it is dictated entirely by our present experience of the world projected back in time, and there is no reason in logic for us to believe that these imaginings in any way constitute the truth of what happened.

ᚷ ᚷ ᚷ

The modern phenomenologist position on prehistory is not far removed from what the Church argued in its dispute with Galileo: there is nothing wrong with constructing hypotheses to explain the planet's arrival at its present state, but it is wrong to assume that because a hypothesis may offer a plausible explanation, it is identical with the truth. At best, hypotheses of prehistory can only "save the appearances," just as both Ptolemy and Copernicus had in the case of the cosmos.

This, then, makes for an interesting interpretation of the long-standing and bitter dispute between Darwinian evolutionists and religious creationists. For a phenomenologist, an appropriate intervention might be, "Who cares?" The best we can hope for in a hypothesis is that it "save the phenomenon"; that is, that it "works" in the sense that we can get results from it, and make useful predictions. To date, Darwinism has proved itself superior in this regard; at some future date another hypothesis will doubtless find favor by virtue of its superior predictive ability and its stronger appeal to reigning common sense.

So we owe it to history to be accommodating in our interpretations, and to try to enter into contemporary reality rather than superimposing our own. Pragmatic people have a useful adage: If it walks like a duck and quacks like a duck, then it is a duck. This was precisely the reasoning employed by the people of fifteenth-century France who believed Joan to be in touch with the divine. Nor should we, as inhabitants of a modern, scientific world, scoff at the apparent naiveté of this outlook. To use just one late twentieth-century example, the controversy over whether true machine intelligence is possible is likely to be decided on exactly these terms. Alan Turing, the British mathematician who invented the modern digital computer in the 1930s, firmly believed that machine intelligence would be a part of our everyday lives before the turn of the century. Since his time the debate over whether such a phenomenon is possible and what it might look like has waxed to the point where it would take a small library to house all of the books pro and con. For Turing, however, all of this speculation was pointless wheel-spinning: he believed that the only way to identify machine intelligence was to employ the duck adage and to this end he proposed what is known as the "Turing test," which has proved remarkably resistant to philosophical attack. It involves placing a human and a computer behind screens, and allowing a person to communicate with each of them via keyboard and printer. The examiner can ask whatever he wishes: if, at the end of day he is unable to determine which of his communicants is human and which machine, the machine is deemed to be "intelligent."

Reality changes slowly because it involves reshaping a broadly based consensus on how we agree to describe our individual perceptions. But it does change, and there is no basis at all for assuming that "newer" means "truer."

More modern = better eg-cars.

South of Limoges we stayed in a picturesque converted mill called Moulin de la Gorce and dined magnificently, and in the morning before a breakfast of fresh yogurt, fruit, boiled eggs, croissants and brioche served under umbrellas by the pond we found Simon, wrinkled and disheveled as usual, sitting in the sun on a mossy boulder beside the babbling mill race engrossed in a copy of Norman Mailer's *Of a Fire on the Moon*. It was a sight to behold. And then Hilary appeared in a spotless white T-shirt and pressed khaki shorts, her hair shimmering in the sunlight, a vision of a different kind. I was quite certain that no Positivist rationalization could account for my feelings for them, or their mother. I was equally confident that those feelings were as real as anything in this world can be.

CHAPTER 7

Brantôme, Rocamadour and the Gîte

DRIVING SOUTH ❧ ROCAMADOUR'S MIRACLES

❧ A STAY IN A CHÂTEAU ❧ OUR COUNTRY *GÎTE*

From a mailbox just down the road from our secluded hotel, I sent off a postcard:

Cher Berkowitz,

Have rented talking car. Spent a night in cave on the Loire. Everything in Paris the same only different. Chartres is software for which we have lost the hardware; a record we don't know how to play, but magnificent even unheard. Offspring are mightily impressed, though not by Joan of Arc who seems to them a character in a comic book. And how is the state of your reality? You may hear beeps in the night (other than the frogs in the pond): power bumps are frequent, and the power back-up boxes for the computers let you know whenever they take over from the AC line current. Hope you're making yourself at home and enjoying the facilities.

Best,

wr

❧ ❧ ❧

For three more days we drove slowly south along secondary roads, enjoying the landscapes which seemed to change dramatically almost every hour. The territory is divided up like a layer cake by three historic rivers flowing from east to west: the idyllic Dronne, on whose banks we discovered the lovely island village of Brantôme and spent a night; the Dordogne with its looming castles harkening back to the days of chivalry; and the Lot, wilder, more primitive, its many medieval towns clinging to cliffs and escarpments, a fitting frontier for the south. Each geographic region has its own domestic and military architectures dictated in part by history and partly by the available building materials, and each has its own agricultural products and industries, its own distinctive cuisine. Settlements along the Dordogne, like Sarlat, a medieval market town, are typically built almost entirely in a rich, golden limestone and roofed with stone slabs; gastronomes flock to the area for its truffles, goose and duck liver patés, strawberries and walnut confections. To the south, sandstone takes over as the primary construction material, the roofs are tiled in clay and the food is more rustic, tending to stews, of which the delicious white bean-based cassoulet is the most famous.

Before we found our *gîte* near Carcassonne and settled in for a week, we had planned one last stopover—the fabled cliffside town of Rocamadour, among the most visited pilgrimage sites in medieval Christendom, renowned throughout the early Middle Ages for its venerable Black Madonna and for the miraculous chapel bell that tolled of its own accord to foretell miracles. It was the banner of Rocamadour, flown at the Battle of Las Navas at Tolosa in Spain, that is said to have sent the Moors into retreat, giving final victory to the Catholic Spanish kings. Breton fishermen invoking the name of the Black Madonna claimed to have been saved from mortal peril at sea through her intercession. At times as many as thirty thousand penitents would gather here and the list of famous pilgrims is very long, including St. Dominic and St. Bernard, Henry Plantagenet, whose inheritance of much of this part of France ignited the Hundred

Years War; Blanche of Castille; St. Louis and a clutch of other early French monarchs.

The town as it was known to the pilgrims of the eleventh century was sacked several times during the Hundred Years War and finally largely destroyed by Protestant zealots during the wars of religion in the sixteenth century at which time the much-venerated body of St. Amadour, still intact after more than five hundred years, was tossed into a fire. But it would not burn and was finally hacked to pieces with a sword. Of the rich treasure and reliquary, only the miracle bell and the Black Madonna were saved: both are there to be seen in the chapel, which like the rest of the town has been "restored" extensively, though perhaps not beyond recognition, down through the centuries.

Nevertheless Rocamadour remains an unforgettable sight, well worth a detour, as Monsieur Bibelot would say. It retains the great advantage of being a living town, home to about 650 people; some of the changes that purists object to, such as the rebuilding of crumbling ruins, are simply necessary to make the village habitable. The unhappy alternative would be to reduce it to the sterile status of museum. Simon and Hilary were shocked to find that vehicles were permitted to drive right down the narrow main street to cramped little parking lots. It seemed somehow a desecration of this place, so hallowed by history. I had had the same reaction on my first visit years earlier, though I had eventually come around to the position that, on the whole, it was wise policy to ensure that historic sites like Rocamadour remain alive and populated by ordinary people living ordinary lives. It seemed the best guarantee of their survival, and anyway, who is to say at what stage of development or decay it is appropriate to "freeze" a historic site for posterity? What is more "real"—the living town or the embalmed corpse? Better to let it evolve as a human settlement, always mindful of what is inviolable and what may responsibly be adapted to modern needs. Rocamadour must be a wonderful place to live, particularly in the off-season: domestic, civil, religious and military structures are piled one upon another in helter-skelter tiers to a

⚔ ⚔ ⚔

height of more than five hundred meters above the gorge, linked by worn and polished stone staircases, some carved right into the rock face, and spectacular views across the valley are never more than a step or two away. Hewn from the living rock about halfway to the top of the escarpment is the sooty little chapel of the Black Madonna, with its small walnut statue of the Virgin Mary dandling an adult-faced Christ child on her knee. Some scholars believe it is the oldest surviving chapel to Mary in Christendom.

That night we dined and slept sumptuously amid decayed luxury in a nearby château of eccentric construction, where Simon and Hilary had a room in a Rapunzel-style turret. Chris and I occupied chambers the owners assured us had been frequented by someone whose name I have forgotten, but who had the singular distinction of having been hairdresser to General Charles de Gaulle. Dinner on the terrace overlooking the woods in the Aizou River valley was a scene from a Fellini movie, with huge white cotton parasols over each of the dozen or so tables lifting like bird wings in the gentlest breath of pine-scented wind and the sun setting like a ball of molten gold.

And then it was on into the true south of straw-colored hills and red-tiled roofs, through fields and fields of nodding sunflowers and vast, carefully groomed vineyards; on to Carcassonne to find our country *gîte*, an apartment in a farmhouse we had reserved sight-unseen through the French Government Tourist Office back home. It was to be our all-purpose headquarters for a week's exploration of the Cathar ruins that dot the countryside in the shadow of the Pyrenees.

We'd bought the largest-scale map we could find of the region, but it did not show the road to our *gîte*; we knew only that, from Carcassonne, it was the "first left turn after the highway overpass on the road to Montréal, 3 km south of Arzen." Even on our 1 centimeter: 1 kilometer map, Arzen was a fly speck. In the late afternoon heat, driving between picket rows of century-old plane trees through shimmering vineyards we missed the turn-off twice before we finally spotted the small green and yellow *gîtes de France* plaque: it was fastened to a post beside a gravel track leading into a sea of grape vines, turning eventually in the direction of a stand of umbrella pines that sheltered a low huddle of tile-roofed farm buildings of oatmeal sandstone. The vision I'd been secretly harboring of a wooden-shod, stubble-chinned owner shooing poultry out of our kitchen in preparation for our arrival became ever more vivid as we approached what revealed itself to be a working farm.

We stopped in front of the farmhouse and climbed stiff-legged from our car, to be greeted by an urbane, middle-aged couple who immediately invited us inside, out of the heat. They were farmers, yes—grape growers—but he was also a reporter for a Carcassonne radio station; she was a chatelaine in the French tradition and an accomplished decorator. Despite our stumbling French and their lack of English, Chris and I felt an instant rapport, and Hilary and Simon were delighted to meet our hosts' daughter Anouk, a pretty Paris university undergrad back for the summer vacation.

Their home, a long, low two-storey structure at one time had been both house and barn, and had been renovated to accommodate both the owners' living quarters and a pair of two-story apartments, newly licensed as *gîtes*. Ours was at the end of the structure, facing the sunrise, and consisted of a fully equipped kitchen and adjoining dining area plus living room (with TV) on the main floor, and two large bedrooms and a bathroom with shower on the second floor. You entered through a gated terrace bordered on two sides by a low stone wall on which ivy and potted geraniums grew, and on a third by chicken coops, swept and whitewashed to a fault and used for storage of bicycles, garden furniture and barbecue gear. There on the terrace we found privacy and shade each morning for our breakfasts of café au lait and the fresh bread, flaky croissants and shiny brioche delivered at 8:45 sharp by the Arzen baker's wife. This was where we planned our daily excursions, poring over our maps, and where we hung our laundered clothes to dry under the hammer of the southern sun.

This, for me, was where the real adventure would begin.

ɣ ɣ ɣ

Carcassonne and the Cathars

LILY DEVÉSE'S SCHOOLROOM ✗ A HISTORY

LESSON ✗ INTRODUCING THE CATHARS ✗

ST. AUGUSTINE AND THE MANICHEANS ✗

THE 'CATHAR INDUSTRY' ✗ MODERNISM

AND CATHARISM

The four of us were sitting on a bench in the front row of Lily Devése's classroom in the high-walled garden behind her house in the heart of fortress Carcassonne. Lily is one of about 150 fortunate people who live and work in the walled city, which may be the most powerfully evocative medieval site in Europe. So astonishing is the result of the enormous mid-nineteenth-century restoration project that saved the city that even Henry James, an adamant opponent of historical reconstructions, was left somewhat ambivalent following his visit at a time when work was still under way:

> In places, as you stand upon it, the great towered and embattled enciente produces an illusion; it looks as if it were still equipped and defended. One vivid challenge, at any rate, it flings down before you;

✗ ✗ ✗

it calls upon you to make up your mind on the matter of restoration. For myself, I have no hesitation; I prefer in every case the ruined, however ruined, to the reconstructed, however splendid. What is left is more precious than what is added; the one is history, the other is fiction; and I like the former the better of the two—it is so much more romantic. One is positive, so far as it goes; the other fills up the void with things more dead than the void itself, inasmuch as they have never had life. After that I am free to say that the restoration of Carcassonne is a splendid achievement.[1]

Lily herself, a tiny fireplug of a woman, seventy-nine years old, zipped into a practical blue polyester smock, the utilitarian effect of which was offset by a narrow-brimmed straw fedora, paced energetically up and down before us, rapping a huge map of the ancient city with an old-fashioned hickory pointer. There was seating for tour groups of perhaps sixty people here, in a long, narrow prefab metal structure with windows along one wall and historical charts and maps covering the others. This evening, though, we were her only students.

"The Romans were here of course very early. In the first century they built a seaport at Narbonne, N-A-R-B-O-N-N-E. Narbonne is here," she said, moving to another map, "and Carcassonne is here. And they built a road, here"—*tap tap*—"called *la via Nar-bon-naise*. And along it on *this* rocky outcropping"—she stamps her sensibly-shod foot several times to indicate she means *right here on this spot*— "they built a castrum, a sort of military outpost, because from here they could keep watch on the via Narbonnaise and on the River Aude and on the very narrow passageway between the Cevenne range and the Pyrenees. And the Romans were never attacked. Never. And they left after the . . ."

She stopped in mid-sentence, fixing me with a gimlet eye.

"Do you know any European history?"

I could feel sweat begin to trickle down my chest.

"A bit . . ."

She gave a little nod that said, *I'll be the judge of that*.

"And so when was the end of the Western Roman Empire."

"Uh, do you mean what year?" I was playing for time. This was a date I should know. This was a date the *kids* should know.

"*What year!?* It was in the fifth century and of course it took place over *many* years. And the Romans left here, and everything was in a good state of preservation because they had never been attacked and the Visigoths who already had a big part of Spain took over and founded their kingdom of Toulouse. In two hundred and fifty years they built nothing and then they were driven out by the Arabs in 725, who had no time to build anything because they were driven back to Spain by Charlemagne's father. Now," she said, planting her feet firmly, grasping the pointer behind her back with both hands like an inspecting sergeant major, "do you know his name? Who was Charlemagne's father?"

I was caught off guard, mentally questioning her assertion that the Visigoths had built nothing. I knew that the many half-round towers along the Cité walls are called "Visigothic towers." Desperately, I ransacked my memory. What would my children think of me?

"Uh . . ."

"Pippin the Short!" she announced triumphantly. "Married to"— a millisecond pause—"married to Bertha Broad Foot. And this lovely couple had a son named Charlemagne who ruled over all of Europe without any trouble at all and was crowned emperor in the year 800. And he divided up the land among his sons and relatives and that was really the beginning of feudalism, but I can see that you are tired and so I will make this short."

"No, not tired at all," I protested.

"It's very interesting," Chris chimed in and Hilary and Simon made positive noises as well.

"I just look at you and know," she continued without skipping a beat. "And so everything was so fine here in the region we call Languedoc, for the language—*langue*—in which the word for 'yes' is

ᴪ ᴪ ᴪ

'oc' rather than 'oïl' as it was in the Northern dialect of Latin which became French; it was so fine it was bound to come to an end and that is where this religion comes in, this Catharism. Do you know about Catharism?"

"A little, yes."

"A little. Well, where did it come from?"

I felt at last I was on solid ground.

"From the north and . . ."

"No."

"But . . ."

"It came from Asia."

"But the Bogomiles . . ."

"Ah! The Bogomiles in Bulgaria were the first in Europe. It existed in Persia before that. It was called Manicheism, for a prophet called Mani who lived in the third century. And do you know what its beliefs were?"

"It was dialectic," I blurted, unable to retrieve the word "dualist" from my pathetic memory, but she accepted this, thank goodness.

"Yes! Correct. They believed that the earth was not created by God but by the devil. Everything material was the devil's work. The spiritual world alone belonged to God. They rejected the sacraments of the Roman Catholic church and had a sacrament of their own called the con-sol-a-men-tum, and once a man or woman received the consolamentum they became a Perfect and were not allowed to kill anything, not even a chicken, and they could not eat meat or milk, only fish and vegetables because human souls could be trapped in animals and they could not have sexual relations because a pregnancy was a disaster since it entangled another soul in a living body made by the devil. And they were called Cathars because . . .?"

"Well, actually because . . ." But I was too slow on the uptake and she jumped in again.

"Because it is the Greek word for pure—'katharos.'"

I could have argued the point with her here, but thought better of it. She was armed, and I was not. But the fact is that modern scholarship indicates that the word "Cathar" was a derogatory term applied to the heretics by orthodox Catholics, one of whom wrote in 1198 that Cathars had been thus named from the Latin for cat, "*cautus*," since, "so it is said, they kiss the hind-quarters of a cat, the form in which Lucifer appears to them." This is an obvious slander, just as in the North of France they were often maligned as "bulgares," a synonym for bugger. The proof of their Christian idealism is in the fact that the Catholic church, in its long campaign against them, was forced to copy at least the form of their principled behavior with the creation of the mendicant preaching orders of the Dominicans and the Franciscans, which essentially mimicked the ascetic way of life of the Cathar Perfecti, which in turn had been modeled on the lives of the Apostles. The Roman church formally called them Albigensians or Albigenses (after the town of Albi), or sometimes "perfect heretics." The members of the sect themselves simply referred to one another as "good people" or "good Christians." They were particularly numerous around Carcassonne, and the city played an important role in their history.

Mani had considered himself successor to Zoroaster, Buddha and Jesus, a great synthesizer, and Manicheism was an aggressive, proselytizing religion that aimed to unite the world under its banner of truth. For this reason it was attacked vigorously by both the Roman state and the Christian church (the state religion), and was driven out of the western Roman Empire during the fifth century, and the eastern empire a century later. Most authorities consider it to have been a Gnostic religion, meaning that its initiated were empowered with secret, occult knowledge of the universe. Gnostic religions are generally placed in direct line of descent from late Greek paganism and in particular the thought of Plato, in which the real and worldly, and the ideal and spiritual, are presented as two distinctly different worlds, the latter to be preferred over the former. In Plato's view, ideal forms that were exclusively spiritual or intellectual formed the

ʮ ʮ ʮ

only reliable reality; the material world accessible to the senses was too transient and misleading to be relied upon for knowledge. It was not a large step from this to a theory of the inherent evil of the material world, an idea which had the not-inconsiderable appeal of offering an explanation for the puzzle of how or why a God of infinite goodness created a world containing evil. Dualist religions said: He did not; the Devil did.

St. Augustine (354–430), bishop of Hippo in North Africa, had been an admirer of Plato and a Manichean himself in his early, wayward years. He attacked both Gnostic and Manichean heresies with all the vigor of the convert, and is revered for having resolved those dangerous conflicts between early Christian theology and the philosophy of Plato. In so doing, he found a place for reason in religion and in doing that he shaped Christianity anew and made of it a philosophy as well as a religion, one that was to deeply permeate all aspects of life in Europe for more than a millennium. To the extent that the threat from Manicheism and Gnosticism forced Augustine and other early Church leaders into developing defensive bulwarks of Christian dogma (including the Nicene Creed) and episcopal organization, within which the authority and purity of dogma could be preserved, the Catholic church bears their indelible imprint, if only in the photographic negative.

Augustine had views on the subject of learning that are quintessentially medieval in character and worth briefly mentioning here: "Seek not to understand that you may believe, but believe that you may understand," he said. "Faith seeks; understanding finds." The role in Christian philosophy of revelation (or revealed truth) contained in the Scriptures, according to Augustine, was to provide a framework or hypothesis within which truth and understanding can be sought in the world of nature. To search without such a road map is to engage in an enterprise with no foreseeable end. If the seeker after truth takes all knowledge in its inexhaustible variety to be his territory, and every fact as being of import, then he is forever in the position of not knowing whether the next "fact" to come to his attention will upset the applecart of his entire previous efforts at knowledge. Thus, trying to understand the world through inductive reason—by reasoning from the specific to the general—seemed to Augustine, and to most of his medieval successors, a pointless, ill-conceived and needlessly harrowing exercise, reminiscent, perhaps, of the labors of Sisyphus. Medieval Christian philosophers, following Augustine, did not object to the investigations of so-called natural philosophy (what we now call science). But they were adamant in their belief that the received wisdom of the Scriptures was necessary to any complete understanding of the natural world.

As we would discover on our travels, a renewed curiosity about the Cathars has spawned a minor industry in the south of France in recent years, one that had grown noticeably even since Chris and I had last visited the area. Bookstores, stationers and tourist kiosks throughout the region display shelves of books in multiple translations, everything from scholarly studies of the origins and doctrines of the heresy to romance novels and superbly illustrated comic books featuring Cathar holy men and the barons and knights who afforded them protection. The British book *The Holy Blood and the Holy Grail* rocketed to international best-seller status in the early 1980s by linking the Cathars to an obscure organization called the Priory of Zion which the book alleged possesses proof that Jesus Christ survived the crucifixion, and what's more, had children, the descendants of whom are still with us. The proof, the book claimed, had been provided when in 1885 an obscure parish priest in the little town of Rennes-les-Châteaux, not far from Carcassonne, had stumbled upon ancient documents concealed in the altar of the local church; the documents led him to a mysterious treasure of some sort; he took its secret to his grave, though it had apparently made him very wealthy while he lived. After exploring the possibilities of its being any of several legendary troves—a hoard of gold buried by Visigoths;

wealth pillaged from the Holy Land during the Crusades and hidden by the Templars; a fabled Cathar treasure—the authors drew on a clutch of conspiracy theories new and old to speculate that the treasure is the Holy Grail. But not the familiar drinking vessel; this Grail was the record of the lineage of Christ's children. The documents containing the bloodlines had been passed along from the Templars to the Cathars, each of whom was doomed by its secret knowledge to violent destruction by the Church. As with any good conspiracy story, there is just enough fact, just enough tantalizing evidence in the yarn to make it a thoroughly entertaining read, and the book and its sequels, along with the related television programs, can claim some of the responsibility for a resurgence of interest in the Cathars, on a scale which has prompted French government tourist authorities to dub the environs of Carcassonne, "Cathar Country," in their tourist handouts.

Ironically, there are no actual "Cathar sites" to be seen: the wonderfully picturesque and evocative ruins that are advertised as such are really representative of the civilization that opposed the heretics, the Roman-Carolingian world that by the twelfth century could with justice call itself Christendom. The complex politics of the south of France led to the Cathars, who were committed to non-violence, being sheltered in the fortified towns and castles of the local feudal rulers, and these are the sites—Carcassonne and its sister ruins— we so admire today. But the Cathars themselves left nothing more than a few scraps of documents and a murky legend . . . and a haunting foretaste of what the world was to become.

The Cathars, I had begun to realize, were the advance guard of modernism in Europe. Strongly tainted by the pre-Christian Gnostic tradition of esoteric knowledge, in which it was believed the devout can have access to the innermost secrets of creation and the universe, they shared the view that would be adopted by modern science that there are no necessary limits to human knowledge. The

ɤ ɤ ɤ

medieval Church, following Augustine, rejected that view, believing that ultimate knowledge was inaccessible to humans (Who can know the mind of God?), and that it was at best a waste of time, and at worst sinful, to go in search of it. A waste of time because such a search was open-ended and therefore endless; sinful because, taken to extremes, it distracted men from the rightful focus of their inquiries and attention: their innermost being. For the Church, understanding and therefore salvation lay ultimately in faith, and not in so-called factual knowledge.

In the dualism of the Cathars lay another harbinger of modernism, a foreshadowing of the fatal undermining of the Catholic doctrines that effectively integrated body and spirit. The material world of the Cathars was not just evil, it was autonomous, and thus existed independent of, and in opposition to, the spiritual realm. Men and women could withdraw from it, as did the Perfect, or indulge themselves in it, as lay followers tended to do: the choice was theirs. However, in the future, if whole societies were to choose the material in preference to the more rigorous spiritual realm in which to focus their lives, the spiritual would be in danger of withering into irrelevancy, reduced to superstition. This was the great, continuing concern of the Church. The war against the Cathars of Languedoc was but an early and remarkably violent episode in the epic cosmological dispute that would climax with the mathematics and astronomy of Galileo, the bloodless philosophy of Descartes, the clockwork science of Newton and the triumphant scientific revolution that changed the world forever.

ꙏ ꙏ ꙏ

Richard and Lily

CARCASSONNE AND ME ❧ RICHARD

HALLIBURTON'S JOURNEY ❧ THE WALLS OF

CARCASSONNE ❧ LILY'S STORY ❧ MONTRÉAL

IN WARTIME ❧ CHOOSING FREEDOM

Carcassonne and I go back a long way. The travel bug bit me early in life, long before my first passport, and it had always seemed to me that one of the most exciting and romantic experiences imaginable must be to walk the grey-stone ramparts of this ancient city, preferably at night and preferably in the autumn. This notion was implanted when, as an adventure-starved Prairie kid in the fifties, I discovered and devoured the books of one of the most popular travel writers of any era, Richard Halliburton. Throughout my adolescence I had a tattered black-and-white photo of the handsome, tow-headed adventurer tacked to my bedroom wall. He is posing at the snowy summit of a volcano in Mexico, a sweat-stained Indiana Jones fedora in one hand and a walking staff in the other. His boots lace up to the knee and his sunburned face is split by an ear-to-ear grin.

In his heyday in the 1920s and 1930s, Halliburton was a household name and his books, from *The Royal Road to Romance* to *Seven League Boots* and *The Flying Carpet*, were perpetual best-sellers thanks to the publicity he generated for them as a wildly successful performer on the lecture circuit. As a writer he had broad popular appeal, but as a lecturer he was especially popular with women, who lined up for hours to get tickets and swooned when he appeared on-stage. He'd discovered early on that what his audience wanted from him was not culture, politics and geography but adventure and, above all, the *romance* of travel. And that is what he gave them. He traveled to the ends of the earth on a shoestring, and when adventure did not present itself, he manufactured it. One example will do: facing destitution in Buenos Aires, while writing the newspaper series that was to become *New Worlds to Conquer*, he spurned an easy bail-out from his publisher and instead talked an Italian organ-grinder into selling him his monkey and hurdy-gurdy. Performing for children in the city's parks and streets earned Halliburton: (*a*) a night in jail for by-law infractions, (*b*) a memorable yarn for the newspapers back home and later his book and (*c*) enough money for his passage all the way north to Rio.

Halliburton blew in to Carcassonne late in 1921 on his first trip to Europe as a young Princeton graduate with literary ambitions, and he wrote about it in *The Royal Road to Romance*, a book I was to be enchanted by nearly forty years later. He was on his way by bicycle and knapsack from Paris to Andorra. The air at the foot of the Pyrenees was sharp and clear . . .

> Late on that glittering November evening I left the modern *ville basse* on foot, crossed the seven-hundred-year-old bridge over the river that separates the fortress from the modern town, looked up the sharp escarpment, and behold, before my eyes, nine centuries disappeared. I became an anachronism, a twentieth-century American living in eleventh-century France. In one sweep the Middle Ages were revealed. A magical moonlit city of walls and towers and battlements, defiant and impregnable, rose before me. . . . Not a person was to be seen, not a light showed, nor a dog barked as I climbed the path and

ℵ ℵ ℵ

walked beneath the massively fortified gate, through the double line of enormous walls, into a strange world. Incredibly ancient houses, dark and ghostly, reeled grotesquely along the crazy streets. My footsteps echoed. There was no other sound. . . .[1]

Halliburton was never far away from me when I was in Carcassonne.

Lily had taken us to a place beside the château with its dry moat and drawbridge, where the various layers of construction in the city's inner wall are clearly visible. A group of schoolgirls were noisily and good-humoredly trying to organize themselves for a photograph. Lily began to tell us about the walls, but then stopped to glare at the girls.

"The French do not know how to behave," she announced. "It has to do with the school system."

We waited a moment more, and then she began in spite of them. She explained to us that in most places the walls go deep beneath the surface as a precaution against mining. Although Carcassonne changed hands several times during the Crusade against Catharism, only once was a siege mounted. Mighty wooden engines that could catapult boulders, rolling siege towers to help storm the walls and other marvels of the military technology of the time were of little use against so well-designed a defensive position and the besieging army found its most promising line of attack to be mining the walls—tunneling under them to cause them to collapse. The defenders countermined successfully, meeting the invading forces far underground and driving them back before they could complete their destruction by firing the timbers that shored their tunnel. As Lily spoke, my mind conjured a vision of the rat-like ferocity of those claustrophobic, clawing struggles in sour air and oily torchlight.

I began to feel a real fondness for Lily. She had enormous energy for a woman of her age, and there was a twinkle in her eye that belied her exterior pugnacity. This was not an easy place to get around in, with its steeply climbing streets, slippery stone stairs and treacherous cobbles, but she navigated it like a youngster. As she led us from location to location, from the Justice Tower where the Inquisition conducted its thumbscrew "interviews" to the upper lists where jousting tournaments were held on the killing ground between the walls, and on to the massive Narbonnaise gate, we chatted about other things. She had come to the city in 1952 to take a job as a substitute teacher: her husband had fallen ill with cancer and was unable to work to support their two children. She'd fallen in love with the place—"I have a passion for these stones"—and had been here ever since, active for much of the time in the protection and restoration of the site.

She had met her husband during the war, when they were both involved in the Resistance. Lily lived with her family in a house opposite the town hall in the village of Montréal, famous for its medieval church in which a famous debate took place between St. Dominic and the Cathar bishop of Toulouse, Guilabert de Castres.

"It was a large house. We lived on the main floor and the Germans took over the top floor for their headquarters," she said. "And in the basement were hiding the Resistance people. We were like a sandwich between the Resistance and the Germans. When the Germans asked me to be their translator and secretary, I asked the Resistance people what to do. 'Yes, yes, you must accept,' they said. They told me I would be able to steal documents for them. And I did. I stole one hundred and twenty-four travel carnets which were used to get people out of France to Allied territory."

I was moved, as I always am, by such stories. "I've always admired the people of the Resistance," I said.

Lily responded with a wry look and a mordant chuckle. "There were a great many more Resistance fighters *after* the war than there were during it. There were not many here at all, in fact. When they offered me a medal after the war I said, 'Give it to one of *them*.' But it was a marvellous experience for a young woman. It made me what I am."

꙼ ꙼ ꙼

The following day we would detour into Montréal to have a look at the house Lily had lived in so precariously, and it was not large at all. It is quite tiny, part of a row of low-ceilinged, two-storey stone houses with heavily shuttered windows and red-tiled roofs. The town hall is tiny as well, and just a few paces away from Lily's front door, across a cobbled street barely wide enough for a car. What had been only imagined seemed suddenly, cloyingly real and I could smell the fear. It was the odor of steel and dirt and wool and vomit and sweat. I had subliminal flashes of pictures half-remembered from my boyhood reading, of burial pits mounded with tangled bodies, of grey-uniformed firing squads, of railway cattle cars stuffed with civilians, of emaciated corpses stacked like cordwood, of warehouse bins of eyeglasses and false teeth and human hair, of soap-making machinery next to crematoria, of lampshades of human skin; images of the methodic horrors that grew out of an unrestrained belief in human beings as the means, rather than ends, of progress.

And yet Lily had said that her own experience had been a liberating one: "It made me what I am." Like material reality, freedom, where it exists at all, exists only *in potentia* until it is actualized, or made concrete. This happens through our making of choices among options: the option we choose becomes real for us, and that, in turn, gives substance and meaning to our freedom. Individual freedom, like democracy, is not a state of being so much as a process. Not all choices we make are equal: some are merely trivial, and some have profound implications and are very difficult to make, as in the case of the proverbial "life or death choice." As a rule, the most difficult choices we are called upon to make, including those involving life and death, are moral choices. There is a direct relationship between the degree of difficulty in a choice, that is, the importance of the implications, and the degree of freedom that is created in making it. That is why the vaunted consumer society of the late twentieth century does not, despite its claims, make free people. Man as consumer has plenty of choices, granted, but almost all of them are trivial, falling as they do into the category of "selections": his freedom is illusory. One's moral choices, on the other hand, repay rich dividends in freedom.

It is possible, of course, to make wrong moral choices: the impact on freedom is the same, in that it remains proportionate to the implications of the choice. It cannot be otherwise if free will is to exist. Fortunately, a majority of us seem to arrive in the world pre-programmed with a strong bias towards the moral over the immoral and an innate sense for distinguishing between the two.

What I liked about Lily, when I thought about it, was that she was her own person, an authentically free spirit. What I had admired about Richard Halliburton was essentially the same thing. I suppose that indicated to me, if only unconsciously, that they were moral peo-ple, as well. Both had earned their freedom by deliberately making it real, in the same way, though not on the same plane, as had the Maid of Orléans. We admire Joan of Arc not, as Anatole France believed, as a martyr or a "symbol of the fatherland in arms," but as a free person who remained free by her own will even as the flames leaped about her at the stake. It is this same determination to be free in the face of the ultimate sanction of civil and religious authority, I believe, that makes the story of the Cathars so seductively appealing.

Three Cathar Castles

THE GALAMUS GORGE ❧ PUILAURENS CASTLE

❧ 'EVERYTHING IS PERMITTED' ❧ CATHARS

AND TROUBADOURS—COURTLY LOVE ❧

CATHARISM'S APPEAL ❧ THE CHURCH'S FEARS

❧ LITERACY AND THE SELF ❧ LIVING IN

THE MATERIAL WORLD ❧ MIGHTY QUÉREBUS

❧ A GOTHIC MYSTERY ❧ 'CARCASSONNE

IN THE SKY'

The next day, we drove south up the Aude River Valley through the low, vine-carpeted hills around Limoux, climbing into the beech and pine forests of the Pyrenees foothills, past the turn-off for Rennes-les-Châteaux, the tiny village made famous by *The Holy Blood and the Holy Grail*. (I had asked Lily Devése what she'd thought of the book: "Hah! I was his [a co-author's] guide and interpreter when he came here for the first time. He didn't speak a word of French. . . . The book is mostly rubbish!").

❧ ❧ ❧

From the lumber and plastics town of Quillan, once known for fashionable felt hats, we followed a loop that took us to three "Cathar" fortresses farther south along the Aude through narrow gorges and then east, up and across the Atlantic-Mediterranean watershed and back through the Galamus Gorge with its hair-raising, two-meter-wide road carved into the limestone nooks and crannies of the precipitous hillside. Clefts in the earth such as this had special significance during pre-Christian times, when the earth was still thought of as a living entity, as a "person," and minerals were organic substances that ripened and matured in the earth's womb. Like the famous fissure at Delphi in Greece, this canyon would have been thought of as a genital opening ("delphi" being the Greek word for vagina). It was in a cave not far from here that the oldest known human skull in Europe was discovered, dating back 450,000 years.

From a small parking area at the gorge's mouth we could see, on a narrow rock shelf halfway down to the roaring, invisible River Agle, a little cottage that once was the home of a Christian hermit and is now a small hostel, surely one of the most memorable in Europe. There was so much history here in this one small circuit, no more than a few hours' ride by car, such varied and spectacular scenery, so many beautiful villages and breathtaking vistas, that it deserved to be seen on foot from the well-maintained hiking trails that lace the region or by bicycle, over a period of weeks, if not months.

We stopped first at Puilaurens, and climbed for half an hour along a well-worn path through the privet, juniper and scrub oak clinging to the limestone, up to the crenelated walls at seven hundred metres, high above the surrounding countryside. It had been built by the local baron as an impregnable redoubt in troubled times of invasion and conquest and had sheltered Cathars midway through its active life.

And like other so-called Cathar sites, Puilaurens is associated with chivalry, courtly love and the romance of troubadours. Early medieval Languedoc had a reputation for religious tolerance, for sexual permissiveness and for egalitarianism that is related to the culture

ϰ ϰ ϰ

of courtly romance fostered by the troubadours, but also, in an odd way, attributable to the very strictness of the moral precepts of Catharism. Because everything material was of the devil, earthly pleasures, including the carnal ones, were forbidden to the Perfecti (as clergy and initiates were called), who were supposed to be celibate and vegetarian, and who fasted frequently. There is a saying the French use when trying to define their national character and it has some application here: "In Germany, everything that is not permitted is forbidden; in France, everything that is not forbidden is permitted." In Cathar Languedoc there existed a third scenario: everything was forbidden, and so everything was permitted. The surviving records of Inquisition interrogations contain many references to this point of view: because sexual relations even within marriage were "of the devil," there was no logical distinction to be drawn between sex within and outside marriage, between intercourse with a prostitute and one's wife. One was as sinful as the other. Since the Cathar doctrines recognized that not everyone could attain the moral standards of the Perfecti, and that in any case sinners could achieve complete redemption if they underwent the consolamentum before death, the practical effect was to encourage a sexual permissiveness that recognized few taboos other than that of incest. Among ordinary Cathar villagers, men and women, sexual relations were defined as right or wrong according to whether or not they involved joy for both partners. At the same time, Languedoc culture accorded an equality of status to women, particularly among the nobility, that was unusual for its time and this was due at least in part to the Cathars' acceptance of women clergy. Several of the most famous Perfecti were female.

Catharism and the troubadour culture seem to have run along parallel tracks rather than being causally connected, though they often seem to have fed off one another. They do share, however, the scent of modernity. The poetry of the troubadours was lyrical, aristocratic, anticlerical and colored with Arab influences, reflecting the increased contact brought about through the Crusades. It is also all

ﻙ ﻙ ﻙ

about self-discipline and self-control, which are thoroughly modern notions. In the best-known of the surviving poetry, love is chaste and unrequited, but much of it is earthy and sensual as well. Nearly 450 troubadours are known to us by name; in this representative poem in the form known as the *alba*, written by a twelfth-century bard, an amorous lady and her lover are heard from in turn:

> Alas, shall he ever again
> stay here in the morning?—
> so that when the night leaves us
> we shall not have to lament,
> "Alas, now it is day,"
> as he lamented
> the last time he lay by me.
> Then the dawn came.
>
> Alas, she kissed me numberless times
> as I lay sleeping.
> Then tears fell
> down and down.
> But I comforted her
> so that she left off weeping
> and embraced me all around.
> Then the dawn came.
>
> Alas, that he has so often
> looked upon me!
> When he took the covers off me
> he wanted to look at poor me
> naked, without clothing.
> It was a great wonder
> that he never grew bored with this.
> Then the dawn came.

ɤ ɤ ɤ

A jaundiced view of the courtly love phenomenon is recorded in the dyspeptic diaries of Giubert of Nogent (1153), a professional preacher. Here he compares contemporary mores with those of the nobles of his mother's day:

O God, thou knowest how hard, almost impossible it would be for women of the present time to keep such chastity as this; whereas there was in those days such modesty that hardly ever was the good name of a married woman smirched by ill report. Ah! how wretchedly have modesty and honor in the state of maidenhood declined from those times to these, and both the reality and the show of a mother's chaperone shrunk to nought. Therefore coarse wit is all that may be noted in their manners and naught but jesting heard, with sly winks and ceaseless chatter. Wantonness shows in their gait, only silliness in their behavior. So much does the extravagance of their dress depart from the old simplicity in the enlargement of their sleeves, the narrowness of their skirts, the distortion of their shoes of cordovan leather with their curling toes, they seem to proclaim that everywhere shame is a castaway. A lack of lovers to admire her is a woman's crowning woe! On her crowds of thronging suitors rests her claim to nobility and courtly pride. In the old days—as God is my witness!—there was greater modesty in married men, who would have blushed to be seen in the company of such women, than there is now in married women.

Nor did contemporary men escape his acid pen:

Women by such shameful conduct encourage men to seek an affair and drive them to haunt the market place and the public street. Indeed, such women have caused far-reaching changes in male mores. No man now blushes for his own levity and licentiousness, because he knows that all are tarred with the same brush, and seeing himself in the same case as all others, why should he be ashamed of pursuits in which he knows all others engage? . . . Listen to the cheers when, with the inherent looseness of his unbridled passions that deserve the doom of eternal silence, he shamelessly broadcasts what ought to have been hidden in shame, what should have burdened his soul with the guilt of ruined chastity and plunged him into the depths of despair. In this and like manner is this age corrupt and corrupting, bespattering men with its evil imaginations, while the filth thereof, spreading to others, goes on increasing without end.

Catharism took root first among disaffected Catholic clergy, the educated and the nobility. It was a predominantly urban phenomenon, which is one of the reasons why it flourished in populous Languedoc (as it did in northern Italy).

The end of the ninth century had seen European economic activity at its lowest ebb, due to the social disorganization and political anarchy that accompanied the barbarian invasions and the collapse of Roman civil order. With the tenth century, a long, slow economic recovery began, which was greatly accelerated in the eleventh century thanks to the reopening of the Mediterranean trade routes by the First Crusade and by traders from the Flemish coast and Venice. A prosperous new merchant class emerged, which became the germ of a rising middle class. The wealth of the aristocracy was balanced by the new wealth of cities, which were able in effect to buy their way out of the old feudal structures. At the same time, serfdom was breaking down as more and more families found economic sustenance in the prosperous towns and villages, and as landowners, faced with strong demand for agricultural products and severe shortages of labor, greatly improved the contractual conditions for tenant farmers. Languedoc by the twelfth century was relatively densely populated, and peppered with flourishing towns, villages and cities. Toulouse was at this time a great city reveling in self-governing independence similar to that of Venice and the other Italian city-states.

Part of Catharism's appeal was certainly economic: its demands for tithes and other taxes were trivial compared to those of the Catholic church, since it had very little administrative overhead and almost no real estate, and its clerics lived on handouts, or by the fruits of their own labors as weavers or doctors or in other well-paid trades. The Cathar Perfecti believed in the discipline of labor (a notion that was largely alien to medieval Europe, but would appear again with the Protestant Reformation) and since they were engaged in crafts important to the prosperity that was developing out of increasing trade in the Mediterranean basin, they could relate to the booming mercantile class better than could the Catholic clergy, who harbored a deep suspicion of trade and secondary economic activity of any kind. St. Jerome had said, "The merchant can please God only with difficulty"; trade, buying low and selling high, seemed to Church authorities to be another form of usury and the official Church was actively hostile to the revival of commerce. Cathars seem to have had no such scruples, and some even engaged in banking (or so the evidence would suggest), a vocation few devout Catholics would consider at that time, since the collection of interest of any kind, however disguised, was condemned as usury.

Beyond the tales of conspiracy and treasure, and the poetry and romance, there is much in Catharism itself as it was practised in Languedoc in the thirteenth century that is attractive, at least superficially, to a modern mind. As champions of individualism, we moderns bridle at the medieval notion of individual identity, or the lack of it. Catholic doctrine saw men and women—Christian men and women—as having their way of life circumscribed by their Christianity, that is, their membership in the Church. The saving grace of this position was that just as the Church was a divine institution, so the Christian was more than simply an ordinary Homo sapiens; membership in the Church, freely available to all through baptism, meant that he or she took part in the attributes and essence of God. Nevertheless, the focus of the Church was on the collective rather than the individual, and while it did offer the individual a special human dignity, it did not recognize inherent individual rights in the modern sense. (Slavery, for instance, was not a pressing issue for the medieval Church.) The Cathars, in dismissing the authority of the Church as it then existed as spurious, or worse, a manifestation of the devil, freed men to act as autonomous agents in a context in which it was increasingly possible, and profitable, to do so. Catharism freed its followers to look after number one.

Nowhere was the difference over the issue of individual identity more starkly drawn than in the case of suicide, which was anathema to the Catholic church, as an interference with the prerogatives of God, but which was tolerated, even sometimes encouraged, among Cathars. Their clerics, the Perfecti, a disproportionate number of whom were also doctors of medicine (a notably modern profession), when giving the deathbed consolamentum to believers encouraged them to refuse food and drink following the ceremony in order to maintain their purity unto the end. This naturally hastened death in some cases; which is not to say that the Cathars actively promoted suicide, but neither did they abhor it, and they certainly did not forbid it. How, indeed, could they, given their belief that the body was the creation of the devil, and that the spirit was in no way reliant on its existence?

The Cathars also promoted the idea of individual access to the Gospels, at a time when the orthodox Church forbade it. In the orthodox view, it was the job of trained and ordained clergy to interpret the Bible to their parishioners; the laity were under no circumstances to be allowed to read the texts for themselves. The idea was to ensure that incorrect interpretations did not lead to the spreading of false doctrines, but even more importantly to avoid the freezing of doctrine at some arbitrary historical date. In Catholic doctrine, divine revelation did not end with the Scriptures, but continued through the medium of the Church, which Christ had given sole authority for safekeeping of the Word. The individual, thus, was obliged to submit his private opinions to the Church for verification. As would the Protestant reformers of the sixteenth century, the Cathars rejected the idea that the Church was a vehicle for revelation, believing that this was merely a rationalization for what was really a strategy to maintain the clergy's monopoly on the power that derived from the authority of the Scriptures. Truth was to be found only in the Bible, which every man could interpret for himself. They translated the New Testament into the local vernacular and set up schools to promote literacy among ordinary folk and their children. This, too, is a very modern idea. And its impact, which the Church only dimly suspected, is much broader and deeper than is even now generally supposed.

Marshall McLuhan and other late twentieth-century media theorists argue that literacy is a very potent catalyst in the development of the idea of "self," and therefore has played a key role in the development of the historically decisive cleavage between subject (self) and object (everything else). Literacy allowed people to take the intensely subjective contents of the mind and lay them out in permanent, unchanging text, which made them available to others as objective information. Media theory suggests that this split began to open up with the invention of the Greek phonetic alphabet sometime around 450 BC, a development which made widespread literacy possible for the first time in human history. Plato certainly seems to have been aware of the phenomenon. His *Republic* may in part be interpreted as an argument against the oral culture of Homeric Greece and in favor of literate culture. In the *Republic*,

> Plato asks of men that . . . they should think about what they say, instead of just saying it. And they should become the "subject" who stands apart from the "object" and reconsiders it and evaluates it, instead of just "imitating" it. . . . This amounts to accepting the premise that there is a "me," a "self," a "soul" or consciousness which is self-governing and which discovers the reason for action in itself rather than in imitation of the poetic experience. The doctrine of autonomous psyche is the counterpart of the rejection of oral culture.[1]

⊻ ⊻ ⊻

McLuhan added:

> A single generation of alphabetic literacy suffices in Africa today, as in
> Gaul two thousand years ago, to release the individual, initially at
> least, from the tribal web. This fact has nothing to do with the con-
> tent of the alphabetized words; it is the result of the sudden breach
> between the auditory and the visual experience of man. Only the pho-
> netic alphabet makes such a sharp division in experience, giving to its
> user an eye for an ear, and freeing him from the tribal trance of res-
> onating word magic and the web of kinship.[2]

At the time of the Cathars, Europe was no longer an entirely oral
civilization, but neither was it any more than fairly started on the road
to literacy. A fondness for books among all but the clergy and scholars
was still unusual enough to cause notice: contemporary chroniclers of
King Louis IX (St. Louis), for instance, never fail to mention his
"exceptional" fondness for books. Historian Regine Pernoud writes,

> The functions of spoken language at that time were less restricted
> than they are today; in a predominantly oral civilization the rich
> resources of speech were used by people who were still far removed
> from our essentially paper-and-ink civilization. As one leafs through
> contemporary documents, one gets a strong impression that everyone in
> the thirteenth, as in the twelfth, century was bilingual if not trilingual.
> Even the rudest peasant was able to mumble a few words of Latin.
> Groups of people of vastly different origins, speaking innumerable
> dialects, were able to communicate with extraordinary ease. James of
> Vitry, for example, a priest from Champagne, landed in Italy and
> preached with such fire to the crowds in churches that even women
> declared themselves Crusaders. But in what language did he pour out
> his eloquence—French or Italian? Just as striking are the many
> poems of this period which alternate between French and Provençal,
> with no indication that the hearers were in the least disturbed.[3]

ᚷ ᚷ ᚷ

In thinking over the impact of literacy, I sometimes wondered whether we should consider Christianity's great role in the Dark Ages and early Middle Ages to have been in minimizing the social chaos that would otherwise have accompanied a too-rapid shift from orality to literacy throughout Europe, not just by acting as a drag on what proved to be an irresistible trend towards the subjective and the idea of the autonomous self, but also in supplying moral restraints that were continuously adapted to the newly subjective environment, albeit often with great difficulty and in the face of divisive controversy.

And the more I learned about Catharism, the more it seemed to me to have been the first of a series of great hammer blows driving the wedge between subject and object ever deeper, until the ultimate divorce was achieved in the sixteenth and seventeenth centuries with the scientific revolution. The heresy's popularity in southern France could be attributed to the fact that it fit well with newly emerging social patterns that included expanded trade and commercial activity, the decline of feudalism and the rise of the middle class. Each of these developments demanded a slackening of traditional Christian restrictions on behavior, and Catharism offered this flexibility to ordinary believers (though not the Perfecti) within the scope of what was nominally a Christian religion.

In its literacy, its work ethic, its rejection of ritual and symbolism, its literalism in interpretation of the Scriptures (it rejected the Old Testament as devoid of interest and probably the work of the devil), its urban-centerdness and its tolerant outlook on secular behavior; in the acceptance of human rights based on natural law that is implied in its egalitarian views on gender—Catharism was thoroughly modern, and we might even say, forward-looking.

At the same time, it made a shambles of the Catholic worldview as it had emerged from Augustine's long labors, incorporating Plato's notion of ideal forms, and built on the bedrock sureties of man's participation in the actualized existence of the material world. The Cathars insisted that the material world was not of God's making:

ɣ ɣ ɣ

how could it be if it contained evil, as it clearly did? But Catholic cosmology saw a hierarchy of existence that *began* in the material world, ascended to man, and then to God. It proposed a transactional reality in which man's consciousness interacted with God's creation to make real a material world that otherwise existed only as a potential: the material world, thus actualized, was explained mainly in its usefulness to man (crops ripened, animals multiplied, the sun shone, for the benefit of man), who in turn justified his existence in a quest for salvation in union with God, the supreme good. Cathar doctrine was sand in the gears of this lovingly crafted philosophy, so carefully and painstakingly elaborated over the previous thousand years and more. In the material world of the Cathars, objects were given form and existence by the devil alone. Man was thus removed from his central place in the material world, and set adrift in a void furnished by completely objectified things; this, too, is an essentially modern view of material reality. The Cathars, of course, added the thoroughly unmodern idea that all of material reality was evil; true modernism, scientific positivism, has dealt with this archaic embarrassment—seemingly unavoidable in dualist worldviews—through the simple expedient of disregarding the spiritual realm. We've copped a plea of "no contest."

From the walls of Puilaurens, shading our eyes against the afternoon sun, we could see far up the verdant Fenouillédes Valley. The environment up here on the wind-scoured rocks seemed so harsh in contrast: what a lonely place it must have been. One of the towers along the interior walls defending the massive keep of Puilaurens is known as the "white tower," after the lady who haunts the ruins, Blanche of Bourbon, granddaughter of Philip the Fair. She had the misfortune to be married to Peter the Cruel, king of Castille at a time when this part of France was in Spanish hands. (Would that our own leaders had such usefully descriptive monickers!) He is said to have smothered her here when her political utility lapsed. Every bit as impressive, though, were the latrines along the north wall, where one placed one's bare bottom over a hole in a bench cantilevered over a sheer, terrifying drop of a quarter of a mile. This small chamber said as much for the constitutions of the people who had lived here as anything else we had seen.

Most of all, we found ourselves unanimous in our awe of the men who had done the initial construction work back in the tenth century: how many of them had died or been horribly injured in terrible falls while putting in place hundreds of thousands of stone blocks to make these massive, dizzying walls rising out of the sheer, native rock? Their work was well done: the castle withstood several attacks during the Albigensian Crusade and finally surrendered only in 1255 or 1256, when all hope had been lost.

Back on the D-117 highway, we followed the Maury River Valley east a few miles to the tiny town of Maury itself, where we turned north on a narrow blacktop road that quickly began a steep ascent out of the rich, alluvial farmland to the fortress of Quérebus. The vistas, once again, were awe-inspiring. To the east, we had glimpses of the distant Mediterranean beyond the broad Rousillon Plain with its market gardens and vineyards. To the northwest, we could see the silhouette of Peyrepertuse castle and to the south, across the river valley far below, beyond a range of chalk-white limestone ridges and still another broad valley, Canigou Peak near the Spanish frontier, its 2,780-meter summit dusted with snow.

A compact structure of roughly cylindrical shape, Quérebus in its geometric precision erupts out of a pinnacle of bare limestone like a massive mineral crystal. So unexpected is it that it seems an optical illusion and we stopped several times on the drive up the steep approach road just to confirm our senses. From the parking area, we sweated out a half-hour climb, much of it on steps hewn into the living stone, before reaching the entrance gate, where a sturdy length of chain has been bolted to the stone wall. It is there because when the wind pipes up it can funnel through the gate with enough force to blow people off their feet, preventing them from entering even on all fours. The chain keeps them from being swept right off the mountain, an occurrence once common enough to have encouraged the local site managers to post wind warnings and to close the site completely if a storm threatens. Thankfully, it was dead calm for our visit as Hilary and Simon, giddy with the altitude and the spectacular vistas of ribbons of road and spaghetti rivers far below, terrified Chris and me by gambolling along the ramparts, oblivious to danger.

There is, in the heart of the massive castle keep, a Gothic chamber supported by a single stone pillar which breaks out into eight ribs across a vaulted ceiling. Three arrow slits, an elegant Gothic window and the remains of a fireplace high on one wall show by their placement that this was a chamber with a cellar, the wooden floor having long since rotted away. The peculiar arrangement of these architectural elements—the fireplace seems high above any probable floor level and the supporting pillar is off-center with respect to both the windows and the rest of the room—have led to much speculation as to the chamber's original purpose. Legends naming Quérebus as one of the Cathars' hiding places for the Holy Grail have further fired imaginations. The historian Fernand Niel studied the chamber and its keep and arrived at the fanciful conclusion that due to the way in which the sun shone through each of the slit windows to hit the central pillar in different seasons, the room was somehow connected with sun worship.

Sun worship or no, the fortress, with its many dank passages and dark chambers illuminated only by arrow slits, is undeniably magical. When the four of us stumbled out of the gloom of one windowless passageway into the dazzling sunlight of the courtyard and looked up, there was a paraglider suspended from a huge wing of yellow hi-tech fabric drifting past perhaps a hundred metres overhead, lifted on the thermals rising from the valley. He was with us for the remainder of our visit, circling the peak silently, effortlessly, like a phantom from an opium dream.

Ɏ Ɏ Ɏ

We stopped for a leisurely lunch in the hilltop village of Cucungnan far below the gaunt walls of Quérebus, in a family-run *auberge* named for the town. In deference to Hilary's incipient vegan sensibilities (chicken or fish is tolerated), we ordered coq au vin rather than *civet de sanglier* or *lapin au saupiquet*, and it was delicious, the rich brown sauce given a unique tanginess by the robustness of the local red wine called Maury.

On the road once again, the air-conditioning mercifully blasting away, we followed the twisting, bucking route upward towards Peyrepertuse, the largest of the Cathar ruins, sometimes called "Carcassonne in the Sky" for its long curtain wall and half-round towers. There are actually two fortresses here on the same razor-backed outcropping, the lower fort shaped like the prow of a ship, and Château St. Georges on a still more precipitous height at about eight hundred metres, sixty metres above the lower fortifications. Together they comprise more than three hundred metres of continuous fortifications and from certain angles resemble a sky-high section of the Great Wall of China. By the time we had negotiated the narrow path along the side of the nearly sheer north face of the peak to the entrance gate, we were bathed in sweat and feeling the results of our day's exertions. We gave the lower castle, its chapel and keep a thorough going-over and admired views no less awe-inspiring than those at Puilaurens and Quérebus; in fact, Quérebus was in plain view to the south, and I wondered what form of signaling had been used between the two garrisons: flags, perhaps, and mirrors. Typically, frontier forts like these would have been occupied by as few as half a dozen knights: it must have been just about the least attractive military duty on earth. Even for a Prairie lad like myself, it is difficult to imagine the severity of the winters in these eagles' nests where, even in summer, a squall will sweep the parapets clean. We had learned from site staff at the parking lot below that just a day earlier a German tourist who had spurned advice to descend when a thunderstorm approached had been struck by lightning and killed.

ꝟ ꝟ ꝟ

Simon asked an interesting question: What would be the modern military equivalent of one of these fortresses in the sky? I thought at first of an aircraft carrier, probably because of the ship-like outlines of Peyrepertuse, and the notion of a heavily defended staging platform for attack sorties. But on reflection, they probably had more in common with the spy satellite, looking down from an inaccessible height on the ant-like creatures going through the motions of daily life on the plains below. Then again, though, there was their role as a sanctuary of last resort, something that does not exist in the modern world of thermonuclear weapons. In this, Peyrepertuse and Quérebus, like the others, had ultimately failed. Peyrepertuse surrendered to a crusading army in 1240, four years before Montségur fell; Quérebus held out until 1255, the last military bastion of Catharism on the planet. There is no record of the fate of the Cathars inside; it seems probable they were allowed to go free in the full knowledge that they were unlikely to escape the long arm of the Inquisition, wherever in Europe they might flee.

We trudged across the grassy esplanade separating the two forts at the summit, to a steep staircase named for Saint Louis (King Louis IX), who had ordered its construction. The sixty-odd steps are carved into the rock in an arc which extends right out over the precipice, and they have been polished to a slippery patina with centuries of weathering and footfalls. My knees wobbled just looking at them. Given the broiling heat and our advancing weariness, it did not seem wise to tempt fate. I knew Chris would be on my side, but to my amazement neither Hilary nor Simon gave us an argument. There were limits to their bravado after all.

Safely back in the car I planned the night's menu at the *gîte*: there were fresh farm eggs and delicious nut-flavored cèpse mushrooms in the fridge, ripe tomatoes on the vine near our little terrace, three kinds of sausage to grill; we'd pick up some fresh *pain de campagne* on the way back. And of course we had cheeses and grapes for dessert, and fresh olive oil of the initial pressing and a bottle or two of the local plonk, quite drinkable at less than two dollars a liter.

Just before turning in, I dashed off a postcard to Berkowitz. It showed an aerial view of Montségur, a wintertime dusting of snow making the ruin and the surrounding rock seem unbearably cold and lonely:

Cher Berkowitz,

The Cathar castles are, like the city of Carcassonne, better in every way than their photographs. No graven image can do them justice. But I am becoming uneasy about the Cathars themselves. I came here thinking of them as romantic paragons and heroes of humanism. They may be all of that but the more I see and read the more they appear to me rather like the Calvinists and Lutherans and other radical Protestant sects who threw out the baby with the bathwater during the Reformation. I wonder if all of this romance stuff didn't go on in spite of them rather than because of them. And I am disturbed by this willingness to commit mass hara-kiri: I don't know quite what it is—something about the value of the life—but it doesn't sit right with me. Still very hot here . . . kids behaving reasonably well, enjoying things a lot, I think.

Best,

wr

ɣ ɣ ɣ

Montségur and Her Martyrs

THE ALBIGENSIAN CRUSADE ⚔

DE MONTFORT'S TACTICS ⚔ THE HOLY GRAIL

⚔ THE SIEGE ⚔ THE IMMOLATION ⚔

THE INQUISITION BEGINS ⚔ A SEARCH FOR

MEANING ⚔ REPRESSION AND FREEDOM

T he surrender of fortress Montségur marks the climax of the protracted war waged by Rome and its allies in northern France to root out and exterminate heresy in the south. The long struggle had begun with the Church's attempts to counter Catharism's popularity through the preaching of St. Bernard and St. Dominic, and great and famous debates were held throughout the land pitting papal champions against the best theologians the Cathar church had to offer. And, aware that part of the appeal of the Cathars was the moral integrity of their clergy, the Church in Rome made serious efforts to reform the local priesthood, notorious for its ignorance and venality. None of this worked, however, and Rome eventually implemented what can only be called its "final solution," in the form of a bloody, forty-five-year crusade against

⚔ ⚔ ⚔

the Cathar heresy—the so-called Albigensian Crusade. This was followed by seventy years of terror under the Inquisition, which did not rest its implacable stenographers or its implements of torture until the very last Cathar cleric had been ferreted out, interrogated and burned alive. Thanks to the cold-blooded efficiency of the Dominican inquisitors, we know his name—Guillaume Bélebaste—and the date of his immolation, August 24, 1321.

Crusading knights and mercenaries from the north of France first responded to the impatient call to arms of Pope Innocent III in 1208. The knights in their armor and the mailed foot soldiers with their pikes and crossbows assembled in Lyon in numbers estimated variously at 50,000 and 130,000, and on a hot July afternoon descended with terrible fury on the Cathar town of Béziers. All 20,000 inhabitants were slaughtered, Catholic and Cathar alike. "Kill them all," the papal legate is alleged to have cried out amid the frenzy, "God will recognize his own!"

This was merely the first of a long series of atrocities committed in the name of the mother Church during the next four decades of warfare, in which southern feudal lords and knights fought to protect not just the Cathar clergy and their followers, but their own lands and independence. The Crusade's military commander, an ambitious baron with a reputation for piety, chastity and personal valor, named Simon de Montfort, hatched a waking nightmare that was designed to weaken the resolve of besieged knights and Cathars holed up in the hilltop fortress of Cabaret, just north of Carcassonne. The particular horror of the story is in its details. De Montfort captured the small fortress at nearby Bram, and mutilated the entire garrison of about two hundred men by slicing off their noses and upper lips and putting out their eyes; one man was left with one good eye, and he was given the task of leading the wailing, stumbling parade up to Cabaret, where, de Montfort correctly anticipated, it would encourage prompt negotiations leading to a surrender. During the course of the Crusade,

Ɐ Ɐ Ɐ

tens of thousands of men, women and children were butchered by the northern papal forces, and thousands of Cathar believers were burned alive at individual stakes or in mass immolations.

All of this has become the stuff of legend, and according to one of these tales the Cathars were in possession of the Holy Grail, not the fanciful genealogy charts of *The Holy Blood and the Holy Grail*, but a drinking vessel that by tradition was used at the Last Supper, and to collect the blood of Christ on the cross. It was the Grail fable as immortalized by a German troubadour, Wolfram von Eschenbach in his epic poem *Parsifal* (adapted for opera by Richard Wagner), that prompted Nazi German forces to set up a small camp in 1943 along the wild and almost impenetrable gorges of the Hers River Valley, which link the fortresses at Montségur and Montaillou. Known as *Gorges de la Frau*, "the gorges of fear," they are said to have sheltered Cathar clergy fleeing the crusaders in the last days of organized resistance. In their search for links to a heroic past of their fantasies, the Nazis hoped to find traces of the fabled "treasure of the Cathars," perhaps the Grail itself. They were soon too busy coping with the realities of the Allied invasion of Normandy to continue their adventure in archaeology.

In this country of grand and elaborate memorials, the monument to the martyrs of Montségur is, to say the least, modest. It is in the shape of a keyhole and about a metre in height: it rests on a simple rock plinth and features a so-called Cathar cross—a highly stylized cross within a stone disc and on the reverse side a five-pointed star, the alchemist's symbol for wisdom. All of the symbology is fanciful, for the Cathars themselves worshiped no symbols and especially abhorred the cross. Nearby there is an enormous boulder on which have been inscribed words which record the bare fact of the tragedy that took place here. The markers stand at the foot of a gigantic upwelling of limestone out of which loom the walls of the ruined castle. Until 1960, when a society of medieval scholars erected the present cairn, there was nothing at all here to commemorate the fact that at or near this spot in the winter of 1248 more than two hundred

Ɣ Ɣ Ɣ

Cathar heretics were burned alive by crusaders. The victims were not tied to stakes; when Montségur finally fell to siege engines of an army ten thousand strong, they had been given the choice of renouncing their beliefs and going free, or death by fire on this little plateau. All of them, men and women, some children, chose the pyre. They leaped into the roaring flames of their own accord.

I stood with Chris looking at the small stone cairn, which was all the more moving for its simplicity. Below us were close-cropped sheep meadows and, beyond, the forested, blue-green mountains of Ariège. The two of us were on our own because after more than a week on the road we needed a little space from the kids. It was Hilary who had made the suggestion that they stay behind at the *gîte* and get to know the owner's daughter. She is the wisest among us; Chris is the smartest, Simon a walking encyclopedia and polymath. I am the best cook and driver.

There is a passage pertinent to the mass immolation in historian Emmanuel LeRoy Ladurie's classic reconstruction of life in the nearby medieval village of Montaillou. The book is based on Inquisition interrogations from about 1290, which he found preserved in the Vatican archives. Two women of Montaillou were overheard chatting, by an informer:

> I was passing [in the street] and I heard them talking. Guillemette Benete was saying to Alazaïs: "How can people manage to bear the pain when they are burning at the stake?"
>
> To which Alazaïs replied, "Ignorant creature! God takes the pain upon himself, of course."[1]

It seemed, in its context, a better explanation than our modern medical description of the physiology of shock and the shutting down of neural connections.

I have had some experience of this myself. One winter when we were clearing the land for the house we now live in, I set fire to a huge pile of branches trimmed from felled trees I'd cut up for fire-wood. It was hard to get going there in the snow, so I splashed some gasoline on it, actually quite a lot of gasoline. The fire flashed back on me and set my clothing alight. I was wearing a leather wind-breaker, gloves and sunglasses. My hair went up like a bonfire, the cloth cuffs and collar of the jacket caught fire: Chris was about fifty yards away up to her knees in snow, talking to an electrician about where to bring the electrical service onto the property. She said I looked like a human torch. I could not breathe because the fire was consuming all the oxygen around me. I fell to the ground and began rolling in the snow. The fire went out quickly and I sat up thinking, *I'm burned*. I scooped up some snow and held it to my face, and then to my neck and wrists. By now Chris was beside me and she helped. I felt fine, but she insisted on driving me to the nearest hospital where they cleaned me up and applied cold packs to the burn areas. I was missing quite a lot of hair, but that grew back, and although I looked a mess for a few months, the only permanent damage was a small scar on my wrist and another at my throat. A year later, you could barely see them. I was very lucky.

The experience taught me that there are worse ways to die. You feel no pain when you're on fire; you feel strangely and powerfully cerebral, as though your mind has expanded beyond your body. And you soon black out from lack of oxygen. It's a bit like drowning, which is supposed to be one of the best ways to go, if you can avoid panicking.

At Montségur there is a steep, half-hour climb up a narrow path along the three-hundred-meter-high cliffs to the ruined walls of the castle, and from there you can see forever across the wind-worn lime-stone Plateau de la Sault from which the castle *pog* erupts like an enormous canine tooth, on to the Aude River Valley, across the forested ranges of the Plantauret and the purple massif of St. Barthélemy. Almost nothing remains of the original "Cathar" fortifi-cations, which were dismantled following the siege: the existing ruins

ꓬ ꓬ ꓬ

date from a new construction in the thirteenth century. This naturally makes problematic a modern theory that a series of arrow slits in the small rectangular keep were the focus of Cathar rites connected to the sun: at the summer solstice the sun shines in through two arrow slits on one wall and straight out through slits on the opposite wall. Almost certainly, both walls antedate the Cathar era.

More affecting than anything else on the summit are the dim traces of homes built on terraced land abutting the castle walls. As many as five or six hundred heretics are thought to have lived here, huddled below the fortifications. During the siege itself, they would have been forced inside the castle walls: the terrible overcrowding this must have caused is evident from the narrowness of the courtyard.

It was in Montségur that many of the black-robed Cathar clergy, as well, sought refuge when it was finally clear that the Crusade would succeed in its military goals. History and legend agree that it was to Montségur that the Perfecti brought the Cathar treasure: what it was, no one knows, but legend has it that it was either a fabulous hoard of gold, or a priceless Christian relic. The first theory is based on the fact that, literate and trustworthy, the Cathar clergy had become bankers in Languedoc, much as the Knights Templar were to the Europe of orthodox Catholicism. Their coffers were further swelled by bequests from the local aristocracy, among whom there were many sympathizers. However, any substantial sum in gold would have been difficult to move about in secrecy, particularly as it would have had to be transported over extremely difficult terrain. On the other hand, given their distaste for symbolism of the cross and the Eucharist, and their abhorrence of relics of saints, it seems unlikely that a relic, even the Grail, had it existed, would have held much interest for the Cathars. In this riddle lie the roots of the theory that the treasure was a document of some sort.

The siege of Montségur is a stirring story of feats of heroism and determination on both sides. For months, sympathetic villagers kept the inhabitants of the fortress supplied with food, slipping through the

Crusader lines and making terrifying nighttime climbs up the almost vertical limestone crags. When the crusading army despaired of starving the garrison out, a handful of volunteers, mountain men, mercenaries from Gascony to the west, scaled the frozen rock face of the *pog* and overcame the defenders of an unfortified height of land on the summit. A desperate counterattack failed with heavy losses, and the Crusaders began assembling a small trebuchet or catapult, piece by piece. It was soon supplemented by a much more powerful machine, which in the depths of winter began pounding the massive walls of the fortress every twenty minutes, day in and day out, with forty-five-kilogram boulders mined on the site. Those that overshot the walls caused terrible carnage among the defenders and their many wards crowded inside.

Early in March, the outcome of the siege was no longer in doubt, and the half-starved, half-frozen fortress defenders agreed to a truce: the terms were that at the end of two weeks' time, the fortress would be handed over; all of the surviving inhabitants would be allowed to go free; Cathars among them would be required to renounce their heretical beliefs and those who did not were to be burned. The peculiar provision of the two-week truce prior to surrender has never been adequately explained, and some authorities argue that the Cathar leaders did not agree to the terms of the truce, which was negotiated by their military defenders. In any case, contemporary accounts say that during the truce several knights and others asked for and received the consolamentum, knowing it would mean certain death. Those who were going to their deaths shared what belongings they had among the men who had defended them. Easter was celebrated in a simple ceremony.

It was during the truce, or shortly before it, that two Cathar priests slipped out of the fortress and down the valley carrying part of the Cathar treasure. Shortly after that, four more Perfecti were secretly lowered to the valley on ropes under cover of darkness: it is these men who, according to legend, were in possession of the Grail, and whose mission it was to carry it safely south across the Pyrenees into Spain. It is thought that all of them escaped by way of the gorges of the Hers River, hiding in some of the many limestone caves in the region. Most of these men are identified in the historical record; at least two were seen years later, in Italy, but what became of their precious cargo, no one knows.

When the fortress was evacuated, the Perfecti were separated from the others who were to be set free and in some cases families were divided in this way. Among the Perfecti was Corba, wife of Raimon de Péreilha, one of the governors of Montségur: she had waited until the last possible moment before taking the consolamentum. She bid goodbye to her husband and two married daughters, her son and her grandchildren, before mounting to the pyre with her mother and an invalid daughter.

History is punctuated by tragic events of sacrifice and courage, though perhaps only Masada matches Montségur in sheer size and drama. The circumstances were similar: at Masada a garrison of Jews, rebels against Roman rule of Palestine, held out for many months against a much larger force of legionnaires. When the Romans finally breached the fortress walls in AD 73, they found that the defenders, who had numbered perhaps a thousand, had killed themselves rather than surrender. Only seven women and children survived, hidden in a water duct.

But perhaps even more interesting than the suicides, and less susceptible to modern answers based on group psychoses and charismatic leaders, is the question of how and why Cathar communities persisted as they did in hilltop villages throughout Languedoc for generations after military action subsided, despite the relentless persecution of the "black and white hounds of the Lord" (*domini canes*)—the Dominicans, and the terrors of the Inquisition.

In establishing the Inquisition as a mopping-up operation to follow the Crusade, Gregory IX was careful to set it up outside the normal framework of canonical law and ecclesiastical courts. It was placed, instead, in the hands of the Dominicans, and to a lesser degree the Franciscans, the new holy orders whose doctrinal zeal was a trademark. They were to report directly to Rome, bypassing normal Church protocol. Unlike local bishops and lesser clerics who could be presumed to have potentially compromising relationships within their communities, the preaching orders could be expected to pursue their assignment with single-minded enthusiasm. And they did.

The Inquisition established procedures which set the pattern for rule by terror in ideological dictatorships down to the present day. The twin cornerstones were the secret accusation and trial and the importance placed on confession. When the Inquisitor arrived in a city or town, he would first issue a proclamation which granted the inhabitants a "period of grace" during which, if they confessed their transgressions, they could expect to be let off lightly, perhaps with some minor penance. At the same time he asked for information on heretics from informers. Anyone who had engaged in heretical activities—or who thought someone might accuse him of such activity—was thus left in the position of either keeping silent and hoping that he would not be reported, thereby risking imprisonment and loss of his property, even death, if he had been, or turning himself in, in the expectation of a lesser punishment. Acquittals were rare in the courts of the Inquisition. The grace period normally lasted about a week, during which frightened people flocked to the Inquisitor to inform on themselves, and on others. In this way, a mountain of information was quickly collected, and as each suspect was hauled in and questioned, more names were added to the Inquisition's carefully cross-referenced files.

At the end of the week's grace period, suspects who had not turned themselves in were arrested. They were interrogated in private, without being told by whom they had been accused. Unless they confessed they were thrown in prison, where they could expect harsh conditions at best and often torture, since the object was to break their resistance and encourage them to provide the confession that was the only definitive demonstration of guilt. Anyone who was released, automatically came in for intense suspicion in the community, since it was known that the inquisitors routinely offered clemency in return for names. The social turmoil caused by all of this is difficult to imagine, unless one has spent time in a modern totalitarian state.

The interrogations themselves were scrupulously transcribed and preserved in archives, many of which have survived, and they make morbidly interesting reading. From a forensic point of view, the difficulty with heresy is that it is an intellectual crime, and therefore difficult to prove: there is seldom any objective evidence. Furthermore, heresy is not heresy unless the error is knowingly embraced. To establish true heresy, then, the inquisitor had to look deep into the heart and mind of the accused. The process was much more akin to psychoanalysis than the kind of questioning that takes place in a modern court trial. The accused were taken through virtually their entire lives, often in great detail, and were questioned closely about all of their important relationships and, of course, their beliefs. In this way, the inquisitors gained a comprehensive picture of life in the community and were better able to judge, in theory at least, which accusations were valid and which were spurious. In this sense, and in terms of the traumatic impact it had on the entire community, the Inquisition can be seen as an exercise in behavior modification as much as a search for truth.

There are important ways, it seems to me, in which the inquisitors had more in common with their Cathar victims than they had with the orthodox Church. In their exquisite organization skills, in their assiduous attention to detail, in their acceptance of the strictly regulated monastic regime, in their obsession with records and procedures and most of all in their willingness to make means subservient to ends, they shared the incipient modernism of the Cathar culture in Languedoc, for none of these characteristics was typical of medieval life as it had evolved through centuries of Church influence. It is at least interesting and probably significant that St. Thomas

Aquinas who, two centuries later, was responsible for committing the Church to conforming to the modern ideals of science, was a Dominican. (In his *Summa theologica* he held that heretics merited not only excommunication, but death, since by their beliefs they had placed themselves beyond the security of the person that only the faithful are entitled to enjoy. To the best of my knowledge, he offered no opinion on the moral efficacy of separating peoples' joints on the rack and hitting them with mallets as a means of eliciting confessions in inquisitorial proceedings.)

The dreadful irony of the Church's having invented modern police-state tactics to destroy a heresy that presaged the soulless "modernism" we currently enjoy, and precisely *because* it contained these tendencies, is richly evident in this passage from a recent, highly scientific, superbly modern book on the Inquisition by Cornell University anthropologist James B. Given, who spent some considerable time with the records of the Languedoc inquisitors, and who gave his work the appropriately ponderous title, *Inquisition and Medieval Society: Power, Discipline and Resistance in Languedoc*. In his scientific detachment he is able to write the following:

> To understand how the inquisitors sought to acquire enough power to accomplish their goals, it is useful to think of their activity as a form of production. Like all other forms of production, political activity is a labor process in which raw materials are transformed into a new commodity . . . the realization of a policy goal. In effect political activity can be understood as a form of technology, as a body of specific techniques for manipulating social relations.

That said, the author goes on to explain that, in the first section of his book, he proposes to "examine the way in which the Inquisition used three different technologies in their pursuit of heresy and heretics: record keeping, coercive forms of interrogation (including imprisonment) and punishment." This approach, of course, allows him to address the issues at hand from a completely value-neutral and therefore rigorously inductive position.

By "punishment," the reader is left to assume he means such tortures as branding irons, slow roasting, the rack and the stake, since the book does not concern itself with these details, although it does supply the reader amply with impressive charts and graphs, including one which illustrates the mean length of incarceration needed to make an accused confess. The word "torture" occurs eight times in 230 pages of text; nowhere is it defined or are measures described. The terror of secret accusations and interrogations, the horrors of the torture chambers, the agonies of imprisonment in dank, filthy, vermin-infested cells, are interpreted this way:

> What the inquisitors had done, and they may have been the first in medieval Europe to have done so, was create a socially delimited space, in which they could isolate individuals from the outer world and subject them without interruption to an enforced and forcible persuasion.

Towards the end of his book the author confesses:

> One cannot read the Languedocian inquisitors' records without coming to feel a grudging admiration for the ingenuity and determination that many of [the inquisitors] displayed in their campaign against heresy.[2]

How, I wonder, can any moral person possibly feel admiration, grudging or otherwise, for the Inquisition and its methods? Professor Given's book, which is here taken as representative of thousands of others like it, penned in increasing quantities by social scientists, puts in high relief the very real justification for the medieval Church's fear that the separation of the material from the spiritual would lead to a kind of hell on earth in which actions could be reduced to "technologies" and evaluated solely according to their productivity or instrumentality.

Ⴟ Ⴟ Ⴟ

The Inquisition created a concentration camp atmosphere throughout Languedoc, which was ultimately fatal to the local culture. Thousands of accused were imprisoned and tortured, and thousands were burned alive; even the dead were exhumed and burned, their property confiscated from their children. And still the heresy persisted through generations, gradually receding to the remotest of mountain villages. How do people survive under such conditions? Certainly they do not survive without values.

I had with me in France a thin volume I had brought along in a duffel bag with our Michelin maps and guidebooks and holiday reading material. I'd come across it among Chris's esoteric collection on our library shelves at home: its title was *Man's Search for Meaning*, and the author was Viktor Frankl. The day after our visit to Montségur, I was up early to make the café au lait for breakfast on the *gîte's* terrace. I fished Frankl's little book out of the bag and sat down to read under our catalpa tree while I waited for the rest of the family to awaken. I read:

> This book does not claim to be an account of facts and events but of personal experiences, experiences which millions of prisoners have suffered time and again. It is the inside story of a concentration camp, told by one of its survivors. The tale is not concerned with the great horrors, which have already been described often enough (though less often believed), but with the multitude of small torments. . . .

Frankl, a psychiatrist, was interned by the Nazis in 1939 along with most of his family. His wife, brother, mother and father all died in the camps or their gas ovens. Frankl himself lived to tell the tale, in fact died only in 1997, well into his nineties. He was a unique witness, and his experiences led him to develop a new strain of psychotherapy, which he called logotherapy, from *logos* = meaning. From observing camp inmates, including himself, Frankl concluded that two apparently very different groups of men had something in common.

On the one hand were those who were brutalized by the experience and became camp guards or "capos," often more vicious than the uniformed guards themselves. On the other were those who simply gave up on life and allowed death to find them in any of the many forms it took at Auschwitz and Dachau. What Frankl discovered they had in common, was that they each had renounced their essential humanity, one group through the rejection of life and the other through a reversion to subhuman behavior.

But what was it that constituted this humanity which was being abandoned? For Frankl, who had been trained in Freudian psychiatry, the surprising answer was "meaning" or purpose in life. Separated from family and loved ones, stripped of every vestige of civilized existence, enslaved in forced labor, identified by number tattoos, beaten, degraded, humiliated, deprived of food and sleep, clothed in filthy rags, often hand-me-downs from gas chamber victims, Frankl found that it was still possible for inmates to hang on to some form of meaning in their lives, and if they managed to do that, they were more likely to survive.

What possible meaning could there be to life as a prisoner in Auschwitz? For most inmates, the question centered on whether they would survive, for if not, their suffering could have no meaning. For them, the prospect of survival was the only thing that could give meaning to their agonies. But for Frankl, the question was different: he struggled to understand whether there could be meaning in the very suffering and death itself, for if not, there could be no meaning in life as a survivor. Only about one in twenty inmates was to escape death, and the selection process was almost purely random, dependent entirely on external forces as unpredictable as the whim of a sadistic guard, or an accounting entry in a commandant's ledger. Frankl concluded that "a life whose meaning depends on such a happenstance—whether one escapes or not—ultimately would not be worth living at all." Meaning in life, he came to believe, is not given, but is something actively created.

✷ ✷ ✷

He recalls a passage from Dostoevsky: "There is only one thing that I dread; not to be worthy of my sufferings." And he continues in his own words:

> The way in which a man accepts his fate and all the suffering it entails, the way in which he takes up his cross, gives him ample opportunity—even under the most difficult circumstances—to add a deeper meaning to his life. It may remain brave, dignified and unselfish. Or in the bitter fight for self-preservation he may forget his human dignity and become no more than an animal. Here lies the chance for a man either to make use of or to forego the opportunities of attaining the moral values that a difficult situation may afford him. And this decides whether he is worthy of his sufferings or not.[3]

This led Frankl to the discovery of the poetic idea which is at the core of his approach to psychotherapy. In order to mitigate the sufferings of the men around him in the camps, he reports,

> [W]e had to learn ourselves and, furthermore, we had to teach the despairing men that it did not really matter what we expected from life, but rather what life expected from us. We needed to stop asking about the meaning of life, and instead to think of ourselves as those who were being questioned by life—daily and hourly. Our answer must consist, not in talk and meditation, but in right action and in right conduct.[4]

Because the circumstances in which men find themselves are always in some way unique, and change over time,

> these tasks [i.e., that which constitutes "right action" and "right conduct"], and therefore the meaning of life, differ from man to man, and from moment to moment. Thus it is impossible to define the

meaning of life in a general way. . . . "Life" does not mean something vague, but something very real and concrete, just as life's tasks are also very real and concrete. They form man's destiny, which is different and unique for each individual.[5]

A new idea in its time, it was also very old. Frankl believed that meaning in life is actively created, moment by moment, but for most of recorded history people have believed that *everything* in this world is actively created—meaning included. What has often been interpreted as fatalism in medieval life is more often an implicit recognition of the fact of man's active participation in the creation of the reality that surrounds him.

In his admirable reconstruction of life in the village of Montaillou, LeRoy Ladurie presents a passage from the Inquisition archives in which a congenial but nominally heretical shepherd named Pierre Maury is chided by a woman friend for failing to avoid the Montaillou district, where the Inquisition was at its most vigilant:

"My son, you should not go back there. Why not stay here with us? You have no son or daughter or anyone to look after except yourself. You could live here quite comfortably. But if you are captured there, you are lost."[6]

To which Maury is reported to have replied, "No, I could not live here [in Catalonia] permanently; and anyhow, no one can take away my fate." He later elaborates,

"I might as well go on living (in the Montaillou district); for no one can take away my fate . . . I cannot do otherwise, for I cannot lead a life different from that for which I was brought up. . . . And I must bear my fate, whether it is here or there."[7]

A well-informed, cosmopolitan and thoroughly engaging character, Pierre Maury thought himself the freest of men, and it was, paradoxically, his acceptance of his fate that set him free in a time of severe religious oppression. He refused to be a fugitive; insisted on being himself and living where and how he wished. His ultimate fate, he well understood, was death. The only issues in question were the relatively trivial matters of timing and means. To the issue of meaning in life, he gave scarcely a second thought: it was manifest in all he did and everything he saw. He created his life, and meaning with it. On this, Cathar and Catholic were in agreement: this was an understanding that underlay all medieval theologies.

Frankl, too, was a heretic. His ideas did not conform to the dominant materialist, positivist worldview; were not, at bottom, scientific. How could they be, since they accepted the reality of values? Freud, the scientist of the psyche, had said: "This alone I know with certainty, namely that men's value judgements are guided absolutely by their desire for happiness, and are therefore merely an attempt to bolster up their illusions by arguments." For him, values could be explained as defence mechanisms, or reaction formulations or sublimations or some other epiphenomenon of a basic animal drive. But Frankl had access to human experience Freud could not have imagined, and he firmly believed, to the contrary, that values are real and furthermore that they do not push people, they pull. People are not driven to moral behavior, rather, they choose it. Love, for Frankl, is not an offshoot of the sexual drive, but a primary phenomenon in itself. "Logos," or meaning, he says at one point, "is deeper than logic." Either statement would be enough to convict him before a modern scientific Inquisition. But Frankl goes further:

[A]s for myself, I would not be willing to live for the sake of my "defense mechanisms," nor would I be ready to die merely for the sake of my "reaction formulations." Man, however, is able to live and even to die for the sake of his ideals and values![8]

꙳ ꙳ ꙳

The argument, baldly stated, is this: The conviction that events in the world are not without meaning, but are informed by an ideal purpose, is the basis of all meaningful lives. This is true not only of the paragons among us, but of the ordinary person who, in whatever he or she does, tries to lead a worthy life, and, so far as he or she is able, to leave the world a better place than it was.

Pierre Maury would have understood Viktor Frankl; he would have thought Freud barking mad.

Toulouse: Dominic and Aquinas

INDUSTRY UNDER THE CATALPA ❧

SPECIALIZATION AMONG THE ANTS ❧

DISCOVERING TOULOUSE ❧ ST. SERNIN ❧

A WARM RAIN ❧ THE JACOBINS ❧ A PLACE

OF MIRACLES

I n the morning following our visit to Montségur, the bread truck arrived at our *gîte* on schedule and I bought two baguettes and half a dozen croissants. With coffee and fresh fruit and our expanding cheese tray, it made a banquet: we now had family-sized chunks of artisan-made Roquefort, ripe Camembert, cheddar-like Cantel (probably the oldest of France's many cheeses), a tangy local goat cheese whose name I've forgotten and heavenly Saint-Marcellin, all bought at what seemed to us absurdly low prices.

Still waiting for Chris and the kids to find their way to the terrace table, now in full sunlight, I was distracted by the ants that seemed to arrive out of nowhere whenever there was food around. They were after the crumbs which fell to the cement, and I watched for long enough to see that the entrance to their underground home, a hole about the diameter of a pencil, was in the small circular plot of soil in which our terrace's little catalpa tree had been planted. Sometimes they worked by themselves, but more often several would cooperate in grappling with a large load. At first, there seemed to be two species, one considerably larger than the other, but after watching for a while I could see that they all belonged to the same colony, and the smaller ants appeared to be the bosses. They moved faster than the bigger cousins, and sometimes would break up a work crew struggling with a large piece of crust, for no apparent reason. The big guys scattered, and the crumb was left, unharvested. Despite the difficulties they faced with the size of the crumbs and having to drag them up over the whitewashed stones bordering the catalpa tree's plot, despite the chaos caused by the aggressiveness of the smaller ants, an amazing amount of bread got shifted to the entrance hole, where work crews cut it to size and manoeuvred it downstairs.

With their shiny exoskeletons, the ants could have been knights in armor. What we regard as technology, tools for doing work, the ant has incorporated into its living being. The body armor, for example, and the powerful mandibles all ants use for fighting and gathering food. Ants even produce different body configurations from the same eggs in order to supply their colonies with the technologies they need to survive: while most ants are workers, some become queens, which are living egg-laying machines. Males exist only for a few days, to perform the single task of fertilizing the queen. Workers of some species grow to different sizes according to the specialized tasks they perform; in one jungle species some workers grow as big (relative to their sisters) as bulldozers, and are used to clear trails for other workers. Some eggs become soldier ants, large, heavily armored, some with huge heads and mandibles, programmed for kamikaze loyalty to the colony. Many ant species have the ability to produce toxic sprays within their bodies, which are used to great effect in combat.

✕ ✕ ✕

In one species, soldiers are walking bombs storing large amounts of toxic chemicals: when pressed in battle, they violently contract their abdomens and explode, spraying the foe with secretions. As I watched them in their highly organized labors, it seemed to me that ants are virtually indistinguishable from their tools.

Chris arrived at last, her long blonde hair wet from the shower, and as she stood by the table for a moment in shorts and a thin cotton top, shading her eyes with a hand and looking out over the vineyards, I could see that she had wiped out a small work crew with her sandaled foot. I said nothing: it would only have upset her, and I had probably done the same a dozen times just that morning, walking back and forth across the terrace, not looking. When Hilary and Simon finally showed up, I pointed out to them the ant drama going on at their feet, and they each watched for a while, dropping bigger and bigger crumbs, trying a little cheese, a little jam, to see what would happen. But before long it was too hot to be comfortable on the terrace and in any case we had to be off on our day's excursion.

An hour later I was behind the wheel again, and Chris had Michelin map number 235 on her lap and was navigating the way to the highway to Toulouse, through vineyards and sunflower fields along pleasant little asphalt roads. Hilary was reading her Anne Rice novel, and Simon had his usual question-per-minute, today mostly about aerodynamics, a subject about which I know practically nothing. He was also on about the cost of new and used motorcycles, something I used to follow before he was born: he appeared to be designing some sort of motorcycle-based aircraft in his head. After a while he retrieved his beat-up Newton from his bag and became absorbed in calculations.

Our guidebooks described Toulouse as a "modern" city and it may indeed be the most modern in France. It is the hub of the French aerospace industry, surrounded by industrial suburbs. It is also very old: treasure pillaged from ancient Delphi was rumored to have been buried here, and in the early Middle Ages, as a rich and important

ɤ ɤ ɤ

crossroads for trade, it was the cultural cockpit of southern Europe. The Moslem invasion of Europe was unable to take Toulouse, though it captured Arles and Avignon and Narbonne; it was unable to plunge north because without Toulouse it could not protect its flank, and so the Moslem defeat owes at least as much to the city as it does to Charles Martel, who won the decisive battle near Muret in 732. Throughout the economic revival of the early Middle Ages the counts of Toulouse were among the greatest lords of Europe, and Count Raymond IV was wealthiest of the lords, taking part in the first Crusade to the Holy Land. Raymond VI of Toulouse married Princess Joan of England, daughter of Henry Plantagenet and Eleanor of Aquitaine and sister of Richard the Lion Heart and King John.

We took the wrong exit off the A-62 and were quickly lost in the industrial wilderness. There was an oily, toxic-looking column of black smoke rising above the power pylons that marched through the jungle of hi-tech factories housed in sprawling, nondescript cement-block structures; a building was on fire somewhere halfway to the horizon in the direction of Aérospatiale and the big Airbus plant. Then we found ourselves in a new subdivision of North American-style bungalows with attached garages and cement drive-ways, the only such houses I have seen in France, where building codes are strict and where normally even new residential construction conforms to traditional, regional architectural styles using either tra-ditional materials or new ones sympathetic in color and texture to the old. These codes are largely responsible for the survival of strik-ing regional identities in France, and for the country's remarkable pastoral beauty. It is a case of community values given precedence over the freedom of the individual to build as he wants.

Eventually we found our way back to the city's ring road, and from there to the Canal du Midi, which we followed until we were close to the old quarter of the city. I parked the car and we walked across a bridge spanning the stagnant waters of the canal. We soon found ourselves in the jumble of cobbled alleyways of the medieval quarter. I don't know if it was the poorest part of the city we chose to walk through, but it was not the wealthiest, and the walls were covered in New York-style graffiti; slogans, names and murals in Day-Glo colors—it looked like thirteenth-century Harlem. Nothing had been spared; ancient carved wooden doors and sculpted capitols and leaded windows, all were defaced, for blocks on end. It was a profoundly shocking sight, something Chris and I had never seen in this country outside the odd bit of vandalism in Paris. Hilary and Simon were as affronted as we were, though Hilary insisted on pausing to photograph some of the more artistic creations. To the rest of us, it seemed somehow wrong to be impressed. The effect of the vandalism was to give the streetscape an edge of menace, of violence, that made us all nervous, even the normally cavalier Simon, and we strode along quickly past shuttered walk-up apartments and Algerian pastry shops, hearing snatches of Arabic music. There was something at work here that ran deeper than the simple issue of vandalism; a whiff of brimstone, a harbinger of the void.

We were headed in the direction of what has been the great tourist attraction of Toulouse for more than eight hundred years, the vast pilgrimage basilica of St. Sernin. The graffiti followed us like the howls of lunatics, though by the time we reached the cathedral square, it was somewhat less ubiquitous.

Saint Sernin, or sometimes Saint Saturninus, the first bishop of Toulouse, was martyred in AD 250 when he was tied to the tail of a bull he had refused to sacrifice to pagan gods; it dragged him down a flight of stone stairs with fatal results. Begun in 1080 and richly endowed with Christian relics by Charlemagne, the enormous brick structure (brick, because there is very little building stone in the Garonne estuary) has been a magnet for pilgrims from all over Europe and North Africa since earliest medieval times. Its treasures include relics of 128 saints, including six Apostles, a piece of the true cross and a thorn from the crown of thorns. We found it surrounded by a stout wrought-iron fence of recent vintage, along which a sad little flea market was in progress, people sitting on blankets or sheets with used shoes and clothing on display before them. In Paris or Lyon, Arles or Dijon or Montpellier, where historic sites are scrubbed and pristine, these people would have been invited to leave, but here they were tolerated. On Sundays, there is a full-blown market with vendors' stalls and carts extending all the way around the basilica. It is a tradition that reaches back to the Middle Ages, when there would have been a circus-like atmosphere as the locals tried to extract a few coins from the throngs of pilgrims.

We entered the building by the great south portal, and were angered to see that the padded leather soundproofing on the backs of the doors had been slashed with a knife, not once but repeatedly, the earlier damage having been repaired with colored tape. The interior is notable more than anything else for the sheer volume of space it encloses, a place big enough to accommodate several thousand people. This was the SkyDome of the eleventh century and remains the largest Romanesque building in France. It must have inspired awe in the pilgrims who stopped here on their way across the Pyrenees, following the Milky Way to Santiago de Compostela. Awe at the power and authority of the Church, certainly, but something more than that as well.

To the medieval mind, the very space contained by St. Sernin would have been animated: empty space was a meaningless concept prior to the scientific revolution of the mid-sixteenth century, and the vastness of the structure would have been inhabited by that ineffable wisdom, or *Logos*, that accounted for the continuing functioning of the universe. This idea of a mind at work in the universe is as old as philosophy. It originates in simple observation of geometric patterns in nature, in particular the regular, apparently circular motions of the planets. How could one account for such regularity of motion in a natural object if not by ascribing it to an overseeing mind? And that mind was everywhere, though nowhere more palpably present than in a great cathedral.

ϒ ϒ ϒ

A few blocks away, and by now completely clear of the creeping fungus of graffiti, we found a quiet street where a violin student was doing much-needed practice on a Bach partita, in an apartment above one of the wonderful little stationery shops found with the frequency of pharmacies in every French town and city. This one had an exceptionally fine selection of pens, art supplies and posters. A warm rain had begun to fall and Simon and I left Chris and Hilary there to browse while we sprinted ahead, umbrellaless, in search of another architectural treasure, the Church of the Jacobins. It was just around the next corner. A fine, massive red-brick structure in the southern Gothic style, it is famous for the graceful octagonal bell tower which relieves the otherwise intimidating exterior of what was a fortified church meant to make a military statement: it was constructed immediately after the Albigensian Crusade in which the city had offered valiant resistance to the northern forces.

This was the mother church of the Dominicans (sometimes called the Jacobins because of their early occupancy of the chapel of St. Jacques in Paris), the black-robed preaching order established by friar Dominic de Guzman (1170–1221) in response to the spreading Cathar heresy. Dominic is a puzzling figure, revered as a man of peace and reviled as a fanatic. Throughout Languedoc he sought to combat Catharism with superior argument in many a debate with Cathar clerics, some of them extending over two weeks or more, but when the Crusade came, he was present at some of the worst slaughters, notably Béziers and the siege of Toulouse, as well as the deciding battle of Muret in which Simon de Montfort defeated the combined forces of the count of Foix and Raymond, count of Toulouse, both suspected Cathars, and their ally King Pedro of Aragon. What Dominic's role was on these occasions, history does not record, although the part played by the clergy in military operations in the Middle Ages was important: it was, for instance, the bishop of Béziers who designed the siege catapult that ultimately broke the resistance of the defenders of Montségur. It is known that Dominic met Simon

ᛉ ᛉ ᛉ

de Montfort in the early days of the Crusade and "a warm friendship sprang up between them."

Six years earlier, in 1203, Dominic had established the nunnery of Prouille to take in Cathar women who had been brought back into the fold of the Church. He had established the building site in a vision of fire while standing on a promontory on the outskirts of the village of Fanjeaux, a Cathar stronghold where he had chosen to live and preach. Chris and I had stopped in Fanjeaux for an hour at siesta time on our way to Montségur earlier in the week. The town is built atop one of the many rocky outcroppings in the region, and was strongly fortified when in the autumn of 1209 Simon de Montfort sent a troop of Aragon mercenaries to destroy it. The inhabitants deserted it en masse rather than face slaughter, and the crusaders burned it to the ground. As we'd walked the shuttered streets towards the high-walled Dominican convent a nun, tiny, stooped, cowled in her long black habit, had scuttled past us to the massive wooden cloister door and, pulling down on its wrought-iron handle, darted inside, dragging the door closed behind her with a squeal of hinges and a clank of locking hardware.

We'd continued up the winding street to St. Dominic's house, a low, stone structure attached on both sides to other dwellings, at a place where the street widens slightly to perhaps twenty feet, close by the massively built Romanesque church which had been raised on the much older Roman ruins of a temple to Jupiter. In one of the church side chapels, there is a length of charred wood, which is said to commemorate the "miracle of fire," one of several miracles attributed to Dominic in his years in Fanjeaux. The story is that at the end of a long debate in nearby Montréal with Cathar adversaries, Dominic summarized his arguments in writing. A Cathar priest later tried to burn the parchment in the fireplace of a friend's home, before several witnesses. Three times the document flew out of the hearth unscathed, the third time setting one of the roof beams alight. It is this piece of scorched wood that is preserved in the church.

ꭓ ꭓ ꭓ

At the end of the lane, street and village concluded abruptly at a steep cliff, and that is where Dominic had his storied vision of balls of fire alighting at the nearby site that would become the Priory of Prouille. We'd looked out over a vast panorama of shimmering saffron fields of sunflowers and blue-green grapevines in a twisting, corkscrew van Gogh landscape punctuated by coppices, farms and estates, and scribbled with roads and highways with tiny, crawling vehicles, the rugged khaki slopes of the Montagne Noir in the distance on the right, and on the left the looming Pyrenees piled high with billowy cumulus clouds. Perhaps thirty kilometers away to the east in the direction of Toulouse were two enormous, white parabolic dish antennas, the earth station for some satellite communications system, perhaps a television network carrying the late twentieth-century version of St. Dominic's fireball visions.

The Church of the Jacobins in Toulouse, where Simon and I were now standing in the warm rain, was begun in 1230, a decade after Dominic's death and the year following the final absorption of Languedoc into the kingdom of France. It was completed just in time to receive the bones of perhaps the most famous of the Dominicans, St. Thomas Aquinas. Probably the most influential of Catholic theologians, he died in 1274 after a life of heroic intellectual effort in the cause of shoring up the beleaguered Church ramparts against erosion from a completely different, and ultimately more dangerous, quarter than dualist heresy.

Simon and I ducked inside the church out of the rain and found ourselves almost alone in a vast nave of an unexpected beauty. The ceiling was double-vaulted, supported by a single row of seven huge, palm-topped columns and almost the entire upper half of each of the exterior walls was made up of stained-glass windows. Most of the interior stonework had been plastered and painted in hues of rose, ochre and grey; the combined effect of the thin light filtering through the ocean of stained glass and the earthy tones of the walls was one of muted warmth that humanized what could otherwise have been an overwhelming space. It is, as some have said, as if the architects had regretted the severity of the exterior dictated by military necessity and made their real statement with the bell tower and the interior. The sight, beneath the marble altar, of the embossed gold chest containing St. Thomas Aquinas' venerable bones had a powerful impact on me for which I was completely unprepared. I had to sit down for a few moments on the cool stone floor, my back against a massive pillar, to take it in.

Toulouse: Aquinas and Galileo

A Saint's Relics ⚲ Dominic's Story ⚲
Aristotle Returns ⚲ Aristotle and
Aquinas ⚲ A Delicate Balance ⚲ 'Doctor
Invincibilis' ⚲ Ockham and Science
⚲ Simon's Questions ⚲ Galileo and the
Church ⚲ Peter Damien's Response

The bones of St. Thomas Aquinas! If only his mind had been preserved in a jar—I wonder what he would have thought of the modern world he played so important a part in creating, the world in which his beloved Church has withered into near irrelevancy under the prolonged onslaught of scientific materialism, an outgrowth of the philosophy of Aristotle which was so carefully preserved through more than a thousand years by the Arabs and newly rediscovered in his own exciting time of intellectual ferment. He thought he could tame the power of Aristotle's cause-and-effect empiricism by welcoming it into Catholic dogma, as

⚲ ⚲ ⚲

Augustine had welcomed Plato a thousand years before. It proved to be a Trojan horse.

Thomas Aquinas (1224/5–1274) was a rebel: he ran away from an aristocratic Italian home to join the newly-created and very fashionable mendicant preaching order, the Dominicans, in 1243, in an age when the Church was under siege from the Cathars and other heretical sects, struggling to reform itself in the face of this new Manichean threat. The Dominicans recognized his talent and sent him to Paris to study with the greatest scholars of the day. Once there, he immersed himself in the most pressing intellectual and theological issue of his era: since Augustine, the Church had been intent on reconciling reason and faith and now a critical juncture had been reached in that process. The problem was how to deal with the newly rediscovered pagan philosophy of Aristotle, whose entire *Logic* was now available in the original, along with his *Metaphysics* and works on science. Aristotelianism had revealed itself to be a philosophical architecture as comprehensive as that developed by Christianity. In fact, it had much in common with Christian theology, as might be expected, given that Aristotle had been a student of Plato. But there were also important contradictions. Since the works of the great philosopher bore an irresistible authority in their own right, it was critically important for the Church to accommodate the differences in a way which would pay due respect to Aristotle while at the same time preserving basic Christian dogma.

The Church had for the first twelve centuries of its existence built its philosophy on the bedrock of Plato as elaborated by his disciple Plotinus and interpreted by St. Augustine; on a belief that universal truths were to be found through contemplation, the denial of worldly things and the ecstasy of revelation, and that once revealed should be accepted as incontrovertible authority. It was the immutable and eternal verities, unaffected by the fickle and ever-changing world of the senses, that gave life meaning and value. And that human life should have meaning and value was of the utmost importance.

⅄ ⅄ ⅄

Now, with the rediscovery of Aristotle, reason was threatening to declare its sovereignty with respect to faith, a separation which would have amounted to a split in human consciousness, a schizophrenia that to Augustinian tradition could only seem terrifying. Aristotle's was not the familiar and comfortable reason of deduction, of figuring out the small details in the context of assumptions or revealed knowledge about the big picture, but an audacious inductive reason built from the bottom up on empirical evidence, that is, on evidence provided by the senses. In the Aristotelian system, the big picture was constructed out of facts derived from sensory experience of the real world.

In Paris, the fiery Siger of Brabant and his followers at the University were openly teaching that, in the light of Aristotle, "there is no state superior to the practice of philosophy," that nothing is added to knowledge by theology and that philosophy, as wisdom itself, was a doctrine of salvation independent of Christian revelation. There was a growing danger that the intellectual life of the Christian world would be torn asunder in a secularization which would sweep Christianity aside and create a moat, a chasm, between what men "knew," on the one hand, and what they "believed," on the other; between philosophy (including what we know as science), and religion. And that could only lead, in the end, to the greatest and most tragic error of all; that of honoring empirical "truth" above the good.

The peril, in the eyes of most historians as well as contemporary Church leaders, was extreme. And, in Thomas Aquinas, history found one of those figures whose unique and prodigious abilities seem to have predestined them to their role. No one doubts his immense intellectual capabilities. His dedication to the great task of his age was no less remarkable. He worked himself to exhaustion, and perhaps to death, before he had reached fifty. In his last three years of work in Paris he produced twelve major commentaries on Aristotle; a landmark commentary on the Gospel of John; a commentary on the Epistles of Paul; the massive *Questiones disputatae* on the virtues, the Incarnation and evil; numerous polemics against Siger of Brabant and

ꭓ ꭓ ꭓ

the final volumes of his giant *Summa theologica*. At the end of it all, in 1273, and while seemingly in full stride, he laid his pen aside and told a colleague, "All that I have written seems to me nothing but straw— compared with what I have seen and what has been revealed to me." And he wrote no more. His *Summa theologica* was left incomplete, an apparently deliberate statement on what he believed to be the essentially inscrutable depths of reality. "This is the extreme of human knowledge of God," he had said, "to know that we do not know God." It was not so much that God and nature were unknowable in the literal sense; on the contrary, they were both so utterly knowable that one never reached the end of knowing; their knowability was inexhaustible. For Thomas this meant above all that theology should not close itself off to exploration of the physical world, to philosophy and science. Along with this openness would inevitably come continuing difficulties in reconciling the two sources of knowledge, but in resolving those tensions both theology and philosophy would be continuously enriched.

In reconciling Aristotle and Scripture he had employed arguments that for all their complexity in elaboration, for all their revolutionary nature, are essentially quite simple. No one has summarized them better than Josef Pieper, whose little volume, *Guide to Thomas Aquinas* I had squirreled away among my rucksack collection:

> Thomas demonstrated that affirmative acceptance of the natural reality of the world and of the natural reality in man himself can be ultimately established and justified only in theological terms. The natural things of the world have a real, self-contained intrinsic being precisely by reason of having been created, precisely because the creative will of God is by its nature being-giving. That is to say that the will of God does not keep being for itself alone but truly communicates it (this alone, is the meaning of 'to create': to communicate being). Precisely because there is a creation, there are independent entities and things which not only 'exist' for themselves, but also, of their own accord, can affect and effect [can act and be acted upon].[1]

Ɐ Ɐ Ɐ

The arguments against Thomas' position were strenuous, from both Church traditionalists on the one side and the militant Aristotelians on the other. The estimable Bonaventura, minister-general to the Franciscans, reminded his friend Thomas that Aristotle was a heathen whose authority must not be ranked with the likes of Augustine; he asked, rhetorically, whether all the philosophy of Aristotle could explain the movement of a star. God, he said, is not a philosophical conclusion but a living presence and the very essence of Being; it was better to feel His presence than to define Him. Aristotle accorded altogether too much autonomy to material objects. To which Thomas replied that the very independence of created things proves the ultimate creativity of God. To the radical Aristotelians Thomas conceded that the natural world is in a sense a reality in its own right, but that in spite of its independence it remained a non-absolute reality, for there would be no reality nor independence without the creative will of God.

Implied in his approach, like a worm in the apple of faith and goodness, was the idea that reason, because it provided complete insight, was the preferred mode of knowledge. Faith, he hastened to add, speaks with a greater authority, and perhaps somewhat para-doxically, results in a greater certitude. But despite his caution and his deeply spiritual nature, Aquinas had thrown open the door to scien-tific inquiry independent of the informing wisdom of religious thought and experience. The intellectual structure he had created to bridge between Aristotle and Christianity, elegant though it might be, was a fragile one, and delicately balanced. Very quickly science would grow to be a robust and then an overwhelming opponent, jealously unwill-ing to share equal status with religion as a pathway to truth in the world, and increasingly disdainful of the ineffable idea of the good.

Just as Descartes' splitting of the subjective and the objective would have the unanticipated effect of consigning God and the spiritual to irrelevancy in everyday life, Aquinas might be said to have laid the ini-tial groundwork for the eventual superseding of religion by science in

ㄨ ㄨ ㄨ

Western culture. In the end, he was perhaps too much a man of his times, in which, everywhere in Europe, naturalism and empirical reason were on the rise: in law, trial by ordeal was being replaced with a renewal of Roman statute law and the weighing of evidence; in government the role of princes was being put to the test with the rise of urban life and the feisty independence of towns and cities. The Aristotelian notion of natural law was used as a weapon by Frederick II in his epic resistance to Rome's push for theocratic world government.

Soon after Thomas' death, William of Ockham (c. 1285–1345), that cantankerous and influential Franciscan theologian, strode straight through the door opened by *Summa theologica* to attack head-on the Platonist and neo-Platonist thought that had been the bedrock of Christian philosophy for twelve centuries and more, and indeed had been so fervently espoused by the Franciscan leader of only a generation earlier, Bonaventura. Riding on the wave of new thinking unleashed by Aristotle and Aquinas, he went far beyond them to insist that universals such as Plato's ideal forms have no real existence, and are merely symbolic representations constructed to aid in the process of thinking. Only the concrete, individual entity or fact was real. He was known to his contemporaries as "Doctor Invincibilis" and in his reasoning he ruthlessly stripped arguments to their bare essentials, a technique of logic which has come down to us as Ockham's razor. For Ockham, all knowledge begins with direct sensory experience, which is followed by intellectual cognition, which may be followed by abstraction, or the construction of universals. He dismissed deductive reasoning, reasoning from the general to the particular; only facts ascertained by the senses are real, so that reality can be neither deduced nor calculated, but only experienced. There was clearly no place for theology in such a system of knowledge, and Ockham insisted on a sharp separation between theology and philosophy: faith and knowledge were entirely separate and distinct, in fact would contaminate one another if not held apart. Thus, in the early fourteenth century the influential doctrines of Ockham

א א א

completed the split between faith and reason Thomas Aquinas had tried so hard to heal. Ockham is the godfather of modern Positivism, which we encountered earlier in the brutally rationalist and uncompromisingly empiricist ideas of Auguste Comte.

In effect, Ockham, in extending Aquinas' thought and denying the existence of Plato's ideal forms—denying as unnecessary and superfluous the very idea of a context in which things existed—had banished ideas from God's mind, leaving a deity that was omnipotent but governed by no law (except that which forbade contradiction, that is, a thing's being both true and not true), and was thus able to behave completely arbitrarily, since values, for example, exist only because of His will and not for any intelligible reason. As well, in Ockham's universe there was no connection between individual things, none of which had anything in common with any other.

Thomas would have thought the idea of a thing considered outside its context to be bizarre and meaningless. His world, for all its intellectual radicalism, had remained solidly medieval in that it was all *about* context, a mutually-supporting hierarchy of existence exhibiting various levels of perfection. For his more conservative contemporaries like Bonaventura, who harkened back to Plato and Augustine, singular things were not even recognizable without the involvement of the minds of God and man. Matter in itself could not be perceived because it depended on its transaction with human consciousness and divine will—that is, on its context—to take shape. The leap taken by Ockham was thus a truly enormous one: Thomas, however unwittingly, had provided the springboard.

Ockham's razor sliced through the umbilicus linking material reality and human consciousness, severing this ancient, organic and endlessly fruitful means of understanding man's relationship to the physical environment, and to God. He replaced it with a world cluttered with autonomous objects, which were accessible to examination and measurement. Reality was no longer a field of transaction on which humans encountered and interpreted the material manifestations of divine ideals, but simply a collection of "things." His world was one of objective fact rather than of intelligible necessity.

It would prove fertile soil for science. Copernicus, Kepler, and finally, Galileo and Newton, in their progressively single-minded insistence on machine-like economy of structure in nature and in the language used to describe it, found themselves at home in Ockham's stripped-down, hard-edged world. It would be but a small step for them to further dismember the complex organic unity of medieval thought by detaching natural philosophy (science) from moral philosophy, leaving the latter rootless, disinherited and increasingly bereft of tangible, understandable premises in nature and life. (Voltaire was to say: "It is given to us to calculate, to weigh, to measure, to observe; this is natural philosophy; almost all the rest is chimera.") It was Ockham's razor at work again, slicing away "irrelevancies" which threatened the smooth functioning of the elegant mental machinery of mathematical reason.

Simon could not escape me. As he gazed around him in awe of the beauty and antiquity of the Jacobins I told him how Napoleon's soldiers were once quartered here, and about the damage done. In the supremely rational era following the French Revolution known as the Enlightenment, like so many other fine churches including Notre-Dame de Paris, the Jacobins in Toulouse had been assigned a sensible, utilitarian function. The interior was divided into two stories, the top floor a barracks for soldiers and the ground level a stable for their horses. Much damage was done and a century-long restoration was completed only twenty years ago.

"Quite a contrast between the mind that dreamed up this place and the mind that saw it as a stable and barracks, don't you think?"

"Yeah," he said, gazing upward at the windows. "Really."

We stood in silence for a while.

"I'd love to be able to go on to Italy from here," I said finally.

"Why Italy?"

"Because it suddenly seems quite plain to me that the key event in this entire millennium was probably the trial of Galileo. That's where everything set in motion by Aquinas came to a head. Have you read about it?"

"Sure. Galileo proved that the earth orbits the sun, by looking through his telescope. The Church said he was wrong, that the sun revolved around the earth, which was supposed to be the center of the universe. The Inquisition found him guilty of heresy and, I don't remember, but I think he was locked up. Typical."

"Well, actually not so typical," I said. "The Pope at the time had been a good friend and admirer of Galileo, before he was Pope and even afterward. And the Church, especially after Aquinas, had nothing against scientific inquiry, and the kind of speculation it led to."

"Well then, why did they throw him in jail?"

"They didn't exactly throw him in jail. Once he'd been found guilty, the law said he had to be locked up, but he was an old man, and he had many admirers within the Church and they managed to have him sentenced to house arrest at his own villa, near where his daughter lived in a convent. And he wasn't found guilty of heresy. The Church said he'd made an agreement years earlier not to publicly advocate the sun-centered solar system idea, and that he'd broken the agreement by publishing a book called *Dialogue on the Two Chief Systems of the World*" in 1632.

"What's the difference? They were still trying to suppress scientific knowledge."

"Yes, they were. And Galileo has been made a kind of martyr to science. But the real story is less black and white, and more interesting. The idea of a heliocentric solar system had been around for centuries before Copernicus and Kepler and Galileo formalized it and put it in mathematical terms. Catholic theologians in general found the idea as interesting as the next guy, and they were even ready to admit that it probably was an accurate description of the way things

χ χ χ

were. What the Church objected to was not the hypothesis, but the idea that it should be accepted as reality just because it fit with what Galileo had seen through his telescope."

Simon laughed: "Well, if that isn't reality, what is?"

"Sounds pretty ridiculous, doesn't it? Especially when you hear about the theologians who actually refused to look through the telescope when Galileo offered them a chance to see for themselves."

Simon slapped his forehead in disbelief: "They wouldn't even look . . .?"

"No, because they believed that whatever it was they would see, it wouldn't be reality. At least, not necessarily. Or, put it this way: they knew beforehand with a great deal of certainty what they would *not* see in it. They were prepared to accept Galileo at his word, that his observations confirmed the Copernican theory. But they also knew that Scripture seemed pretty clear in placing the earth at the center of things. That was problem number one. Problem number two was that the medieval Church had always known with perfect confidence what reality was, and it was *not* something that could be grasped via the senses and their contacts with the physical world—in other words, by observation. At least not completely. What your senses told you was just a sort of surface reality, a superficial representation of something much deeper. Ultimate reality existed as ideal forms or ideas *behind* the physical representations of things. Reality in this sense was the mind of God, or the expression of God's will. Even Aquinas, for all his flirting with science, said that revelation is a higher truth than observation. So, all that was expected of a scientific hypothesis like the ordering of the planets was that it explain people's experience of nature in a satisfying and maybe even useful way, or, as they used to say, that it could 'save the appearances.' Don't forget that the astronomy of Ptolemy, even though it had the earth at the center and was a real Rube Goldberg affair with epicycles galore, was perfectly capable of accounting for the motions of the planets, and it was able to predict eclipses, for example, with complete accuracy. From the Church's point of view at that time, the only advantage that anybody could claim for Galileo's hypothesis was that it was simpler."

"Yeah, but it was *right!*"

"Well, it certainly seemed to be right. But that wasn't the point. The Church thought it was much more important to establish what was good, rather than what was true."

Simon rolled his eyes.

"Hang on now," I said. "Hear me out. It might well be that Galileo's observations were correct, but the Church wasn't willing to accept his conclusions at face value without long and detailed study, because Scripture seemed to contradict them. And even Aquinas would have argued that since there was no possible contradiction between correct science and the revelation recorded in Scripture, it was necessary to find ways of reconciling the two. This was a process that normally took decades, not months or years. Galileo was not prepared to wait, and so we ended up with this real tragedy on our hands."

"What do you mean 'tragedy.' He won in the end, didn't he?"

"That's the tragedy. It would have been much better for everyone concerned if it had been possible to negotiate some sort of a deal that would have worked for both sides."

"Oh, come on . . ."

"Well, think about it. Galileo was insisting that his version of things was Truth with a capital T. But for the Church to agree to call his hypothesis 'reality' on the basis of observation alone would involve incredible dangers to the entire metaphysical system that focused on God as ultimate goodness. That was anything but a trivial matter. It was a system of great antiquity and one which had been defended against all sorts of heresies, including the Cathars. Bloody wars had been fought to defend it. Martyrs had died. Human salvation depended on its continuing integrity, or so it was believed by just about everybody.

⅄ ⅄ ⅄

"Look at it this way. In Christian cosmology, motion was supposed to be caused by God's will and therefore was always towards a greater good. Mathematics could have nothing to say about motion in this system, because there is no mention of the good in mathematics. But the essence of Galileo's cosmology was a planetary system that was based on the rules of geometry, and the relationships between the heavenly bodies were mathematical rather than spiritual. For Galileo, the real world existed in the mathematical relationships discoverable in it: the real world was one of quantities, rather than qualities. In his own words, 'The book of nature is written in the language of mathematics.' Just think about what that means. Not only does the whole idea of 'the good' as a focus of everything go into limbo somewhere, because it's irrelevant, but it means that nature operates according to rigid laws. And that in turn means that there must be restrictions on God's freedom of choice, to prevent Him from messing with the laws of nature. So if we accept Galileo's observations as truth, and the conclusions he draws from them as laws of nature, we no longer have an omnipotent God. And 'good' is off somewhere in limbo. You can see, can't you, why the Church would be so cautious?"

"I suppose so . . ."

"Well, it gets even worse for the Church. Galileo was a good and faithful Catholic and he did not deny the existence of God. But it was a slippery slope he'd set out upon, because if the universe operated on the basis of mathematics and logic and laws of nature, what was God's role in it? Galileo had an answer, one that had in fact been accepted by Aquinas, that God was the 'prime mover.' In other words, if it takes a push to move something, something must have given the first push to the first thing that moved and got everything else moving. That was fine, but then God could no longer be at the same time the 'final cause,' the ultimate meaning of things, because mathematics *had* no ultimate meaning. Still doesn't, in fact."

I stood up to stretch my legs, and Simon stood with me.

ꓫ ꓫ ꓫ

157

"You could say," I said, "that the Church was defending a universe in which 'true' equalled 'the good' against a new one in which 'true' equalled, I dunno, something like 'accurate' or 'instrumentally useful.' It was bad enough that Aquinas here, and Ockham, had split philosophy into natural philosophy and moral philosophy, but now Galileo was insisting on giving precedence to natural philosophy—which he said was nothing but arithmetic—and that was downright scary."

"Huh. That's interesting. I mean, it really is interesting. But, in the end, Galileo was right."

"I think I could give you a pretty good argument that he was wrong and that science has come round to admitting the fact, if only quietly, in books nobody reads—you certainly won't see it in your school texts! Not that anyone thinks he was wrong about the solar system, but he was wrong about the nature of reality. That's really what the whole dispute was about, anyway."

As we looked for the last time at St. Thomas' relics, a memory came to me from out of nowhere, as they do, miraculously.

"There was a Catholic theologian named Peter Damien, who lived nearly six hundred years before Galileo, and he put the Church's position about as well as it's ever been stated, I think. Listen to this. He said that 'the nature of things' is not some ultimate reality, because behind it there is a 'nature of the nature of things.' Scientific theories and so-called laws relate not to this ultimate 'nature of nature' but merely to the 'nature of things.' As an analogy he said, think of an absolute ruler, a lawgiver, on earth. The 'nature of nature' relates to the laws of nature as we normally think of them, in the same way as the will of the lawgiver relates to the laws of his kingdom. The laws he makes constitute a legal order for his subjects, but he is always free to override them with a command of his own. Damien said that what appear to us as laws in nature are really signs of obedience. He said that the supposed 'order of nature' was really just an order of words, in other words a human construction that had only a second-hand relationship to the underlying reality. It's really a sophisticated, elegant

ℵ ℵ ℵ

argument when you look at it closely, and he wrote it right about the turn of the last millennium. It blew my mind the first time I read it."

"So that's what caused the damage!" Simon couldn't quite manage a deadpan delivery.

"Very funny. As proof of his argument, wise guy, Damien pointed to miracles, which he said are the 'stigmata' of the world's creation from nothingness. The lingering marks that remind us what's what and where we came from. A nifty image, don't you think? Anyway, Hilary and your mom will be wondering what's happened to us. We'd better get back."

We took a final walk round the church ambulatory as we left. Standing in that magical ancient space, trying to contemplate the kind of sensibility that would see fit to desecrate one of the finest pieces of southern Gothic architecture in existence, I found it hard to resist comparing Voltaire's intellectual offspring, all children of Descartes, with the vandals of today's Toulouse. Only someone who can see nothing but stone and brick and mortar in such an edifice would be capable of despoiling it, someone either so vain or so bereft of imagination as to be certain of being right, of being entitled above all to the last word.

compares new thought to vandals

Science and Reality

A Trip to the Supermarket ⚭ Objects and

Idols ⚭ God and Newton ⚭ Science

and Mathematics ⚭ Faith, Metaphysics

and Science ⚭ Einstein's World ⚭

Reflections on Alienation

The following afternoon found us once again in Carcassonne, in the lower town, where Hilary needed to buy a telephone card so that she could check with her agency in Toronto about a modeling contract she was expecting. On a whim, we pulled in to a supermarket, to see how it compared to what we have at home. At the back of the store, beyond the dairy section with its overwhelming selection of cheeses, yogurts, creams, milks and eggs, past the long aisles of wines and liquors, past the vast selection of fresh produce (a dozen varieties of garlic to choose from), was the long, long meat counter. Nothing was wrapped in plastic here, just carefully arranged and displayed on large white-enameled trays and there was everything from standard cuts of beef and pork to fresh fowl with heads and feet intact to unattached pigs'

⚭ ⚭ ⚭

heads and feet and whole suckling piglets and various internal organs of which the French are fond.

Hilary and Simon reacted simultaneously in unison: "Oh, *gross!* That's *disgusting!*" Hilary demanded that we leave, immediately.

I had to chuckle at their reaction and my mind spooled back to a similar occasion perhaps ten years earlier. One desperate night on the way home from a long day at work I'd picked up a bucket of Kentucky Fried Chicken (now known officially as KFC so as to submerge the fact that the chicken is fried in oil). Simon, especially, loved it. Smacking his lips over a breast held in his small fingers he'd asked, "Mom, what is this crispy stuff on the outside. It's *so* good."

"It's the skin," Chris had replied.

We were both nonplussed to see the color drain from his face as he carefully put down the breast, got up and left the table. He did not return, and I have never again brought home KFC.

This time, when I caught up with them at the front of the store, I said: "You guys watch too much television."

"Dad, we hardly watch any television and, anyway, that's got nothing to do with what's back there. It's just plain disgusting," Hilary retorted.

"But there is a connection, you know. You're not used to seeing things as they really are. We have most of what's on display there in supermarkets back home. It's just that it's packaged so that you can't see what it really is. All the parts that identify the dead animal are cut off."

"Dad, do we *have* to keep *talking* about it. You're making me *sick,*" she said.

We were already attracting the attention of other shoppers so I shut up, still smiling to myself, glad to have had the two of them reminded what meat is, to have been exposed to a bit of reality. Their shared reaction, I was pretty sure, illustrated the fact that we have not completely lost our ability to participate in the reality of material objects in the way peoples of antiquity did, though perhaps it was

❧ ❧ ❧

now limited mostly to other living things, and maybe even to animal life. And perhaps, as children, they had lost less of this ability than Christine or me, because in the poet's words, they were still young enough to be "trailing clouds of glory." Anyone who has closely watched kids develop will suspect that they "participate" in reality in a way that animates the world and thoroughly delights them, for as long as we allow them to. Eventually, of course, they are taught directly and through a thousand subtle paths that what they perceive as being connected to themselves, even a part of themselves, is "in fact" entirely outside them. In other words, they are taught to objectify the material world, and their life thereafter is missing much of its magic. They no longer see angels, nor monsters, and can face such an object as fried chicken skin with the equanimity that comes with assurance that it has nothing to do with them.

That of course does not change the fact that there *is* a connection between their consciousness and the existence of the objects of their perception. It is in fact characteristic of modern perception that it hides or denies this fact, and it is sometimes denied in theory as well. It is no longer part of our "common sense."

The British philosopher Owen Barfield, who has written lucidly about perception and the transaction between consciousness and matter *in potentia*, has an interesting word for material objects for which we insist on assigning an existence independent of ourselves. He calls them "idols"—an idol being a representation of a real object, which is itself taken to be real—for instance, a statue of a god. Barfield's point is that when we recognize an object as having an autonomous existence we are perceiving the representation as reality, when it is only a *re-presentation* of reality. Hence, we are creating an idol.

"Idol" is of course a word that carries with it a lot of religious freight, and perhaps it would be better to use a synonym, such as "icon." The important point is that, in the process of ignoring or denying our own involvement in the reality of the material world, we are *falsely* objectifying it. The consequences of this error can scarcely

ᚷ ᚷ ᚷ

be overstated. They revealed themselves in concert with the unfolding of the scientific revolution begun in the seventeenth century.

In the year in which Galileo died, still under house arrest as ordered by the Inquisition, Isaac Newton was born into a world just a generation older, but completely transformed. If Galileo had suffered persecution for his ideas, Newton was worshiped by his contemporaries. In an epitaph intended for the scientist's grave, the poet Alexander Pope wrote,

Nature and nature's laws lay hid in night;
God said, "Let Newton be," and all was light.

The revolutionary and supremely rational universe described by Newton with his laws of motion and elegantly simple formula for universal gravity fit perfectly with Aquinas' protoscientific worldview, with its divine "Prime Mover," and with Ockham's emphasis on cold, hard fact. By describing the phenomenon of gravitational attraction as a straightforward mathematical relationship between mass and distance, Newton had provided a blueprint for the workings of the universe which seemed as reliable and predictable as a mechanical clock, and in so doing he realized the worst nightmares of the medieval Church, as they had found expression in the controversy surrounding Galileo's trial. God's intervention in this new materialist universe was limited to providing the initial wind-up to get it all going, and the important consequence of that was that it could then carry on running without benefit of clergy. To be sure, it would take many generations for the fall of God to be complete, but once the common sense reason for his existence was removed, His downfall was inevitable. Augustine's notion of the "belief" that necessarily preceded understanding became, more and more, a kind of theatrical suspension of disbelief instead, and even that would become more and more difficult to achieve for ordinary people in their day-to-day lives.

With Newton (again, following on Galileo), reality was confined

꙰ ꙰ ꙰

to those aspects of nature that were quantifiable, or translatable into the language of mathematics, for only through mathematics could reliable knowledge of the world be had. Newton further refined the position by stating that all non-quantifiable phenomena, including those which appeal to the senses and are often more prominent than the underlying mathematical relationships, are mere "secondary" qualities which reside in the observer rather than in the object observed. They are subjective qualities which the viewer projects onto the object and in that sense are not as "real" as the quantifiable, mathematical aspects of nature.

The science that followed Newton and the technology that grew up alongside it was of course enormously successful. Along the way, however, people lost track of the fact that—as Aquinas knew—science describes, it does not explain. To say that the earth and the moon attract each other with forces proportional to their masses, and that it is the moon's momentum fighting against the earth's gravitational attraction that keeps it in its orbit, is to describe the relationship between the two bodies. However, had anyone asked Newton *why* they attract one another, he would have been unable to answer. He would also, particularly in his later years, have been *unwilling* to answer because such a question could not be answered in mathematical terms and was thus not a part of his science. Dogged by criticism of his work for its fuzzy and often contradictory metaphysical content, Newton retreated into a position of banning all hypothesis or metaphysical speculation—questions of "why"—from his science, confining himself rigorously to discovery and verification of exactly quantifiable properties and laws. There, he could make satisfying progress. In the same way all questions of value, big and small, all equally and embarrassingly unanswerable by science, were eventually to be dismissed with increasing impatience as irrelevant and unimportant.

For Newton, then, and for all the succeeding generations of scientists in all of the fields of inquiry science has touched, science

ﾒ ﾒ ﾒ

was nothing more nor less than the exact mathematical formulation of the processes of the natural world. Indeed, this focus on the quantifiable was so all-pervasive that, over time, it ceased to be remarked upon, and gradually came to be part of the territory, accepted without question or reflection.

The warnings of Peter Damien were forgotten. As Europe had begun to emerge from the turmoil of the collapse of Roman imperial social order into the relative stability of the early Middle Ages, he had written that man is misled by language and his methods of inquiry into asking questions to which he can only find false answers. The forms of thought and observation that have proved reliable on earth, he said, cannot be projected onto the heterogeneous metaphysical world in which truth is to be found.

The notion has a decidedly "postmodern" ring to it and sure enough, nearly a thousand years after Damien was in the grave, in our own century, a kind of confirmation appeared. Science was finally confronted with the full irony of its being wedded so intimately in its substance and fabric, in its very methods of observation, to mathematics—which is itself a purely intellectual construct and anything but "objective" or "empirical" in the sense those words carry of having been derived from the observed workings of nature. When in 1931 mathematician Kurt Gödel derived the long-overdue proof that mathematics could make no claims to proving anything outside its own logical framework—could prove nothing about the wider universe and was merely one more metaphor for reality—the claims of science to access to "truth" were shattered. Mathematics became the first science to define its own limitations, and in doing so gave strong clues to the limits of all mathematics-based disciplines within the sciences. Science can have no opinion on the possibility or reality of things outside the system of rules and conventions that defines it, for there is no reason in logic for assuming that the unknown is governed by the same rules as the known.

Here was confirmation of the suspicions long harbored outside

⊻ ⊻ ⊻

science, that hypotheses like Newton's universal law of gravity and Maxwell's electromagnetic fields are in fact metaphysical concepts themselves, camouflaged in the mathematical language of physics. (They can be "proved" because science is a formal system, a game played according to a finite set of rules, and those rules are set by scientists. Furthermore, they are changed frequently to accommodate new hypotheses.) As such, scientific hypotheses have no automatic priority in terms of truth and are legitimately subject to critical comparison with other, competing metaphysical postulates.

Nor—despite hundreds of years of protestations to the contrary—is faith alien to science. Even the simplest of scientific inquiries are worth carrying out *only* because the inquirer has faith that the workings of the universe are amenable to some sort of intellectual understanding, in other words, are not completely random and haphazard. Every scientist must believe, must have faith, at some level, that there is order in the universe, or else his work would be pointless and fruitless. And order, inescapably, implies purpose. Augustine was right when he advised, "Seek not to understand that you may believe, but believe that you may understand." Faith is a necessary and unavoidable prerequisite to understanding, which means that faith and reason cannot be divorced.

What science did, beginning with Galileo, was deconstruct the medieval idea of reality and replace it with what can only be called a synthetic version. First, the notion of human consciousness' involvement in the construction of the reality of the material world was denied, through the stratagem of separating the material world into primary and secondary characteristics, as I've already related. The primary characteristics, those which were mathematically quantifiable, were the exclusive domain of truth. Secondary characteristics were interesting, perhaps, but unquantifiable and therefore unreliable and not suitable subject matter for scientific inquiry. In other words, science attempted to define itself as being concerned exclusively with areas of experience which did not rely on consciousness for their existence. The idea, however, of matter existing *in potentia* was not entirely lost: *In science the activating agent which made reality of matter existing* in potentia *was not consciousness, but mathematics.*

And here, in plain view, is the recursive sophistry of the scientific argument, because mathematics, which replaced consciousness, is merely a human construct. Mathematics does not derive its laws or its processes from nature. It is as possible, for example, to construct a geometry in which parallel lines meet, as it was to construct the one we are more familiar with in which they cannot. (It's called spherical geometry.) And yet mathematics forms the indispensable foundation of science, in fact is used to delimit the legitimate boundaries of scientific inquiry. This is the truth that Gödel's theorem exposed.

But science at its best is nothing if not honest in its inquiries and so it was inevitable that it would eventually uncover its own limitations through inquiry and experimentation. This process began early in the nineteenth century with the work of Michael Faraday who first studied the phenomenon he called electromagnetic force fields. But the full impact of Faraday's experimental findings did not come until James Clerk Maxwell translated them into mathematical formulae. It was these formulae defining the electromagnetic spectrum that challenged the seemingly watertight vessel of Newtonian physics by demonstrating that Faraday's force fields had a "real"—real in terms of mathematics—existence. Albert Einstein, as a bored young customs clerk, wondered how both Newton and Maxwell could be right. The pursuit of that question led in 1902 to his publishing the Special Theory of Relativity, another mathematical construct that was finally and permanently to bury the decomposing corpus of Newtonian law.

In the brave new Einsteinian world, subatomic entities such as photons exist simultaneously as both particles and waves; it is impossible to know the speed and location of a given particle at the same time; particles can communicate with one another at superluminal speeds, instantly from one side of the universe to the other; effects can sometimes precede their causes, and so on down through the long

༐ ༐ ༐

catalog of mysteries and paradoxes written by quantum physicists and proved empirically in a thousand experiments that have been monitored and reported on by the very latest in observational technologies.

Most significantly of all, we are informed by experimental physicists that neither waves nor particles at the subatomic level have any real existence in time and space until they are observed by an observer, in other words until they are seen and acknowledged by a conscious entity. Until then they are mere "probability waves." And what is a probability wave? According to Werner Heisenberg, one of the founders of modern physics, "… it is a tendency for something. It [is] a quantitative version of the old concept of 'potentia' in Aristotelian philosophy. It introduce[s] something standing in the middle between possibility and reality."

Heisenberg is stating, in other words, that the science of the late twentieth century has determined that material reality exists only *in potentia* until it is actualized by a conscious observer. Which is more or less identical with the position taken by a long, long line of thinkers stretching from the Church scholars and thinkers of the sixteenth century back through Augustine all the way to ancient Greece: reality is a process that involves our active participation in the actualizing of potential, and to that extent each of us continually "participates" in the existence of the material world.

And so we have arrived at a position today in which science's dead, static, synthetic reality, which we have come to call objective reality, is revealed as being illusory, if not impossible. And yet we have lost touch with the earlier notion of reality as a living, dynamic construct of human consciousness in cooperation with material *in potentia* that had proved so serviceable for two thousand years, until the scientific revolution, and which permitted the secure placement of man in a cosmos that also had room for an ultimate good.

As I suggested to Simon at the Jacobins, no one who has studied the history of science and scientific thought can avoid wondering what the world might be like today had Galileo been a little more

ɣ ɣ ɣ

willing to reach some sort of reasoned accommodation with the Church fathers back in the seventeenth century. If, in the late twentieth century, we have accepted the essential truth of the ancient idea of our intimate involvement with the existence of the rest of the material world, and if we have accepted that scientific fact can make no claim to being truth, should we not ask how much of the rest of the cosmology that grew out of these medieval insights might better fit the world than our own? Which is likely to take the human mind further: the idea that man exists in a cosmos of wisdom in which everything proceeds towards an ultimate good; or that the universe is unknowable in its smallest constituents, finite but unbounded, and meaningless in its operations?

That night the sky was clear and the Milky Way stood out, marking the ancient pilgrims' route to Compostela just across the Pyrenees. Chris and I sat at our terrace table sipping chilled rosé while Hilary and Simon deciphered a French movie on television. I tried to imagine what it must have been like for medieval people to sit under a sky like this, to see the zodiacs and the planets and know they were sending down their influences, to bask in the comforting understanding that their motion, in its regularity, was clear evidence of a supernatural mind at work, to know that "empty" space was filled with intelligence, to feel gravity as the effect of matter's desire for its preferred place at the center of the earth, to know that in my own body was a microcosm of the world at large, with the four elements being mirrored internally as the four humors; to feel, not isolated within my skin, but connected, integrated, in a thousand ways with the rest of the universe. I wondered what it would feel like not to be alienated.

We have, it seemed to me, good reason to suspect that there may be many ways of explaining and organizing what nature offers to our understanding, and that the most important condition for choosing among them is something within ourselves, rather than in the "outside" world.

CHAPTER 15

The Ant and the Grasshopper

A VISIT TO THE BAKERY ❧ SOME MEDIEVAL

TOWNS ❧ HIGHLY SOCIAL INSECTS ❧

A FABLE AND ITS MORAL ❧ ETHICS AND ANTS

❧ A WARNING

I t was another glorious morning of perfumed zephyrs and rau-
cous squawks from crow-like birds I couldn't identify, and
rather than wait for the baker's wife to make her delivery, I
drove the three kilometers to Arzen, through vineyards, along
a narrow, winding asphalt road, past the old co-op wine processing
facilities on the outskirts with their ivy-covered bulk-storage tanks
of concrete, up the hill past a sprinkling of modern stucco and orange
roof-tiled houses with fences hung with pots of red geraniums into the
village square just below the thirteenth century stone church, which
commands the high ground.

Too small to be more than a footnote in the history books (its population numbers only a few hundred), Arzen would almost certainly
have been a centre of Catharism, which would mean that the church
was probably improved and refurbished during the Inquisition that
followed the Albigensian Crusade, as Rome poured its resources into
reclaiming this war-ravaged territory for orthodoxy. Here in the square

❧ ❧ ❧

or nearby on streets where the cobbles have not been covered in asphalt are all the necessities of a pleasant life: the bakery, the butcher shop, the combination grocery, wine and cheese store, the *tabac* with its racks of newspapers and magazines, the bar and restaurant where workers dropped in on their way to and from farms for a quick *pastis* and espresso. And in the narrow streets that twist and turn up the hill from the square to the church, lined with shuttered two-story stone houses, you can find a walled monastery, these days used for retreats and conferences, and the modest little *Marie* with its tricolor hanging limp in the morning stillness and its modest cairn of remembrance to the dead of this century's two great European wars.

I found myself fourth in line in the low-ceilinged bakery shop, a utilitarian, cement-floored space big enough to accommodate half a dozen customers, a wooden counter topped with a single broad plank which had been rubbed to a satiny patina by decades, perhaps centuries of use, equally old bread bins and racks on the whitewashed wall separating the shop from the actual bakery beyond, a cash register and a streamlined, touch-tone telephone. The aroma of freshly baked bread was heavenly. The three men in front of me, locals all, each purchased two baguettes; one asked for half a dozen egg-glazed brioches as well. They did not stop to gossip but headed straight out the door with the breakfast bread fresh from the oven. I imagined their wives busy in kitchens nearby opening the shutters, putting eggs on to boil, heating milk for the coffee. I imagined them not in aprons but in business attire, checking their quartz wristwatches.

The girl behind the counter was eleven or twelve years old; bright, alert and efficient in jeans and a crisp white T-shirt with an Apple computer logo on the front. I saw with relief there were still a few croissants left and bought them all, along with a baguette of perfect crustiness, still warm to the cheek.

The sun was by now high enough to begin bathing the streets and doorways of the houses as I walked back to my car, which I'd parked down the hill where the farmers' market is held once a week and where the regional bus line has a small passenger shelter. Already, it was getting hot. Commuters were setting out on the air-conditioned drive in to Carcassonne or to the fields and offices of the big wine domains nearby, or perhaps to Toulouse, less than an hour's drive on the A-61, the *Autoroute des Deux Mers* that followed the path of the Roman via Narbonnaise. Arzen shares with all surviving medieval towns an organic beauty and human scale, unexpected nooks and crannies, higgledy-piggledy lanes and alleys, sensual, hand-made shapes and textures, central focus-points of commerce, community and religion, a compact and self-sufficient intimacy. Today's Arzen is like a community of chambered nautilus shells, long abandoned by their patient makers, taken over by scuttling hermit crabs.

It is in towns like this, or in Montréal a few miles down the road, or a little further south and west in the *bastide* of Mirepoix, with its wonderful half-timbered houses spilling out over arcades surrounding the ancient central square; it is in places like these that you are confronted with the fact that medieval life, for all its hardships and injustices, was essentially humane in ways that our own civilization is not. The clue is that it feels so undeniably comfortable to be there. Remembered at a café table in the plaza of, say, Fanjeaux, the antiseptic grid-pattern streets of a typical modern suburb seem an alien environment, indeed.

Arzen, Fanjeaux, Mirepoix, Carcassonne are all, simply put, homey places to be in. You feel at home. These human settlements are very clearly bottom-up constructs: no chief planner or despot imposed an efficient grid structure on the streets: they evolved according to people's needs. And they evolved into streetscapes we recognize as beautiful; as enfolding rather than alienating. They are anarchistic in their lack of formal structure but in spite of that somehow integrated into a satisfying whole. They convey a strong sense of community, of shared values.

Winston Churchill, in insisting that the bombed-out British House of Commons be restored rather than replaced with a larger, more efficient space, argued that men and their ideas are shaped by the structures they inhabit. But the reverse is also true, and medieval settlements embody in their very stones the notion of Christian brotherhood and equality, and of human existence in a universal nation of deities, people, animals and plants, all seeking rest in their appointed places under a benevolent, watchful and eternal sky.

Medieval towns and cities express the values of an era in which man's closest analogy for himself was God, both in an abstract spiritual sense and in the person of Jesus Christ. Prior to that, the analogy had been to the Roman pantheon of deities and the Greek gods of Olympus. We look back on medieval people and their artifacts from the very different point of view of a scientific civilization that finds its closest analogies for man in machines, in the clockwork mechanisms of Descartes and Newton, or in more recent robot and computer-based analogies. Our own urban landscapes are more machine-like than organic for that reason. They reflect our civilization's preference for scientific over metaphysical truth and above all for reason over intuition. They embody the idea of efficiency as opposed to goodness. Personally, no matter how much I tell myself I ought to be comfortable amid the technically sophisticated amenities of a Bauhaus-inspired building or cityscape, I still *feel* more comfortable, more at home, in medieval spaces.

Probably this is due to my innate romanticism and, as Simon and Hilary would have been quick to assure me, I would have been decidedly *un*comfortable had I been transported back to the authentic medieval world, in the absence of all that science has provided in the intervening centuries. But, on the other hand, that was not really what was at issue. The real question, it seemed to me, was this: Were people born into that time and place more, or less, happy than we are in ours?

Back at the *gîte*, I parked the car in its accustomed place beneath the parasol pines. Chris was in the shower and Simon and Hilary were still sleeping as I laid out the breakfast bread and croissants and

⅄ ⅄ ⅄

cheese and honey on the terrace table while the coffee was brewing and the milk was heating on the stove. I was careful to avoid stepping on the few ants I could see; they were busily foraging, apparently having forgotten yesterday's downsizing. Though it is doubtful whether individual ants have much of a memory for events like that, it is at least conceivable that the colony may, as an entity. It is a semi-respectable scientific and intuitively appealing notion that colonies of "highly social" insects—some bees, some wasps, all termites and all ants—behave like a single organism, exhibiting a kind of group consciousness that seems to emerge out of thousands of individual interactions. A hive of bees or wasps will swarm an intruder, or migrate to form a colony, in a closely packed mass that seems to obey a single mind. Army ants forage like organized battalions of Janissaries. They all accomplish these marvels of cooperative behavior through communication. Bees communicate by dancing. Ants have a rudimentary language based on a vocabulary of about twenty pheromones, odors secreted from scent glands. The smells themselves convey basic ideas such as attraction, alarm, recruitment, identification and recognition. They are modified by complementary signals provided by body movement, touching and sounds, to create a language complex enough to have made ants the most successful animal in creation, barring only, perhaps, Homo sapiens. The living biomass of ants on earth probably matches that of humans, and is half the total insect biomass. Their evolutionary success seems clearly to have been based on their cooperative social behavior which is in turn based on their ability to communicate relatively complex ideas. Modern information specialists, observing how seemingly intelligent computer programs are the result of layer upon layer of increasingly complex language, starting with the basic binary machine language of 1's and 0's, speculate that intelligence may be an emergent property of complexity. It is not much of a leap from that position to the idea of a hive consciousness, which would imply a hive memory as well. Or anthill memory.

ɣ ɣ ɣ

Standing by the breakfast table I tore off a piece of baguette and sliced it open, spreading it with soft Brie and all the while showering the ground with a tiny miracle of the loaves. The industrious creatures at my feet brought to mind a fable I grew up with, and which I passed on to Hilary and Simon at bedtime reading, the story of the grasshopper and the ant. The assiduous ant toils all summer long gathering food and fuel while the grasshopper enjoys life playing his fiddle and dancing. Come the winter, the ant is cozy in his nest with its woodpile and its well-stocked larder, enjoying a bowl of porridge before his blazing fireplace, and in a lull in the howl of the wind outside he hears a faint scratching at his door. He opens it to be greeted by a blast of snow, and there on his stoop, half-frozen, is the grasshopper, pathetically begging to be fed. The ant takes him in, lectures him as he thaws, and it is a properly chastened grasshopper who greets the next summer ready and eager to put his fiddle aside and work hard all the livelong day.

Like all fables, it has a moral and like all morals, this one's meaning shifts according to the context in which the story is told. The fable made sense in the setting of the agrarian society in which it was first told (it is attributed to the Greek slave Æsop). Of course it is incumbent upon each of us to look to his own provisioning, to do the work necessary to put aside stores against hard times and bleak seasons. Perhaps it was a necessary admonition to the Greeks, given their famous aversion to manual labor, which they preferred to have done by slaves.

It might have served the same purpose in the Middle Ages, when myths, fables and allegories were extremely popular, and when by all accounts most people needed encouragement to engage in toil beyond that which was made absolutely necessary by a landlord or tithe collector or the needs of the immediate family. There was no urge to work more than was required to maintain the traditional standard of living; the workaholic was palpably insane and probably

☓ ☓ ☓

unscrupulous to boot. Life was for living, whether that meant the sociable pastimes of the peasant or the "nobler" occupations of the cleric or scholar. Menial toil only interrupted that process. The ant and grasshopper fable was a salutary reminder that at least the minimum must be done. And by now it had taken on the further import of a lesson in Christian charity.

But the view from this side of the great divide called the Industrial Revolution is far different from the medieval view. With the Industrial Revolution and the rise of the factory system of production in the late eighteenth and nineteenth centuries came the revolutionary concept of the job. As I interpreted the fable, and as it was presented to me in my own childhood, the ant had a job and the grasshopper did not. Indeed, how else was I to interpret it? How did one "earn a living" except through a job? The ant, a social insect, was a worker in the anthill that employed him.

The idea of the ant's having a job and the grasshopper's not having one turns the story into a fable of freedom, in which the issues are much less clear-cut. Imagine for a moment that the ant represents the person with a steady corporate job with a reliable paycheck, and the grasshopper is the freelancer who literally or figuratively sings for his supper when necessary. Consider that corporate employment requires of the employee that he or she conform to the market-value criteria current for human resources. Psychoanalyst and social critic Erich Fromm observed of the job market:

> Here as in the commodity market, *use* value is not sufficient to determine *exchange* value. The "personality factor" takes precedence over skills . . . [with the result that] man's attitude towards himself is conditioned by these standards for success. His feeling of self-esteem is not based primarily on the value of his powers and the use he makes of them in a given society. It depends on his salability in the market . . . he experiences himself as a commodity.[1]

A commodity is, by definition, an object. For a commodity, freedom is not an issue. It does not exist. The question posed by the fable then becomes: Was the grasshopper right to prefer freedom to material security? My instincts have always led me to vote for the grasshopper over the ant, although I must confess to having frequently coveted the security of a steady income with dental plan and pension benefits, and to chastising myself during lean periods for my grasshopper fecklessness. The irony is that there is no longer such a thing as a "secure job," as my friend Berkowitz and millions like him have learned to their dismay; perhaps there never was in an existential sense. This is so well understood today that I need not elaborate beyond the simple statement of fact. "Job security" is a chimera. Nowadays self-employment, not jobs, provides security.

There is also lurking in the fable as I knew it (in which the grasshopper plays the fiddle; in the original he is merely idle) a suggestion that work which is pleasurable is less worthwhile than toil that is not, or perhaps that what is pleasurable cannot be work, which implies that work is a moral end in itself. This is definitely not a medieval notion, nor is it an idea of Æsop's time in Classical Greece; it has more the odor of a concept coming out of the Industrial Revolution when it became important to organize workers under military-style discipline, synchronized by mechanical timekeeping, within factories located near the resources they used.

Clearly, though, neither Æsop nor the modern interpreters of the fable had much knowledge of the insect world. For the single most significant difference between grasshoppers and ants is not even hinted at, and that is that grasshoppers are solitary insects while ants are highly social. The fact is, the individual ant is in almost every way the inferior of the grasshopper: in size and mobility, it doesn't hold a candle, and, most important of all, the vast majority of ants are sterile, relying on the queen back at the colony to provide offspring, while every female grasshopper can produce eggs. The secret of the

✷ ✷ ✷

ant's success is social cooperation based on a fairly complex ability to communicate. The ant does not succeed because it is morally superior, or because there is ethical content inherent in work, but because it cooperates, however blindly.

For humans, however, cooperation is an ethical value, as everyone would agree. Here, then, is one example of how values can arise out of nature, out of our interaction with our natural surroundings. What began as behavior that provided an evolutionary edge to the species becomes an abstract idea that can be incorporated into a philosophical schema defining a good life. It does not lose its Darwinian survival value, but it takes on an extra, intellectual value, and the two combine to create moral value.

But if ants cooperate, why isn't their behavior moral, too? Objectively, ants behave in decidedly immoral ways. The great ant experts Edward O. Wilson and Bert Hölldobler say this of the animal they've devoted much of their lives to studying:

> Ants . . . are arguably the most aggressive and warlike of all animals. They far exceed human beings in organized nastiness; our species is by comparison gentle and sweet-tempered. The foreign policy aim of ants can be summed up as follows: restless aggression, territorial conquest, and genocidal annihilation of neighboring colonies wherever possible. If ants had nuclear weapons, they would probably end the world in a week.[2]

What is missing for the ants, and not surprisingly since their brains are about the size of a grain of salt, is the intellectual dimension that amplifies and shapes survival values into something greater, by placing them in a wider context of experience. The example of the ants and other highly social insects demonstrates that not all cooperation is equal in moral terms. Broadly speaking, there are two kinds of cooperation: that which is forced upon us from outside agencies such as police, parents or other authority figures, through rules and regulations—or in the ants' case by what we loosely call "instinct"—and the kind that we undertake spontaneously, without coercion or the threat of it. The latter might be called true cooperation; the former is more akin to conformity. Most people would agree that the latter bears more ethical weight than the former—that virtue must be chosen, not imposed—and that in the case of the ants, there is no ethical weight at all to their behavior because it is strictly instinctual, in other words, effected entirely by means of an outside agency: they have no choice.

In fact, they have no individual identity; they are incomplete. That is the great sacrifice the species has made in order to achieve the evolutionary benefits of social cooperation on the basis of limited intelligence. That, it seemed to me—as the sun crept higher over our terrace amid the grape vines and the Pyrenees turned from violet to blue-green—that was the real message the ant world held for us humans: beware of specialization; beware of single-minded focus on material productivity, for it makes tools of the living and, as Aristotle said, living tools are slaves.

Progress and Salvation: On to Avignon

'WONDER PEOPLE' ❧ HILARY AND SIMON'S
ADVENTURE ❧ ECONOMICS AND LUST ❧
FAREWELL TO THE *GÎTE* ❧ THE QUESTION
OF SALVATION ❧ WHY? VS. HOW? ❧ A HISTORY
OF PROGRESS ❧ A VISIT TO THE BEACH ❧
PONT-DU-GARD

I was inspired to dash off an aerogram to Berkowitz:

Cher B.

I have today learned the following from *oc*-speaking ants of my acquaintance. There is no moral to the fable of the grasshopper and the ant. How could there be, since ants have no free will? What can be said is this: the scientific revolution set in motion by Galileo found its practical expression through the Industrial Revolution. For most of recorded history up until that event, most people were self-employed most of the time, though they survived and flourished through

❧ ❧ ❧

cooperation. The "job" with all its overt and subtle financial and psychological instruments of coercion is an innovation designed to meet the requirements of industrial capitalism. In the same way as Wonder Bread is not really bread at all but a bread substitute engineered to meet the specifications of mass production machinery, the industrial worker is a resource that, as worker, is something other, something less, than a whole human being. Because he lacks freedom—the market makes of him a commodity, an object to which freedom is a non sequitur—he is something less of a fully developed human and something more of an ant than are truly free people. Hence the term "human resources." We might as well substitute "Wonder People." The ants tell me they look upon scientific man with increasing admiration, as a species moving in the right direction. Soon, thanks to the march of science, procreation will be accomplished much more rationally, communication will be reduced to that which involves only our most fundamental urges and requirements, technology will be incorporated into our very bodies, we will in turn be integrated into our technologies and specialization will be so complete as to make survival impossible in the absence of hoards of others of our species. We will have joined the great nation of the ants.

I can only presume that they are unaware of, or seriously deficient in their knowledge of, television, MS-DOS, trans-species organ transplants and genetic engineering, and university academics.

The weather here has been perfect, I hope the same applies where you are. I'll probably e-mail you from Paris to confirm our arrival time.

Ciao,

wr

That done, I went back inside the *gîte* to find a stamp and to rummage in my book bag in search of a battered volume I've hung on to since my university days, Tawney's *Religion and the Rise of Capitalism*.

ꙮ ꙮ ꙮ

It was somewhere in the rucksack with the rest of my small medieval collection. Chris was descending the pine staircase from the bedroom loft, barefoot in a long, full cotton skirt and white T-shirt, Nikon in hand, a towel piled high on her head. She stepped gracefully outside onto the terrace.

"Mmm. It's beautiful again today."

"You should have seen the sun coming up over the village. I went in for bread."

"Oh, lovely." I heard the scrape of her chair being pulled up to the table, and she added, "Watch out for the ants when you come out."

I joined her at the table, leafing through Tawney for a half-remembered passage.

"The kids are still asleep. They must have been wiped out by all the excitement yesterday." She was adding steaming milk to her coffee while she talked.

We both smiled at the recollection, though it hadn't seemed funny at the time. There was a thunderstorm, and Hilary and Simon had been caught out in it while jogging along the machinery trails among the grapevines. They had lost their way, and it was after ten and pitch dark out before they turned up, wet, scratched and exhausted.

Excited to the point of bursting, the told us their story in turns:

". . . there was an *awesome* moon, did you see it? We thought it would be easy to get back, and then all of a sudden it was raining!"

After many wrong turns and false starts down little asphalt roads and gravel trails they had had to give up and find some place to ask directions. At a farmhouse, they'd managed to convince an old woman that they were not dangerous, and although she hadn't let them inside to use her telephone, she'd given them directions home.

". . . and, oh, there was this, like, giant dog, freaked me out totally . . ."

They'd apparently been about three kilometers away, in the general direction of Arzen.

ᴥ ᴥ ᴥ

"Holy cow, did you see the lightning? Wicked! Is there anything left to eat around here?"

I'd made some scrambled eggs, and brought out the cheese tray.

While Chris sipped her morning coffee, I finally found my passage in Tawney I'd been looking for, and read it aloud to her.

"Listen to this, he's talking about the difference between modern capitalism and the medieval attitude to economics. He's got a line in here which is beautiful, somewhere towards the end of the passage. He starts off by saying that there were two main assumptions about economic life in medieval times":

> . . . that economic interests are subordinate to the real business of life, which is salvation, and that economic conduct is one aspect of personal conduct, upon which as on other parts of it, the rules of morality are binding. . . . It is right for a man to seek such wealth as is necessary for a livelihood in his station. To seek more is not enterprise, but avarice—and avarice is a deadly sin. Trade is legitimate; the different resources of different countries show that it was intended by Providence. But it is a dangerous business. A man must be sure that he carries it on for the public benefit, and that the profits which he takes are no more than the wages of his labor. . . . There is no place in medieval theory for economic activity which is not related to a moral end, and to found a science . . .

"Here it is," I said, "here's the line":

> . . . *and to found a science of society upon the assumption that the appetite for economic gain is a constant and measurable force, to be accepted like other natural forces, as an inevitable and self-evident datum, would have appeared to the medieval thinker as hardly less irrational and less immoral than to make the premise of social philosophy the unrestrained operation of such necessary human attributes as pugnacity and the sexual instinct.*

"That's so great. Can't you just imagine an economic system based on lust?"

"I don't have to imagine it," said Chris.

We left our *gîte* at week's end with real regret, not simply because it meant we would be leaving Cathar country and starting the return trip north, but because it had been such a pleasant experience playing house in such exotic surroundings. We'd do it again in a flash. Our hosts presented us with a bottle of local wine and their daughter Anouk had hugs for Hilary and Simon and the offer of floor space in her Paris flat should they return on their own.

The Laguna stuffed to the gills with luggage and memorabilia, we set out east, to the Mediterranean. As I drove, a question rattled around in my mind like one of those jingles you can't shut off: namely, if the central focus, the defining goal, of medieval culture was salvation as Tawney had said, what could "salvation" have meant?

I asked Chris: "Remember that piece I read you from Tawney about how medieval people saw salvation as the central goal of life?"

"Yes . . ."

"What do you suppose they meant by 'salvation'?"

Hilary piped up: "It means to be saved, obviously."

"Saved from what, though?" I asked.

"It means to be taken up to some fictional place called Heaven to float around on clouds and feel warm and fuzzy," Simon offered.

"I don't know," Chris said, "but I don't think it could have been something as simple as going to paradise after death, because you couldn't get a whole civilization, top to bottom, to buy into that. Not the way medieval people did."

"I agree," I said. "It wasn't just church leaders and elites who thought that way, it was practically everybody, at least according to everything I've read. It was built right into their social structure. My theory is that it had something to do with understanding. In other words, you were 'saved' if you figured out what life was all about, why we were put on the planet, and what that meant about how you were to conduct your life and so on."

"Oh, great," said Simon. "So you got to go to heaven if you bought the Church's story about how the world was created in six days in the year four thousand whatever BC and all that!"

Chris sighed: "If you understand the truth, Simon, then you're saved. I think that's what it means. And the reason you have the stories about heaven and hell and so on is because the truth is so far beyond our experience that it is unexplainable in ordinary language, and so it has to be described through analogies and metaphors."

"Just like science," I interjected. "Science is another metaphor."

"It's a big mistake," Chris continued, raising her voice to override Simon's spluttered objections, "it's a big mistake to assume that because people lived before us they were stupid or naive. I'm quite sure, Simon, that there were plenty of people around who were just as smart as you are."

"The medieval Church was big on analogy," I said. "And even Augustine said that the Scriptures weren't meant to be taken absolutely literally. I think people generally understood that there was some deeper meaning behind the analogies. It's not surprising, because they basically thought of all material reality as a sort of analogy to a more perfect version in God's mind."

"Hmm," Simon said.

"Well, brainiac, what's your answer?" Hilary pestered.

"Answer to what!?"

"He's allowed to think, Hilary," I said. "It's permissible."

We drove on in silence.

Our own age dismisses such notions as salvation and redemption as quaintly superstitious examples of the backward, pre-scientific worldview. But medieval people, no less intelligent than we, also had a great deal more time to think than we have. Work, beyond what was necessary to maintain an adequate standard of life, was not at the top of their agendas. There were about ninety statutory holidays in the thirteenth-century calendar. People had time on their hands and they loved to use it for discussion and argument on matters moral and theological. Whenever they had the chance, they listened to debates, lectures and sermons of not only the great Cathar preachers, but also the mendicant friars of the orthodox Church, among them superstars of the calibre of St. Dominic and St. Bernard. This was a society not nearly so highly stratified as our own; we are not speaking here of merely the clergy and the aristocracy. In his memoirs, a scholar of the time, Amiel Bernard, records that as he was passing by the hospice of Laurac, he heard "two tramps, doubtless belonging to this house for beggars, debating on the Eucharist. One of them maintained that, provided one had faith, it would be just as good to eat a leaf of a tree or even dung to receive the consecrated species; the other tramp denied this."

Christian salvation as it was understood in thirteenth-century Languedoc by Catholics and Cathars alike is derived from both Judaism and Hellenism, and it is an interesting tale of the evolution of a metaphysical idea. It began, on the one hand, as a tribal or political concept involving the preservation of Israel from her enemies. Israel was favored by God, who acted to protect the community of "chosen people." For its part, Israel sought to understand, and progressively discover, God, his character and intentions. In the Old Testament, in fact, "knowledge of God," by which we may understand "enlightenment," is a synonym for salvation. The God of Israel was primarily a God of "the people," considered as a social organism, a community; inasmuch as individuals were God's concern, it was in ensuring that parts of that organism or community were properly disposed to one another. With the Exile and the destruction of the nation of Israel, the relationship of God to the nation became problematic and emphasis was put on a new covenant between God and His people, in which the subjects were individual human souls. Salvation was no longer communal, but individual, dependent on man's fidelity and confidence in divine power, and on his complete acceptance of the authority of God's will. It is not until the second century BC that the idea of an afterlife appears for the first time in connection with salvation.

The other current of thought leading to Christian ideas of salvation was Greek, and it followed a parallel development from communal to personal, in which knowledge of God or supreme good or truth—enlightenment—was the route to salvation. Early Greek philosophy was centered on the improvement of man's lot on earth through rules of conduct and government, and was displaced by a more personal focus with the decline of the city-state. When Greek political power passed into the hands of the Macedonians, philosophy looked more and more to personal virtue and individual salvation as opposed to the construction of the ideal state. As well, though it may seem an issue remote from spiritual concerns, the widespread literacy that arrived with the user-friendly phonetic alphabet in about 450 BC had played an important role here, even more important than the loss of political autonomy. Marshall McLuhan, Harold Innis and others have argued that the new ability to, as it were, expose the contents of one's mind, to lay it out in text in a document for all to see and comment upon, led to the strongly accelerated development of the idea of "self," in other words, of the individual's separate consciousness as distinct from that of others of the same tribe or species. In a broad sense the process led to a sharper separation between the subject "in here" and the objective world "out there."

The idea of the transactional nature of reality, or reality as a collaborative construct of matter existing *in potentia* and human consciousness, also played a role in the evolving nature of salvation. In the Neoplatonic thought that developed out of Plato in the late Hellenistic period and so heavily influenced St. Augustine and other early Christian philosophers, it was believed that the soul, which was the locus of understanding, was directly influenced and shaped by the objects of its perception. The impact was inevitable, because of the way in which the two mingled in the interactive process of creating reality. In other words, what you thought about played an important role in shaping what you were. (This in fact sounded a lot like the argument Chris and I and many other parents have used to deter their children from watching too much television!) The more time an individual spent in contemplation of the spiritual as opposed to the material content of the world, the closer he and his soul would be drawn to salvation.

In any case, for the Greeks and the Jews, the idea of personal salvation seems to have evolved in large measure as a refuge made necessary by the collapse of once-paramount community values. With the coming of Jesus Christ, the idea of salvation remained personal, but became much more potent: it was not to take place at some future date amid the splendor of the Apocalypse, but was available and effective here and now. Jesus taught that he was empowered by God to forgive sin: this meant that the power of salvation, God's redemptive power, was now operational through Jesus. But at the same time, the sense of community that had been lost by the Jews with the Exile, and the Greeks with the collapse of the city-states, was gradually revived throughout the Dark Ages and early Middle Ages in the idea of Christian governance. In other words, government according to Christian ideals, out of which evolved the whole notion of Christendom and world theocracy. Individual and community salvation had merged in a powerful new ethic.

This last iteration, what might be called the Augustinian doctrine of salvation, remained pretty much intact through the Middle Ages, right down to Thomas Aquinas. And then it became one more area of vulnerability to the Aristotelian, scientific approach to the understanding of nature, one more doctrine apparently in need of revision. With Aquinas begins the concretizing of the material world foreshadowed by the Manicheans and the Cathars and accomplished definitively by Galileo, Descartes and Newton. And that profoundly altered the nature of the processes by which salvation was made accessible.

ℵ ℵ ℵ

Augustine had said "Seek not to understand that you may believe . . ."but that was exactly the approach now being sanctioned by Aquinas in his incorporation of Aristotle into Church doctrine. More and more, belief—faith—came to be supplanted by knowledge as the source of enlightenment and the intimate connection drawn by Augustine between faith and the achievement of true understanding (". . . but believe that you may understand.") was lost.

It bears repeating that the worst fears of the medieval Scholastics who opposed Thomas Aquinas seem to have in fact been fully realized in our era. The question of meaning, of enlightenment, is "why?", which is ultimately a question of faith or belief, however modern cosmology, rooted exclusively in the material world of knowledge and facts, confines itself to asking "how?" Modern Western civilization's search for meaning, to the extent that it survives at all, is therefore doomed to failure, because the dominant, scientific worldview offers no ultimates. "Meaning" is not on its agenda.

Inescapably, however, it is the desire to understand, to find meaning, that distinguishes Homo sapiens from the rest of the animal kingdom, that defines the species. And philosophers and psychoanalysts alike talk of the destructive, existential anxiety that can result from an inability to resolve the question of man's place in nature. In fact, few issues have generated such philosophical unanimity: from classical Greece onward, there is a very strong consensus that, in Socrates' phrase as reported by Plato, "the unexamined life is not worth living."

There have been times other than our own in which the comforting assurances of age-old systems of thought have seemed to break down and lose their authority as pathways to understanding, and the happiness that comes with that understanding. The one which seems most relevant to our own is the time of late Hellenism in the early years of the Christian era, when the history of Greek philosophy had climaxed in a plethora of conflicting schools: the Skeptics and Cynics, the Epicureans and the Stoics. The pursuit of astrology was widespread. Given the absolute and unquestioned certainty that the way to life's fulfillment lay in the possession of the truth, a kind of apathy arose in the face of philosophy's evident failure to get at that truth in a clear and unequivocal way. It seemed the human claim to happiness was in vain.

> The age was one in which a man who had money and no desire for power could enjoy a very pleasant life—always assuming that no marauding army happened to come his way. Learned men who found favor with some prince could enjoy a high degree of luxury, provided they were adroit flatterers and did not mind being the butt of ignorant royal witticisms. *But there was no such thing as security.* [Emphasis added.] A palace revolution might displace the sycophantic sage's patron; the Galatians might destroy a rich man's villa; one's city might be sacked as an incident in a dynastic war. . . . There seemed nothing rational in the ordering of human affairs. . . . Except to adventurous self-seekers, there was no longer any incentive to take an interest in public affairs. . . . The man whose virtue has no source except a purely terrestrial prudence will, in such a world, become an adventurer if he has the courage, and, if not, will seek obscurity as a timid time-server.[1]

The contemporary Athenian dramatist, Menander, wrote:

> So many cases have I known
> Of men who, though not naturally rogues,
> Became so, through misfortune, by constraint.

It was the existential insecurity and the disillusionment with pagan systems of thought that gave Christianity its historic opportunity to blossom. But there were other, competing religions afoot in the world of the Mediterranean basin, notably Gnosticism, which claimed to have the keys to esoteric knowledge of the innermost workings of the universe. It was, most authorities agree, the single most serious threat to the continued survival and growth of the Christian church in the first two centuries after Christ. If knowledge was the key to human happiness, then Gnosticism could offer it in literally infinite quantity. Adept at absorbing features of other religions, the Gnostics adapted Christ to their system, as a messenger—not human but entirely spiritual—from a previously unknown supreme God. Christ's knowledge of the path to intimacy with God was said to have been preserved and passed down to a select few Gnostic initiates, in secret, by the Apostles.

In its claim to potentially limitless knowledge of Creation and its workings, Gnosticism bears a revealing resemblance to modern science. It had mostly died away by the end of the third century, supplanted by Christianity, not, in the main, through force of arms but by dint of superior argument, a process in which St. Augustine played a definitive role. The main philosophical case against Gnosticism, according to the Christians, was that its quest for spiritual fulfillment through knowledge had no end, and was therefore ultimately and literally pointless. In Christianity, the quest was guided by faith and ended in a kind of stable equilibrium, or peace, with God and in Christ.

In our own time, humanity continues to be neither equipped nor predisposed to abandon the search for meaning, which it has for so long equated with salvation. But like our Mediterranean ancestors a thousand years ago we, too, live in a time of confusion and apathy brought about by a spiritual vacuum. Where our ancestors turned to Christianity and faith, we have, by and large, placed our bets on science and knowledge as the winning path. We have redefined the quest, the Grail, in terms of an idea that fits better with the modern outlook. For modern man, salvation as both a social and individual quest is equated with the unending pursuit of knowledge that we call "progress."

Progress, it has been said, was the great discovery of the late eighteenth century and the dawning of the Industrial Revolution, and it has dominated our historical and political thought ever since. The notion, in its familiar modern guise, seems to have arisen out of the enormous increases in power made available to people through their new machines, and techniques they developed for organizing people in groups, so that they could efficiently serve those machines. It seemed as though nothing in nature could stand in the way of the modern engineer and his patron the industrialist, and that no traditional way of life or mode of belief could withstand the impact of modern education, propaganda and behavior modification. Nothing was any longer immune to change.

The impact and direction of this frame of mind was greatly influenced by Charles Darwin. By compiling an overwhelming body of evidence in support of the theory of evolution of complex organisms from simpler organisms, and by describing the mechanism for evolution as, in effect, survival of those organisms best suited to their environment, he provided a model in which nature itself seemed bent on progress.

There was a time, during the confident optimism of the Victorian and Edwardian eras, when it could be argued reasonably that the progress newly central to our culture meant not simply material progress brought about through mechanization and industrialization and regimentation, but moral progress as well, and to some extent it was true. One of the great accomplishments of the Industrial Revolution and the liberal, materialist philosophy that accompanied it was the eradication of the worldwide slave trade. Another was the gradual elimination of child labor. Both of these ends were, it is true, made economically attractive through the introduction of machines as a substitute for human labor, but they remain moral victories nonetheless.

In fact, however, the moral content of "Darwinian" progress was of a highly dubious nature. It was no doubt natural and comforting for the upper echelons of society to subscribe to a theory which told them that they held their lofty positions due to their genetically inherited superiority rather than to any accident of privilege. Closer examination, however, showed this argument to be a simple tautology (as is the "survival of the fittest" notion itself): viz. the rich and powerful

ᕁ ᕁ ᕁ

are where they are because they are fittest; we know they are fittest because they are where they are. No moral content can cling for long to so flawed a web of reason.

The enormous popularity of so-called social Darwinism in the United States in the late nineteenth century was due largely to the writings of the pioneering British sociologist Herbert Spencer, who coined the phrase "survival of the fittest" in interpreting (or rather misinterpreting) his mentor, and who achieved Messianic status all over America. The potential for political and social mischief inherent in what might be called Spencer's Darwinist fundamentalism is evident in this single excerpt from his writings:

> Partly by weeding out those of lowest development and partly by subjecting those who remain to the never ceasing discipline of experience, nature secures the growth of a race who shall both understand the conditions of existence, and be able to act up to them. It is impossible in any degree to suspend this discipline by stepping in between ignorance and its consequences, without, to a corresponding degree, suspending progress. If to be ignorant were as safe as to be wise, no one would be wise.[2]

The rich, in other words, were the innocent beneficiaries of their own superiority, and the poor must not be shielded too much from the harsh but ultimately rewarding experience of squalor. Charity, both individual and social or governmental, was a problem for Spencer and his legions of followers: it obviously interfered with the weeding-out process, but at the same time it was ennobling for the donor. In the end he decided reluctantly it should not be forbidden.

Much of the so-called progress made under the influence of such ideas is less than commendable in retrospect: in this category we can include much of what went on in the name of colonialism throughout Africa, Asia and Latin America, the tragic after-effects of which haunt us to this day.

✗ ✗ ✗

On another level, the great error of the Victorians was in equating human happiness with material comfort. It did not occur to them that people could be "comfortable yet not happy, happy yet not comfortable. . . .

> The measure of happiness is not, as the Utilitarians fancied, material prosperity, but fullness of life. . . . the manifest fact that, every day and all day long, men and women sacrifice comfort, health, and economic gain in the pursuit of truth, goodness and beauty, welcoming any burden so long as it affords scope for high activity, shows the irrelevance of material welfare as a criterion of progress.[3]

Today, in the shell-shocked, post-Industrial Revolution, post-First and Second World War, post-Hiroshima, post-Holocaust world, it would be hard to find more than a few hard-core Positivist ideologues who believe that material progress automatically brings with it moral progress; in fact, a majority of us have begun to suspect, with our medieval ancestors, that beyond some sustainable level of comfort, the opposite may be true. An idea that arose in the eighteenth century as offering hope of salvation in a better future, "progress" has degenerated into a bemused fatalism in our own time, having lost what slender claim to moral content it once could assert. In popular usage it has come to mean simply material or technical advancement, a process we believe is literally unstoppable regardless of its consequences. In its original conception, progress as salvation was a self-contained process, the material victories driving the moral ones. It didn't work out that way. And we are left with an ideology of salvation which can accurately be called half-baked, devoid as it is of moral purpose, which is now deemed to be an external issue, a field for specialists on the fringe of the mainstream of economic, social and scientific processes in society. As Augustine would have said, we have chosen to search, endlessly, rather than to find.

There is one other important consequence to this that needs to be mentioned here because it gets very little attention, though it seems to me to have direct bearing on the nature of the helter-skelter lives we lead.

That little-known fact is that time, in the era of "progress," has ceased to be morally neutral.[4] Throughout history, societies have accepted that quality and merit were as likely to be found in the past as in the future. The retrospective honor accorded the cultures of classical Greece and Rome throughout most of Western European history is only the most obvious example of this. For the past two hundred years, however, we have tended more and more to equate the past with "bad" or "backward" and the future with "good" or "progressive," which is the distinguishing characteristic of a culture deeply devoted to the idea of progress. History has nothing to teach us; we live on an inclined plane. Living on an upward slope is exhausting in itself; living on an upward slope with no crest in sight can lead to serious psychoses.

For medieval people, time was morally neutral, but it differed from our own understanding of it in another interesting and important way as well. As occupants of the centre of the universe, it was natural for the people of the Middle Ages to think of time as coming to them, rather than having to be pursued. Medieval society stood rock solid, immovable, and the future was continuously absorbed into the present. This view was fatally undermined by the scientific revolution, in which time became a mathematical construct, a continuum stretching infinitely into both the eventful past and the uncharted, untraveled future, which is a view of things we accept more or less unchallenged today. But what does that make of the present, in which all of us are living our individual lives? If time moves from the past into the future (as opposed to being absorbed into the present), the present is nothing but a moving point of no dimension, setting out the boundary between the two. It has no actuality. It cannot be lived. All is becoming. Present existence, because

ϗ ϗ ϗ

it has no real substance, is easy to sacrifice to the future, to progress. And not just present existence, but those who are trapped in it.

This was a discussion I had often had with Hilary when she was consumed with the terrible anxieties and regrets that accompany emerging adulthood, and I would try to console her.

"You have to live in the present," I would say to her. "You can't change what's happened in the past, and the future doesn't exist, so don't let either of them ruin the only real life you have, which is right now, in the present."

"Dad," she would say, "I *have* to worry about the future or I'll make a mess of it. Can't you see that? And how can I just forget about the past? It's not possible!"

The present to her seemed to have little meaning, although as our trip progressed I began to see occasional signs that that might be changing. Perhaps it is simply a question of maturity and experience of life.

By lunchtime we had made our way east to the wonderful old university city of Montpellier where Chris and I hoped to drop in on a high school chum of hers, a free spirit who'd backpacked here in the seventies, met a local girl, acquired a life and stayed on. But our friends were on holiday in Switzerland and so we decided to drive back down to the Mediterranean to spend a couple of hours at the seaside. According to our guide book we had a choice of several resort areas just a few minutes' drive away: nude or conventional. We chose conventional, but it didn't seem to make much difference. Poor Simon—no doubt he would have been happy enough to explore the beaches, crowded as they were with topless, G-stringed Parisiennes, had he been on his own, but it was not the sort of thing one does comfortably with one's parents. While Hilary and I took turns struggling into our bathing suits in the back seat of the car and Chris found a space amid the exposed flesh to spread a towel on the sand, Simon planted himself on the parking lot curb, his back to the sea, and determinedly read a book. Hilary, for her part, went

꙳ ꙳ ꙳

for a long stroll along the water's edge. She returned a little wide-eyed, I thought.

Later that afternoon, sticky with sea salt, we were in Avignon, another thoroughly enchanting city, where we left the car in the shade of a plane tree in a municipal parking lot and strolled to the grand plaza of the papal palace. Clement V, a Frenchman and weary of the continual feudal warfare around Rome, in 1309 moved the papacy to a substantial tract of territory just north of Avignon that had been ceded to the Holy See as part of the spoils of the Albigensian Crusade. Successors, preferring the bustle of urban life, had built the magnificent palace here in the city. In the blistering afternoon heat we trudged across the square and up a hill to the gardens overlooking the Rhône, from where we could see what remains of the famous bridge that inspired the children's song *"Sur Le Pont d'Avignon."* The story of its construction is a typical medieval tale: a young shepherd named Bénézet was commanded by voices from heaven to build a bridge across the river at a point indicated to him by an angel. His story was not believed, until he demonstrated its truth by miraculously lifting a huge building stone. With that, a brotherhood was formed to oversee construction and money and materials poured in from Church and laity alike. Within eleven years it was complete, with twenty-two separate stone arches, of which four remain.

From Avignon we struck out north, following the N-7 up the Rhône Valley towards Lyon. France's largest river, the Rhône has been corralled, channeled, harnessed and engineered to a fare-thee-well since 1933, when the Compagnie Nationale du Rhône was set up to systematically exploit its potential. This enormous public works project involved nineteen hydroelectric stations and dredging and canal works to accommodate fleets of 150-foot river barges that carry millions of tons of freight each year, and it has turned the valley into one of the economic powerhouses of Europe. Natural and human geography are incredibly varied along the Rhône Valley, and the travelog playing outside the car windows ranged from the salt flats and

꙰ ꙰ ꙰

rice fields of the Camargue Plain south of Avignon to irrigated orchards and vegetable farms, to industrial plants and refineries, and every few kilometers along the route in the high hills and mountain ridges overlooking the valley, fortified towns, castles and châteaux stood out against the sky.

The Rhône's bridges tell a story of their own: the Romans built two, one of wood at Arles and another of stone at Vienne. Three more were built in medieval times, including the Pont-Saint-Bénézet at Avignon. During the golden age of civil engineering in the nineteenth century, seventeen bridges were built, every one of which was destroyed in the Second World War. These have been replaced by prosaic reinforced concrete spans and suspension bridges.

Against my better judgement, because it was August and the height of the summer holiday season, we took the short detour off the N-7 to see Pont-du-Gard. The magnificent three-tiered Roman aqueduct spans a minor tributary of the Rhône a little west of Avignon, and has stood there in its tawny-gold splendor for nearly two thousand years. More than the amphitheater of Arles or the theatre and commemorative arch in Orange and other surviving Roman architecture in urban Provençe, the Pont-du-Gard speaks of the optimistic mien of Roman civilization, of a secure knowledge of man's place in the order of things and the enduring values of public investment for the general welfare. Such sanguine confidence in manifest human destiny was not to be seen in Europe again until the era of Victoria and *pax Britannica*, when public engineering works strongly resembled the Romans' in their enormous scale, their sturdy, broad-shouldered symmetry and elegant proportions—and when all those bridges were thrown across the Rhône. The optimism of the nineteenth century, however, was fated to be short-lived because it was built on the wobbly foundation of salvation through never-ending progress. Two world wars and the subsequent period of preparation for a war of global extermination effectively destroyed it. Nowadays little of what we build is built to last, so tentative is our faith in the continuity of

✗ ✗ ✗

human values, or even human existence, in what seems an increasingly hostile universe.

The parking lot was a dust-choked zoo of ice-cream and souvenir vendors and the aqueduct itself was swarming with sightseers. In the river below, unsinkable yellow plastic kayaks rented by the dozen from an outfitter somewhere upstream were elbowing their way past one another, their sunburned occupants gawping upward at the 160-foot-high span. I felt obliged to apologize to Simon and Hilary: I wondered then, and still do, whether it might have been better not to have shown them this noble, dignified relic in such demeaning circumstances, and let them instead discover it for themselves on some later trip, in a better season. Nevertheless we walked across the lower span, touched the Volkswagen-sized stone blocks, hewn on orders of Marcus Vipsanius Agrippa—who had campaigned in Egypt against Antony and Cleopatra—barged here from quarries up the river and fastened together with iron cleats in the public-spirited reign of Caesar Augustus, whose boast it was to have found Rome a city of brick and left it a city of marble, an accomplishment we are able to enjoy to this day (though, it must be said, the marble is being dissolved by acid rain).

✕ ✕ ✕

CHAPTER 17

Culture and Cuisine: Georges Blanc

THE MEANING OF RITUAL ⚲ THE FIRST RESTAURANTS ⚲ POPULAR AND ERUDITE CUISINE ⚲ DISCOVERING GEORGE BLANC ⚲ THE BLANC FAMILY'S STORY ⚲ THE ZEN OF DINING ⚲ AN AUDIENCE WITH THE MAESTRO ⚲ HOW TO BUY A MOTORCYCLE

W e had raised Simon and Hilary in a culture that too often mistakes the menu for the meal and it seemed to us that having them partake of a meal in the most exalted French tradition of gastronomy might help them to see that there is a difference, and understand its nature. To that end, after we had showed them Lyon, to my mind the most inviting and enjoyable city in France (always excepting, of course, Paris), we took them out for a once-in-a-lifetime dinner, at Georges Blanc.

⚲ ⚲ ⚲

In cuisine, as in all the arts, there is among the French an appreciation of a certain kind of perfection, of the achieved form, of knowing one's job and doing it well, that allows art to thrive.[1] Georges Blanc, the man and the eponymous restaurant, had for several years past represented the pinnacle of that tradition. There is much to be learned from such a man, and in such an establishment. It is a place where the ancient idea of reality as a joint project of matter and consciousness survives, where our identity with the material world that succors us is not denied, but celebrated. It is a place where subject and object are not seen in alienating opposition to one another, but as unified, through the senses. In a country where the spiritualism of the Age of Faith is palpable in thousands of medieval cathedrals, churches, abbeys, châteaux, hilltop fortresses and walled towns and villages, fine dining has evolved into a eucharistic celebration of life, a secular ritual rich in symbolic references to history, patriotism and the miraculous fecundity of the soil. Even the tall chefs' toques, designed to draw heat away from the head in furnace-like kitchens of yore, are reminiscent of bishops' miters. But as important as the ritual is in its transformative power, at the heart of everything is the food, the sacrament.

The artistry, the careful, knowing craft and the physical sensations that it creates, communicates information of a non-literal kind, the sort of information that is also transferred by music or visual art. This is often very rich stuff, mined from the deepest and purest veins of cultural wisdom and indispensable to the enjoyment of a full life. You might say that this is a kind of information that helps to make sense of the purely statistical data provided by our scientific inquiries. Indeed, without it, science makes no sense at all, because it exists in a vacuum of symbolic, mathematical language, with no roots in the real world. It is the non-literal or intuitive stream of information that gives meaning to science's symbolic language. The two are, or ought to be, inseparable.

⅄ ⅄ ⅄

In any culture, these intuitive or non-factual insights (some would call them spiritual insights) are often communicated through ritual. In ritual, as in art, communication takes place at a level beyond the rational, and thus it is an appropriate medium for the transfer of intuitive insight. The American philosopher Susanne Langer called ritual "the most primitive reflection of serious thought, a slow deposit, as it were, of people's imaginative insight into life."[2] Which is why it often seems so solemn, whether it is religious or secular; whether it is a priest with a communion cup or a sommelier decanting a fine wine over a candle flame. It was ritual in this sense we wanted Hilary and Simon to experience, so that they could see and understand how value is implicit in the humblest of human activities, and how, by making that value—or moral content—the focus of one's attention in participating in those activities, they can be lifted out of the strictly animal realm, into the spiritual. And since we were in France, food was the obvious vehicle; in no other culture, except the Chinese, is the ritual of dining so highly refined.

It begins with the simple fulfilling of a need for sustenance, which is common to all animals. Humans very early took it beyond the instinctual, to the social: cave paintings in Ariège only a few miles south of Montségur depict Stone Age families enjoying a meal together around a fire. Refined aesthetics of preparation and pre-sentation had added anticipatory delight and gustatory excitement at least two millennia before Christ; more recently, the classical Greeks had seventy-two varieties of bread (according to Athenaeus) and were gourmands of such exquisitely refined taste that they were capable of identifying the river from which a fish had been taken or the leg on which a quail habitually stood while sleeping.

Hospitality and sociability were ritualized to further heighten the pleasures of dining, but also to express more fully the meaning behind the getting and eating of food, the act which more than any other connects us to the rest of nature. It is a two-way street: the art and rit-ual in turn created meaning beyond the immediate basic fulfilling of

ᚷ ᚷ ᚷ

needs. Thus, in a felicitous phrase of Lewis Mumford, we entered "by this useful back door, into the domain of beauty and significance . . . [where] every instinctual need is broadened, yet partially concealed, by a social form, as the naked body is soon covered by decorations or clothes."[3] In this way, values grow out of needs and their fulfillment, because in "the domain of beauty and significance," it is the metaphysical questions framed by Socrates that make sense.

Restaurants themselves are a relatively recent innovation. The great French gastronome Jean-Anthleme Brillat-Savarin wrote in the early years of the nineteenth century that prior to about 1770 the aristocracy had had a monopoly on fine food. Travelers had been forced to make do with whatever was provided by their hotel; those who craved a good meal but whose household establishment did not include a cook resorted to caterers. With the opening of the earliest restaurants in Paris, he says:

> Anyone with fifteen pistoles at his disposal, who sits down at the table of a first-class restaurateur, eats well and even better than if he were at the table of a prince; for the feast which is offered him is just as splendid and moreover, having every conceivable dish at his command, he is undisturbed by personal consideration.

Menus in those days often ran to scores, even hundreds of dishes. The fare offered in a typical restaurant might include a dozen soups, two dozen hors d'oeuvres, fifteen or twenty beef entrées, twenty of mutton, thirty of chicken and game, sixteen or twenty veal dishes, a dozen pastry dishes, two dozen fish offerings, fifteen roasts, fifty side dishes and fifty desserts. In the face of such abundance, Brillat-Savarin wryly warned that,

> the availability and attraction of the restaurateur's wares may lead many people to indulge themselves beyond the limit of their faculties, and . . . this may cause indigestion, in the case of delicate stomachs, and some untimely sacrifices to the basest of Venuses.[4]

Humor is a common attribute among the great chefs and gastronomes. Fernand Point, the patron saint of modern Burgundian cooking, for many years plied his trade at La Pyramide just outside Lyon. Asked once about his weight by an impertinent journalist, he'd replied: "My weight is confidential. However if you wish to obtain my volume, you have only to multiply the surface of my base by my height and divide by three."

What are the insights communicated by the rituals of fine dining? They have to do with the pleasures of existence in this world, and at a deeper level with the paradox of our being both animal and spiritual beings. A great chef takes the basic foodstuffs of his environment and uses them in ways that enhance their essences, as historian Jean-François Revel says: "[He] knows how to extract their aromas and flavors and set off their consistencies, but he does so by transposing them into a new register, where they disappear only to be reborn as a whole that owes its existence to intelligence."[5] The chef raises the ordinary material substances with which he works to a level somewhere closer to Plato's ideal, as it exists in the mind's eye of the Creator: to dine well in France, or in any culture with a strong culinary tradition, is to be in touch with the gods.

I find it interesting that Revel's definition of gastronomy bears a strong resemblance to the definition of "knowledge" frequently found in discussions of information technology and society: knowledge = information + intelligence + experience.[6] In a knowledge-based economy, knowledge may be used to add value to products by, for instance, controlling production functions, or it may be produced as an end product in itself. Knowledge, in this latter case, is a commodity with economic value that is created "out of thin air" by combining a raw resource with human intellect and experience. In this sense gastronomy is clearly a part of what is commonly called "the information economy." Like other sources of value in the information economy, it has the very important advantage of creating high value with a relatively small impact on the planet's natural systems, while at the same time adding materially to quality of life. And the improvements to quality of life apply not just to the consumer of the product, but to its producers as well, since they enjoy the satisfactions of creative, ecologically ethical work.

According to Revel, cuisine comes from two sources: the popular and erudite. By the first he means the traditional fare of the family hearth and by the second he means the cuisine of the professional, "that [which] only chefs fanatically devoted to their art have the time and the knowledge to practise."

> The first type of cuisine has the advantage of being linked to the soil, of being able to exploit the products of various regions and different seasons in close accord with nature, of being based on age-old skills transmitted unconsciously by way of imitation and habit, of applying methods of cooking patiently tested and associated with certain cooking utensils and recipients prescribed by long tradition . . . The second cuisine, the erudite, is based by contrast on invention, renewal, experimentation.

With the formation of the urban middle classes in the eighteenth and nineteenth centuries, the unconsciously transmitted and the deliberately created cuisines began to merge in France to form what is known as bourgeois cuisine, which is what most of us recognize as classic French cooking, and which "retains the heartiness and the savor of peasant cuisine while at the same time introducing into it the subtlety and the 'distinction' of *haute gastronomie*, in sauces, for instance."

While "erudite" cooking has led to the blossoming of an international cuisine that borrows elements from the four corners of the earth, regional cuisine, in general, rooted in the very soil as it is, does not travel well. Hence the very best of the chefs in France tend to be regional chauvinists, fiercely dedicated to their local culinary traditions. Their cooking arises out of those traditions, but of course transcends them or, as Revel would say, transposes them to a new register.

To get to Georges Blanc, you must drive sixty kilometers north from Lyon, or a similar distance west from Geneva or south from Dijon, or four hundred kilometers southeast from Paris. It is quite deliberately a destination unto itself, determinedly rural, in the heart of the great vineyards of Burgundy—Beaujolais, Mâcon, Chablis, Côtes de Beaune. There is no direct access by highway; to reach the village of Vonnas (population 2,381) where the restaurant-hotel is located we had to slow down and enjoy a few kilometers of winding, tree-lined road through small, mixed farms, up and around orchards, down across streams. It is here and in the surrounding region that the toothsome, blue-legged *poulet de Bresse* are produced; grain- and milk-fed chickens bred and raised as carefully as Kentucky thoroughbreds (and about as expensive). They have been renowned for two hundred years and more: Brillat-Savarin wrote in 1825:

> Three districts of old-world France dispute the honor of furnishing
> the best fowls, namely, Caux, Le Mans and Bresse. As regards capons
> there is some doubt as to which is superior; and as a rule the one we
> are eating seems better than the rest; but as for pullets there are none
> to compare with those of Bresse, known as *poulardes fines*; they are as
> round as an apple and all too rare in Paris . . .[7]

As one might expect at this sine qua non of restaurants, the idea of the welcome, *le bon accueil*, which is considered by the French to be of critical importance in the ritual of hospitality, is here taken to its logical conclusion. The village, when it appears around a bend in the road, across a low stone bridge, is scrubbed, swept and alive with color, every square inch of land not devoted to some other purpose having been planted with flowers. And before you can absorb all of this, you are in the town square, which is dominated on three sides by the properties that make up the Georges Blanc establishment: the half-timbered brick hotel and restaurant; the *Ancienne Auberge*, a reproduction of the original Blanc family restaurant featuring a modestly-priced menu; and the store, which sells baked goods, preserves and charcuterie, fine china and flatware, cooking tools and utensils, wine and gifts. We learned later from the maestro himself that he spends a great deal of money each year to create and maintain this atmosphere of serenity in Vonnas; if you're looking for a typical Burgundian village, look elsewhere—Vonnas is all about Georges Blanc and Georges Blanc is all about creating the perfect atmosphere for the appreciation of what strives to be France's best cuisine.

Chef Blanc would later tell Chris and me with characteristic modesty that thanks to a purchase made that summer, he now owns *all* of the properties facing onto the town square. "It was necessary . . . we would not want someone to open a pizza parlor, for example. It would spoil the atmosphere," he explained apologetically.

Even the hotel (thirty-two rooms, six apartments) is simply a necessary adjunct to a dining room that is so far from major centers that some sated clients will need a place to sleep. Naturally, the rooms must match the quality of the dining, which means that they are sumptuously comfortable and absolutely quiet. Behind the hotel is a large pool and beyond that, in manicured parkland, a helipad.

All this, as I say, is ancillary to the food, which is the main event and the source of the Blanc family fame and fortune for generations. Jean-Louis Blanc and his wife opened the first restaurant and hotel at the fairgrounds in Vonnas in 1872, where they served poultry dealers who appeared each Thursday for the market. They provided the hearty fare that in the nineteenth century distinguished kitchens in rural, middle-class homes where, especially around Lyon, "meals were copious and cooked with loving artistry, since as Balzac pointed out, the lack of occupation and monotony of life in the provinces concentrated attention on the kitchen."[8] By the time their son Adolph took over the business in 1902 it had attained a modicum of fame.

Adolph installed his new wife Elisa in the kitchen at "La Mère Blanc," and it is she who earned the passionate admiration of the great chef and gastronome, Curnonsky. He so admired her frogs' legs in herbs, her Bresse chicken in cream and her crêpes Vonnaissiennes that he described her, in 1933, as "nothing less than the finest cook in the world." National recognition followed, and son Jean brought home a bride, Paulette, a baker's daughter, who would in her time inherit the kitchen from her famous mother-in-law.

In January of 1943 a son, Georges, was born to Jean and Paulette, a prodigy who was destined to be the most renowned Blanc of them all. Succeeding to the family business in 1968 after rigorous training in some of the best kitchens in France, he began the transformation of the simple country inn he had inherited, aiming at a membership in Relais and Châteaux. By 1981 he had achieved the pinnacle of culinary success, a third Michelin star. Gault and Millau give him 19.5 out of 20, their highest rating. There were other prizes, including the Légion d'Honneur. Success was prodigious, and it permitted him to purchase a vineyard which he planted with the finest Chardonnay vines; to open a fine restaurant overlooking an ancient bridge on the river Saône in the town of Mâcon; to buy a twelfth-century château on the outskirts of Vonnas and turn it into a lavish convention centre. And now his sons Frédéric and Alexandre are being groomed in the kitchens and business offices of Vonnas, the fifth generation in this remarkable dynasty.

There was a transcendent, Zen-like quality to the evening that was fascinating; a seamless coming together of the various elements of a memorable experience. It was hot when we'd arrived in Vonnas, and we were all pretty tired. Chris and I showered and dressed in diffident silence and descended to the hotel lobby, where I flopped in a leather chair and picked up a crisp copy of the *Herald Tribune* from a coffee table. Then Hilary arrived, looking so gorgeous in the black sheath she'd brought along just for this occasion that I melted a bit.

Ӿ Ӿ Ӿ

Then Simon, in tie and jacket, rumpled like a poet, long hair slicked back with water.

I stood, a compliment on my lips, but before I could say anything, Georges Blanc and his wife appeared out of nowhere, to ask us if we had found our rooms adequate (adequate?!) and to escort us to the bar, which adjoins the dining room. This was no accidental encounter: they had been discreetly waiting for us to assemble as a family group. (Madame Blanc's office, from which she helps to stage-manage each evening, contains several video monitors, including one which watches the hotel reception area.) We were conducted down a long, carpeted corridor past plate-glass windows looking into a very large, ultra-modern kitchen of white ceramic and stainless steel where we could see white-smocked cooks of every rank working over ovens and ranges, cutting blocks and pastry tables. Georges Blanc employs 125 people; a goodly number of them seemed to be on hand in the kitchen at that moment.

By the time we had reached the bar (maroon leather barrel chairs, tapestries, hand-hewn beams), we had all been thoroughly distracted from whatever mundane thoughts we might have been nursing. Aperitifs were ordered, and we were presented with menus. Small pre-dinner appetizers began appearing before us on our low coffee table, so artfully concocted and presented they made us smile. There was, for instance, a miniature veal stew served in an eggcup. As our appetites swelled, we discussed the menu with the maestro himself, who was quietly moving from table to table, giving each of his patrons for the evening the same personal treatment, now and then signing a menu with a flourish, or autographing a copy of one of his books on cuisine. A waiter took our orders, and another tiny appetizer arrived, even more clever than the last.

The bar is a carefully conceived decompression chamber, which prepares patrons to get maximum enjoyment from the main event to come: another step in the crafting of the complete experience.

Ɣ Ɣ Ɣ

The preparation of the food was one thing: just as important for the transaction that would shape the ultimate reality of the dining experience was the preparation of the diner's consciousness, or in other words, the setting of the mood. The effect was irresistible. By the time we were seated in the dining room with its timbered ceiling and floor of varnished brick, Christine and I were smiling, congratulating one another on how well our children had turned out; the kids were complimenting her on her good looks and laughing indulgently at my jokes. We were ready, at last, to eat.

With four of us ordering three courses from an extensive menu, a description of the food would be much too long for the context here, and in any case after years of reading what is sometimes described as gastro-porn, those effusive restaurant reviews larded with adjectives like "succulent" and "orgasmic," there is something about describing cuisine of this calibre that makes me uncomfortable. Words simply cannot do it justice. I ordered, for example, the famous *cuisses de grenouilles sautés comme en Dombes* (frogs' legs) and a main course of *poulet de Bresse à la crème façon Grand-mère Blanc*, two of the dishes that had made the Blanc name famous; Chris had *croustillant de foie gras de canard et petite salade potagère* (a duck pâté salad) and *gâteau de crabe aux sucs de champignons et truffes* (truffled crab in pastry). The duck liver pâté and the creamy crab with mushrooms and truffles were not, strictly speaking, dishes native to this region, having their roots farther to the south and west in Perigord, the part of France Chris likes best of all. My dishes, though, were solidly in the tradition of Bresse cooking, which is deceptively simple in its essence. It is the attention to detail—the inspiration and intelligence behind its preparation—that lifts it out of the ordinary. Pastry shells are so flaky you can cut them with a sharp look; vegetables are so fresh and so perfectly prepared that they are almost unfamiliar. Sauces are bursting with the flavor and aroma of just-picked herbs. The chicken, its texture and flavor, is unrecognizable unless you happen to have grown up on a farm back in the days when the birds were left to roam the barnyard.

⊻ ⊻ ⊻

And above all, Grand-mère Blanc's tiny masterpieces, the little crêpes Vonnaissiennes, feather-light potato pancakes spiked with caviar and smoked salmon. The presentation was impeccable, each plate bringing murmurs of surprise and delight, as a stage setting sometimes does when the curtain lifts. Then, the dessert trolley, which groaned under the weight of a dozen spectacular offerings concocted of the freshest cream and eggs, the finest chocolate, the tenderest pastry and the freshest, plumpest fruits and berries the region has to offer. The cheese tray was a smorgasbord with everything from creamy artisan-made Roquefort to tart local chèvres. Finally there were tiny petits fours which the pastry chefs regard as a test of their creative mettle and are irresistible even after so lavish a feast. I am quite certain Brillat-Savarin would heartily have approved of it all.

Was there music? I can't remember. I do remember lavish bouquets of cut flowers, brocade upholstery, gilt mirrors, the sparkle of fine china, crystal and silver, a sensation of warmth and conviviality. Since, once we'd ordered, there was no more real need to speak to a waiter, dinner proceeded seamlessly from start to finish: glasses were filled, cutlery was changed, dishes arrived and empty plates departed . . . and never was there an interruption to our conversation; nothing was permitted to invade our dome of pleasure.

Hilary and Simon discussed our wine like connoisseurs.

"It's quite spicy, not at all like the one we had last night," Hilary said.

"Yeah, it was definitely fruitier," said Simon, withdrawing his nose from his glass.

To Chris, Hilary said, "This is a whole other world, isn't it?"

Chris, in her element, smiled back dreamily.

Hilary and Simon, I observed with satisfaction, were on their way to becoming gourmands (a word I prefer to the synonymous but ugly "gastronome"), though it would be a long time before they could claim full fellowship in that singularly French expression of enthusiasm for fine food and interest in its preparation. (Gastronomy, like

ɤ ɤ ɤ

coquetry, the French like to boast, is a French innovation, and both words are used untranslated in every European language.) In his classic *Culture and Cuisine*, Jean-François Revel speaks of the gastronome (or gourmand) this way:

> The gastronome is at once curious and suspicious, venturesome and timid; he explores, but he does so faintheartedly. He seeks new sensations and at the same time fears them. He spends half his time recalling past satisfactions and the other half making skeptical conjectures as to possibilities to come. The Maréchal de Richelieu . . . declared: "I have never rejected happy innovations; but with the exception of bisques made from a purée of small crabs, timbales with quail eggs and glazes of whole-wheat bread alternating with glazes of fresh butter, I can assure you that nothing satisfying or distinguished has been invented in the seventy-five years that I have been eating and inviting others to eat with me."[9]

Brillat-Savarin, writing two-and-a-half centuries before Richelieu, paints a less emotionally fraught and more wholesomely enthusiastic picture. While insisting that gourmandism is the enemy of excess, he defines the word as referring to

> an impassioned, reasoned, and habitual preference for everything which gratifies the organ of taste. . . . From the moral point of view, it shows implicit obedience to the commands of the Creator, whom when He ordered us to eat in order to live, gave us the inducement of appetite, the encouragement of savor, and the reward of pleasure. . . . Social gourmandism . . . combines the elegance of Athens, the luxury of Rome, and the delicacy of France, and . . . unites careful planning with skilled performance, gustatory zeal and wise discrimination; a precious quality, which might well be called a virtue, and is at least the source of our purest pleasures.[10]

Ɣ Ɣ Ɣ

Towards the end of our meal Hilary mused, to no one in particular, "Food like this makes time stand still."

"I know what you mean," I said. "I think what it does is help you to exist, for a while, self-consciously in the present. And that's a gift, isn't it?"

Her face lit up: "I never thought of it before, but if you always lived in the present, time *would* stand still, wouldn't it? You'd be immortal!"

"Immortally enjoying *poulet de Bresse à la crème façon Grand-mère Blanc*. Maybe that's what's meant by heaven."

She laughed: "No—an infinite dessert trolley!"

"It'd be the cheese tray for me," Chris offered.

Simon took a great interest in the logistics of the affair, noting with approval the discreet professionalism of the servers. The complexities of the stemware and cutlery were the kind of challenge he enjoys, and he allowed after a suitable period of reflection and analysis that it was the best food he'd ever eaten.

"Or are ever *likely* to eat," I assured him.

We could not hear the conversation from other tables; the nearest was ten feet away from us. But Chris drew our attention to an older man and his young daughter (granddaughter?) as a small cake was being presented to her, a birthday cake with a sparkler.

"I guess this won't be like East Side Mario's," Simon grinned. "You know, when all the staff gets together around the table and sing 'Hap-hap-happy birthday.'"

I had to laugh at the image: if they had, it would have resembled a serenade by the Mormon Tabernacle Choir.

After dinner, Hilary and Simon went for a late-night swim in the pool, Chris and I took a walk under the trees in the square before bed. Our room had been prepared: the bed was turned down, the electrically-operated shutters on the windows closed and heavy curtains drawn. No sound could be heard.

ᴚ ᴚ ᴚ

In the morning the two of us enjoyed coffee, fresh yogurt and cheeses, fruit and baked goods in the sunny, homey breakfast room while Hilary and Simon were still sleeping, and then we met Georges Blanc in his office, a large paneled room dominated by a wall of books and a vast, cluttered desk, home to a flock of telephones, computer, modem, electronic notebook, calculator and other hi-tech bric-a-brac. While he showed us the half-dozen books he had authored, one by one, we struggled to fend off his big, affectionate golden Lab, who was all over us. A son popped his head in the door to ask a question and we were introduced: Alexandre, short, slim, intense, in kitchen whites. There was a brief exchange in rapid-fire French and Alexandre disappeared back to the kitchen.

We had wondered how such a busy entrepreneur managed to maintain his focus on food, and asked about that. Plainly puzzled at the question, he responded with an eloquent shrug that the cuisine is his passion. How could one fail to be focused on one's passion? (We had heard that word "*passion*" often from restaurateurs and hoteliers we'd chatted with in France; I was beginning to think that in this context it might better be translated as "a calling.") It was as if the question was a non sequitur for him. Though the syntax is identical, there is after all a difference between asking "What is the purpose of preheating the oven?" and "What is the purpose of life?" The answers draw on two different wells of information, as Socrates made plain. Though the appurtenances of his office showed him to be a thoroughly modern man in some respects, George Blanc had retained a Socratic mindset.

We continued to chat while Chris took some pictures, and he told us that an important influence in his life and art had been industrial designer Raymond Lowey, a long-time family friend. Lowey was born in Paris but went to New York in 1919. He will be remembered as one of the century's leading industrial designers, responsible for the Studebaker car, the Lucky Strike cigarette pack, Coca-Cola soda fountain dispensers, Electrolux vacuum cleaners. Lowey was not of the mid-century's fashionable functionalist school of design led by Walter Gropius and his church of functionalism, the Bauhaus: he wondered with many others what was so functional about sitting on a hard steel chair in a bare room lit with an exposed light bulb.

On the other hand, Lowey was no purveyor of ersatz "styling" like that of his automotive competitor Harley Earle, long-time GM designer and instigator of the finned and chrome-encrusted Detroit land yachts of the sixties and seventies. Lowey understood that design is more than style *or* function; it is an attitude to a product's intrinsic qualities, and is thus as much a moral as aesthetic process.

It was this clear understanding of the moral and aesthetic dimensions of what are otherwise, let's face it, mundane products—food and lodging—that helped Georges Blanc transform his family business into a diversified, multimillion-dollar industry, without sacrificing quality, without losing sight of the original goals. As Lowey might have said, it is the chef's respect for the integrity of his ingredients and his attitude to the purposes of dining that make great food, just as it is the attitude to the basic purpose and necessities of lodging that makes a great hotelier. But I think there is a more profound truth at work here as well, and that is that there can be no distinction between means and ends; that bad means lead inevitably to corrupted ends. Or, to frame the same thought in positive terms, enlightenment in the sense in which I've used the word, and the enlightened values that go with it, are good for business just as they help transpose every other aspect of life into a higher register.

In the busy, meticulously preserved heart of nearby Dijon that afternoon, we stopped for lunch and a stroll through the winding, cobbled lanes of the pedestrian precinct with its many food and wine stores and antique shops before resuming our trip back to Paris. Throughout the fourteenth and fifteenth centuries the city was the resplendent capital of the Dukes of Burgundy—frequent allies of the English in the Hundred Years War—and one of the jewels of Europe. Reflections

ϰ ϰ ϰ

of that faded glory are everywhere to be seen, though by now we were all, I think, a little overstuffed on rich medieval fare. Or perhaps it was just the indulgences of the previous night, but for whatever reason we did not stay long enough to do the place justice. I dropped a complimentary Georges Blanc postcard to Berkowitz in a mailbox:

Cher B.

I won't torment you with the details of dinner at G.B., except to say that it was a transcendent experience in every way. The guy is an alchemist with food. Who would have thought dining could be spiritually enriching! Leads me to believe there might be something to the Eucharist thing after all—that chicken I ate had definitely been lifted to a higher order of being! If it hasn't rained there and you find you have to water the grass, remember to turn the tap off at the hydrant on the well, or you'll end up with sand in the household water. Chin up!

Regards,
wr

As all French towns and cities do, Dijon has an abundance of fabulous lingerie boutiques, which I have always found as difficult to pass by as bookstores. Fortunately, Chris shares my interest (I am old-fashioned enough to be reluctant to be discovered in one without female accompaniment), and of course Hilary was agog at the quality and style they offered compared to stores back home. Only Simon was a recalcitrant browser, and I felt for him in his adolescent male embarrassment. But after all, we'd brought him all the way to France to help him break out of some of the North American culture's childishness. I walked back to where he was stationed by the door, arms crossed, cheeks flushed, gaze fixed on the street outside.

"You know, this place is a lot like Georges Blanc," I said.

No response.

"It is, you know. It's the same attitude to form and to the world of

✗ ✗ ✗

the senses. You can see it if you look at how the things they sell here are designed and sewn so carefully, and the materials are selected for exactly the right feel, the right amount of clinginess or drape or transparency, and they're cut perfectly to show not too much and not too little. . . . You should try having a look around from a design point of view."

I knew full well that this last suggestion was completely bogus, because to look at French lingerie through the lens of a design engineer is to miss the whole point. Its appeal exists in the realm of the instinctual, not the mathematical; its purpose is to take you beyond the body as object, to the ideal form beyond it. But I thought it might get him to see that here was a way to celebrate *la differénce*, a way to display and savor the female form that is not pornographic, but still powerfully sensual. At the very least, it might help him rationalize to himself a curiosity that otherwise embarrassed him. He was a bit too young.

A kind of strangled grunt was the best he could manage in reply.

"Come on outside," I said.

He gulped down the fresh air.

"Have you ever thought, Simon, that when you have strong experiences that involve the senses, like, for instance, dinner last night, you're actually learning at a tremendous rate? Later on your mind can sort it all out and organize it rationally, but the actual learning takes place when you're tasting or looking and just absorbing it all."

"Learning about what?"

"About yourself, ultimately. Because you're a part of everything out there, and vice versa. It's a way of breaking down the subject and object barrier, short-circuiting it, so that you can absorb knowledge directly."

I thought I'd get an argument here about the objective nature of reality, but all he said was, "So?"

"So, that's why travel is a good thing and why you should keep yourself open to new experiences and indulge your senses now and then. That's all."

Silence.

"When we get back to the car, let's keep an eye out for a good motorcycle shop. There's a ton of models here you never get to see in North America, and the shops are different, too. They have a whole different attitude to bikes."

"How's that?" He'd perked up a bit.

"Well, for one thing there are a whole lot of road bikes available in the 250- to 650-cc range, whereas back home it's hard to find anything other than 1,100-cc behemoths that cost as much as a car and you need a crane to pick up if they ever fall over on you. You could pull a horse trailer with them. To me, that's a dumb idea of a bike, the exact opposite of what they ought to be."

"Why? What do you mean?"

"I mean, it's a trap rather than a freedom machine. You need to be rich to own one and even richer to maintain it, and it's only good for paved highways. It's just a car pretending to be something else. You buy one because *you're* pretending to be something other than what you are; if you're a car person, get a car. Because the more you keep pretending, the less free you are because you're more and more bound up in illusions."

"All that, from buying the wrong motorcycle?" he asked with a patient smile.

"Absolutely!"

An hour later he spotted a motorcycle megastore as we drove through a light rain in the city's industrial suburbs, on our way back to the highway to Paris. We pulled in to the parking lot and Hilary groaned and reached for her book, but Chris joined Simon and me and we had a fine time examining the merchandise, trying out the saddles, squeezing brake levers and cranking back on throttles, smelling the new rubber, admiring the engineering of the frames and engines and the styling of the fairings, checking out the leathers and the helmets. There is integrity, and knowledge, to be found in the best of these machines as well.

CHAPTER 18

Dijon to Paris

SEEING AND BELIEVING ❧ BELIEVING AND

SEEING ❧ A PIT STOP ❧ MY LETTER TO

BERKOWITZ ❧ THE SMOKING CAR

"I wonder how the wedding went."

Chris smiled back at me. We had just passed a road sign pointing to the little village of St. Julien about an hour's drive south of Paris. You could just see the church steeple peeking over the crest of a green hill that had been cropped by pearly Charolais cattle. This was where the old woman we'd chatted with when we'd arrived in France had told us she and her noseless husband were going to be staying.

"I imagine they had a wonderful time. She seemed such a warm person."

"Once you got to know her a bit."

Hilary piped up from the back seat, "She looked *grotesque* when I first saw her on the plane."

"Just goes to show," I said, "seeing isn't always believing."

"Yes, because she turned out to be really nice."

Simon, always alert for irrational sentimentality, snorted impatience. "What do you mean, 'seeing isn't belicving'?"

"I mean that your frame of mind has a lot to do with what you see, and if you don't keep an open mind, you'll often be misled by appearances."

❧ ❧ ❧

"Of course seeing is believing. In fact," he moved forward, straining against his seat belt, "you told us we were going to Georges Blanc because you wanted us to see how *tasting* is believing. So what's the difference? There is no difference!"

"Ah."

He had me there. I had to think for a moment. A big BMW bike with two leather-clad figures aboard swept past us as if we were standing still.

"It actually works both ways, doesn't it. I mean, it is correct to say that seeing is believing, when you mean that when your senses are in contact with something you get good, concrete information about it that you can generally rely on. But it's also true to say, 'Believing is seeing,' because often you see what you expect to see rather than what's really there. You expected the old lady to be one thing because of her appearance and her husband and so on, and we found she was something else altogether."

"All that means is that your mind can delude you and you should always look for empirical evidence before you believe something." Score one for Simon and for Positivism.

I thought it best to let it go at that. Approaching Paris at 140 kilometers per hour on the A-5 is not the best time or place to wade into contentious philosophical waters. But the more I thought about it, the more interesting the phenomenon of the reversibility of the expression "seeing is believing" became. It seemed to penetrate to the heart of the question of perception.

St. Augustine said, "Seek not to understand that you may believe, but believe that you may understand." In other words, he came down on the side of "believing is seeing." On the other hand, the Scholastic theologians of the fourteenth century, on the cusp of the modern, scientific outlook, had said, "About things eaten, there can be no argument," which might be paraphrased as "Seeing is believing." And that is certainly the modern scientific view of things.

ℵ ℵ ℵ

To the modern mind there is a paradox in this magical palindrome, worthy of Magritte; the two statements seem to contradict one another. But to the pre-scientific outlook, there is no contradiction at all, because the model of reality as a transaction between mind and matter, between consciousness and objects *in potentia*, covers both perspectives. Both statements are true, depending on which end of the transaction you're looking at.

Had he lived in our own times, St. Augustine might have added by way of explanation of his dictum about belief preceding understanding that by "belief" he meant having a hypothesis. A hypothesis is a framework for observation or reasoning, and it is also a way of seeing. If you do not know of or believe in a thing's existence, you are unlikely to see evidence of its existence, or if you do stumble upon evidence, you will in all likelihood misinterpret it. However, if you do know of (or believe in) the existence of the thing, then you will readily see and recognize the evidence of its existence. And you will also now see other entities in terms of their relationship to it, and that will change your understanding of those other entities in turn. The best examples of this process come from science, where, for instance, Faraday's discovery of force fields made Newtonian mechanics obsolete, and Darwin stood the world on its ear with his idea of evolution by natural selection. Once these phenomena had been described, evidence for their existence was recognized on every hand. Until very recently, medical science was certain that babies do not feel physical pain, and so circumcisions and other minor surgical procedures were conducted without anaesthetic. Now that we realize that this idea was incorrect, evidence abounds, not only of reaction to pain, but of the long-term post-traumatic effects. And now that we recognize our mistake, it is hard to understand how we could have been so blind as to not see the evidence in the first place (which in the latter case included the screaming of the babies). In this sense a valid belief, though it may be "unprovable" in scientific terms, can be like a good

ﭏ ﭏ ﭏ

scientific theory, in that it can help to make the world a more understandable place; a valid belief, like a good hypothesis, is a great aid in solving any problem. A bad one, on the other hand, can lead to a completely delusional life. The job of philosophy and religion might be said to be the development of "good" hypotheses and beliefs about the nature of existence.

Simon and Hilary were dozing in the back seat, and so that they would not miss the entire ride back into Paris, we pulled into a toll route gas station to stretch our legs and buy coffee and snacks. While highway pitstops and truck stops in North America more often than not, in a word, are disgusting, here they are a place where one can eat well and cheaply. This one was clean and efficient, and the food was fresh, varied and on the whole remarkably good. There was a bar, of course, which both kids found quite astonishing.

While Simon and Hilary ate and explored the souvenir shop and Chris browsed in the big magazine stand, I rapped out a few final paragraphs of an e-mail to Berkowitz. I'd been working on it for the past several days when I should have been making travel notes to myself, so that I'd be able to send it off when we reached our hotel. It was the kind of stuff he would enjoy thinking about, but I was doing it as much for myself as for him, to keep some ideas from slipping away before they'd had a chance to jell.

Cher Berkowitz,
I've been feeling guilty lo these many months for saying I'd have some helpful thoughts about your predicament. I know you never took me seriously, but I did (take me seriously). It's been bugging me. So here are some ideas for you to chew on.
    The mind-body duality that came out of the scientific revolution, and especially from those mathematical paragons Descartes and Leibniz, was undeniably a bad hypothesis that became a destructive belief. It took the healthy development of the self that began with the Greeks and alphabetic literacy (remember?) and made of it an

ᛣ ᛣ ᛣ

obsessive pathology. It did this by insisting on the radically objective nature of reality, opening up a chasm between subject and object, between the perceiver and the thing perceived, between "in here" and "out there." Whereas we had once been active participants in the existence of the world around us, we were henceforth to be isolated, self-contained entities.

But as sealed-in entities, what role could we play in the cosmos, in the great scheme of things, which science had reduced to mathematical rules and formulae? The only possible role remaining to us was that of spectator. Where once we had been at the very center of the universe, at the heart of its being, we were now merely accidental tourists of no greater or lesser importance than anything else under the sun. Not puppets of the Gods, but beings suspended ridiculously, as Arthur Koestler said, by our chromosomes.

I ask you, Berkowitz, does this make sense? Does it sound right to you? In your heart of hearts, do you really buy the idea that we are of such infinitesimal significance in the overall scheme of things? Or is there not a sense in which we really are at the center of the universe, or should be? Surely, if we create reality, including the universe, then we *are* at its center, in a real and important sense. And we *do* create reality, every bit as much in the scientific age as in Augustine's day.

I don't know if you got around to reading E. A. Burtt, the philosopher of science I recommended in class, but this is how he described the shift in outlook that came with the overthrow of the old Scholastic worldview in favor of the scientific, dualist perspective of the new science:

> The Scholastic scientist looked out upon the world of nature and it appeared to him a quite sociable and human world. It was finite in extent. It was created to serve his needs. It was clearly and fully intelligible, being immediately present to the rational powers of the mind; it was composed fundamentally of, and was intelligible through, those qualities which were most vivid and intense in his

own immediate experience—color, sound, beauty, joy, heat, cold, fragrance, and its plasticity to purpose and ideal. Now [he means, post-Galileo and post-Descartes], the world is an infinite and monotonous machine. Not only is his high place in a cosmic theology lost, but all those things which were the very substance of the physical world to the Scholastic—the things that made it alive and lovely and spiritual—are lumped together and crowded into the . . . human nervous and circulatory systems. . . .[1]

That last sentence is a reference to the way Galileo and, following him, Newton, divided characteristics of matter into the primary and the secondary. The primary were those qualities that could be quantified and turned into mathematical expressions, things such as dimension, mass and velocity. Secondary characteristics were those things Burtt talks about as being "most vivid and intense in his own imagination," in other words, the qualities that are recorded by the senses in concert with an interpreting mind. Galileo and Newton rejected these qualities as unreliable since they were products of the senses, which are obviously capable of being fooled and misled in a thousand ways. The only reliable information, in the view of science, was mathematics, because it was purely intellectual.

And so what science did was make a language of mathematics, and insist that this was the language spoken by nature. Anything in nature that could not be weighed or measured was not worth talking about. That may seem to limit the horizons of science rather severely, but in fact it did not. Here's why: science made sure that virtually everything *could* be weighed and measured, and it did this by using a trick you should be familiar with, because it is the same method that's used to make digital audio recordings out of analog music. It made the bits of unruly nature it was investigating into digital systems. Anything can be quantified that way. Take, for example, a stream of water gushing out of a spring—how on earth can you measure its flow rate? The answer is, you don't; you set up a digital system and measure

⤧ ⤧ ⤧

that instead. In the case of the digital recording process, you take continuous samples of the audio waveform and assign each sample a series of numbers that describe its amplitude, frequency and so on. The playback machine converts those numbers, which have been stored on a CD, back into analogue form via loudspeakers. In the case of the spring, you make a little paddle wheel and insert that in the water flow and then count the number of revolutions per minute the paddle makes. Then you estimate as closely as you can how much water it takes to make the paddle go through one revolution. Presto— multiply one result by the other and you have the flow rate. But, and this is important, it is never completely accurate, because you've only been able to approximate how much water it takes to move the paddle. In the same way a digital recording is never one hundred percent true to the analog original, because it can only take a finite number of samples—some information invariably gets left out.

So, science weighs and measures everything, it is true, but whenever it can, which is most of the time, it prefers to measure its own digital reproductions rather than the real thing. Real things present too many problems! This is especially true of processes, as opposed to structures. But even with structures, there are problems. For instance, scale matters: what may be a close approximation at a macro level can be wildly off base at the micro level. And even small inaccuracies get big when whatever it is that is being measured is multiplied, because the error gets multiplied as well. So when science claims accuracy, what it usually means is that it is accurate within the parameters of the digital system, and not the actual natural phenomenon being examined. In the case of the spring, for example, it can be perfectly accurate in counting the number of revolutions the paddle makes. But if you actually captured the water leaving the ground and weighed it carefully and measured its volume, you'd get a different result. Thus science, to the extent that it uses measurement and mathematics, studies not nature itself, but a simulation or reconstruction of nature, one that it manufactures, in digital form. Sometimes the model is a close reflection of the real thing; often it's not. Put that in your pipe and smoke it!

Nicholas of Cusa, a Church scholar of the late Middle Ages, used this analogy: he said you can draw equilateral triangles within a circle and join their apexes till the cows come home, but no matter how many triangles you draw, you will never get a real circle by joining the apexes: the best you will be able to get will be a very close approximation. Science draws the triangles; nature is the circle. No matter how closely science manages to approximate reality, truth will continue to withdraw from it.

Why did we end up buying into the scientific worldview back in the seventeenth century? That's a deep question, but it certainly was *not* because scientific rationalism is somehow an innate feature of human nature. If it were, it would have emerged long before it did. Whatever the historical reasons may have been—the loss of faith in the benign essence of nature due to the great European plagues; the impact of the Reformation and so on—the fact we're facing today is that science has made itself seem to be necessary for our very survival, and that gives it an unbeatable edge in arguments with opposing worldviews.

Anyway, to get to the point, the objectifying process started in the seventeenth century has finally enveloped mankind, or rather individual men and women and made of them "human resources." Science has mostly forgotten that what it measures when it studies humans is not real people, but the only-approximately-accurate Frankenstein monsters it slaps together as digital entities to represent real humans. All the messy (i.e. essentially human) bits get bracketed and ignored so that manageable equations can be developed. Of course we have to give credit, too, to the impact in our own century of the dehumanizing propaganda of war and the equally dehumanizing advertising that supports consumerism. But can you imagine what people of the Middle Ages would have thought of the notion of a human resource?

Ӿ Ӿ Ӿ

It would've been so alien to their world that it would have seemed insane. It would, in fact, have *been* insane in that culture.

There is another element in all of this that is a huge subject all on its own, and that is the role of the corporation, and in particular that of capitalist corporations. If you were looking for a vehicle through which to transfer the objectivism of science into the mainstream of economic life, you would invent a joint stock corporation. Why? Because corporations have no souls and no consciences. They are engines for reducing economic intercourse to a single objective: maximizing profit. Whether this works to the long-term benefit of society or not is arguable, but beside the point in any case. The point is that this very human social activity—economic activity, I mean—is now carried on in an artificially constructed and essentially inhuman framework of statistics, balance sheets and mathematical formulae. The human value content has been removed in exactly the same way as it was extracted from physical science beginning with Galileo and his "primary and secondary characteristics" notion. Human participation in the economy is limited to the value-empty roles of "consumer" at the one end of the production process and "human resource" at the other; in these roles human wants and needs (but not values) can at least in some rough way be quantified and responded to by adjusting flow rates and resource allocation and so on. Inevitably, attention has tended to focus more and more on the wellbeing of the economic machine itself, on the assumption that its health is essential to our survival and that almost any sacrifice in favor of its welfare is justified.

You and I know how pervasive and influential the notion of human resource has become; the other great goal of late twentieth-century economics is the shaping of consumer desires and aspirations, through what's called "marketing," to fit with the mathematically constructed model of an ideal economic system. I hope you'll remember how commercial broadcast media continually condition human behavior to make it fit the requirements of the economic machine. (Remember?

Ɏ Ɏ Ɏ

"We don't watch television; television watches us." And: "Television is not a window on the world; it is a window on the consumer.")

And so, what happens when economists and politicians and business leaders "rationalize" a social system like the economy and force it to conform to the norms of scientific inquiry—in other words, transform it into a manageable digital simulacrum? Well, of course, there's that built-in error difficulty, which is no small issue when it comes to economic processes. But the real problem is that they slowly lose track of the human goals and aspirations that went into organizing the system in the first place: you can't quantify the values that make us human. And then, heaven help us, the rationalizers and objectifiers start talking about government as if *it* were just another business enterprise. We become more and more ant-like as objectification progresses; we are all scurrying workers and soldiers with mandibles snapping in the service of a queen who is nothing more than a procreating machine, each and every one of us under the cybernetic control of an all-but-inescapable hive consciousness that we've created out of our own reason and which unfortunately seems to have a life of its own and an insatiable capacity for absorption of newcomers.

So where is the good news in all of this? Well, I can't be sure but it seems to me that the worm is beginning to turn and that even science itself is waking up to the fact that it does not have all the answers and in fact has been excluded from metaphysical truth by its own rules. Maybe it's just wishful thinking, but I have the feeling that ordinary people everywhere have had just about enough of being treated as factors of production to be disposed of when their presence on the payroll is inconvenient or even just unfashionable for accounting purposes. If enough people see the connection between the misery wrought by objectifying humans and the possibility of other modes of perception than the scientific, then we can hope for some change. Sounds naive, I know, but being here makes you aware of history, and one thing you learn from history is that things can and do change.

X X X

You know, it always seems to those caught up in it that the status quo is eternal, but of course any status quo is only a temporary adaptation. Change *is* possible in our time, even change on the scale of the revolution wrought by Galileo and Descartes and the rest. In fact, it is inevitable. Ideas change things like moving tectonic plates, with a series of tremors and then a truly big quake. We've given the big shifts names like the Age of Pericles, the Age of Faith, the Renaissance, the Reformation, the Age of Reason and so on. I have the strong sense that we are overdue for such a continental shift right now. The Big One. Ideas are percolating: we've finally got the means to share them without authority figures in the way, mediating, censoring, filtering. I mean the Net, of course. Until now our most powerful communications media were broadcast, top-down, point-to-multipoint affairs that were and are essentially authoritarian. They tell us what to think and do. But the Net isn't like that: it is multipoint-to-multipoint, the intelligence is distributed more or less evenly throughout the system and it's been designed from the bottom up by and for people who want to decide for themselves, through discussion and consensus, what to think and do. The Net, I believe, is a potent facilitator of democracy at every level of our social and economic activity. I believe it will free people to make more sensible choices than they've made over the past couple of hundred years.

Anyway, I'm thinking seriously of doing a book on all, or maybe just some, of this. It's a huge subject, but I don't see how else I can get it off my chest. If I do, I'll give you a mention in the acknowledgements. Big deal, eh? I'm thinking of calling it *In a Time of Miracles* or something along those lines to get across the idea that the world is a kind of miracle that we construct. Or maybe I should call it *Ockham's Razor*; I'm not sure. What this will do to the travel book I'd planned I do not know. To tell you the truth, though, Chris and I have spent so much time riding herd on Hilary and Simon and worrying about them that I haven't paid as much attention to the travel bits as I ought to have. Nothing is ever simple, is it? "Bairns are

ϒ ϒ ϒ

a certain joy, but nae sma' care," as Granny Berkowitz doubtless used to say.

Speaking of simple, a homely pleasure we really enjoy is to start a fire in the wood stove in the kitchen now and then when it's raining and a little chilly in the morning. Feel free. The woodpile is at your disposal; just be sure to keep the tarp in place.

Yours,

wr

Back on the A-5, Simon and Hilary alert once again, we were passed by a small Peugeot that must have been doing 160 kilometers per hour, and blue smoke was pouring from underneath the chassis.

"He'll never make it to Paris," I observed.

"Is it on fire?" Chris asked.

"No, just burning a lot of oil."

"My God!" Hilary said. "We should tell him! Dad, speed up so we can warn him!"

"Warn him how?" asked Simon.

"We can make a sign," said Hilary, rummaging in her bag for some paper. "Mom, quick, I need a marking pen."

"Hilary," I said, "I'm already doing one hundred and forty, which is about the limit for this car weighed down the way it is with all of us and our luggage. I am not going to risk our necks to catch up with him."

She ignored me. "What should we say? How do you say 'Your car is smoking' in French? Quick, Simon! You've got the dictionary, look it up!"

Moments later she had produced a sign which read: "*Attention! Votre voiture est fumer!*"

"Dad, speed up! He's almost out of sight."

"Hilary, I told you I'm not about to kill us all trying to save his crankshaft bearings. Anyway, I couldn't catch him if I wanted to. He's too far ahead."

"Darn," she said, "I went to all this effort to make a sign and now it's wasted."

I thought for a moment: "It needn't be wasted. Show it to some other car."

Chris shot me a cautionary "You're corrupting the kids again" look but smiled. Hilary and Simon laughed, but had the good sense not to do it.

"All right, then" I said, "not that sign, but how about one that says, 'Ceci n'est pas une automobile.'"

"That'd get them thinking," Chris observed.

"Dad, don't be stupid," said Hilary.

Simon had fallen asleep again.

Paris and Perpetual Motion

T H E   M A G N I F I C E N T   C R I L L O N   ❧   P R O G R E S S   A N D

M E D I A   ❧   P A R I S   T H R O U G H   F R E S H   E Y E S

❧   A R C H I T E C T U R E   A N D   O B J E C T I F I C A T I O N   ❧

R E F L E C T I O N S   O N   M U S E U M S   ❧   A   P A R I S

O F   O N E ' S   O W N

I n Paris we stayed, like pampered royalty, at the Crillon, the only hotel *grande luxe* remaining in French hands, and the flagship of the Relais and Château group. We pulled up at the front door, handed car keys and rental agreement to a liveried doorman, and that was the last we saw of either car or luggage until we reached our rooms and found our suitcases waiting for us. The car simply vanished and we received a receipt in the mail a week after we got home. We were very early for check-in; either for that reason or through some other error, our names were not in the computer: the receptionist assured us immediately that rooms would be made available, and ordered up champagne for us in the palatial gold-leaf-and-marble lobby bar while we waited for the problem to be sorted out.

❧ ❧ ❧

When we reached our rooms, there were bouquets of roses and chocolates in shiny black-and-gold Crillon gift boxes.

Waiting for Chris to shower and change, I plugged my Powerbook into the phone line in our small brocade and walnut sitting room and while my letter to Berkowitz was uploading I flipped on the television set and watched a few minutes of CNN. After three weeks of immersion in medieval culture, it was a revealing experience, an epiphany into the fundamental psychic pathology of our time. Trapped as we are in an untenable cosmology, frustrated in our search for understanding of our place in the universe, modern civilization has taken to an obsessive, compulsive gathering of fact, which science has promised will produce progress, the "progress" which has replaced salvation as the human project. Philosopher Susanne Langer described the process like this: "Hoping to find something without looking for it, expecting to obtain final answers to life's riddle by resolutely refusing to ask questions—the oddest attempt ever made to get something for nothing."[1] Victor Hugo was as skeptical a century earlier: "Science searches for perpetual motion. It has found it; in itself."

CNN is symptomatic of this obsessional behavior; a never-ending barrage of fact without context. Many people find it comforting to have CNN playing in the background in their homes and offices while they go about their daily routine, as reassuring evidence of the ongoing accumulation of fact. It is comforting because the accumulation of fact is evidence of continuing progress. What the process really represents is something much more prosaic and casual, that is, continuous change, which is not quite the same thing as progress: change requires a goal in order to be progress and our cosmology has no place for such qualitative notions as ultimate goals.

Himalayan Buddhists for centuries have built devices called prayer wheels, containers like lottery or bingo drums stuffed with scraps of paper on which prayers are written. As the drums are rotated with hand cranks, or sometimes by wind power, the tumbling prayers are thought to be activated. There in the Crillon, awash in a river of sound bites and video clips and animated graphics and text tickers, it seemed to me that CNN and its sister all-news services the world over are modern Western culture's version of the prayer wheel. Like Tibetan Buddhists, we have automated the quest for salvation. Unlike the Buddhist contrivance, our hi-tech machine is lacking a crucial component—an ultimate object and thus a reason for being.

Chris and I collected Simon and Hilary from their room and we all went for a long, last walk to say goodbye to the city. Outside our front door was Place de la Concorde, a vast and justly famous space that began life as Place Louis XV and later became Place de la Revolution. Here, only a few yards from where we stood, the guillotine was in action more or less continuously for two years, severing the heads of 1,343 victims of The Terror, prominent among them Marie-Antoinette and Louis XVI. When the machine was finally dismantled in 1795, the Directory scrubbed away the blood and renamed the square, apparently without irony, Place de la Concorde, as if changing its name could change its history. Like a million travelers before us, we stood at the obelisk in the center of the square and looked up the Champs-Elysées to the Arc de Triomphe, and down through the Jardin des Tuileries towards the Louvre. To the north, rue Royale was framed by our hotel on one side and the French navy headquarters on the other, and in the distance were the enormous marble pillars of the Madeleine. To the south, across the Seine, was the classical façade of the National Assembly. It all looked different than it had just a couple of weeks earlier.

The monumental, magnificent buildings on view in every direction from Place de la Concorde, as in so many other places in the Paris of the Bourbons and Napoleon, are undeniably captivating. And yet to my eyes, fresh from the medieval south, there seemed something alien about all of this magnificence, something swollen, monstrous, disturbingly out of scale, like a seven-foot mushroom or a thirty-pound honey bee. It would take a while to readjust to the materialist Enlightenment vision that treated objects as fetishes and buildings

ϫ ϫ ϫ

as symbols and thus created these extraordinary, dazzling, faintly unhuman structures.

We walked up rue Boissy d'Anglais, past the American Embassy towards rue du Faubourg St. Honoré and on past boutiques for the fabulously rich to rue Royale and up to the Madeleine. An oversized copy of a Roman temple on a plinth nearly thirty feet high, the Madeleine seemed to me to be the most preposterous building in Paris. So stupidly out of context with everything around it, it is in both literal and figurative senses a monument to the excesses of eighteenth century Rationalism with its blindness to the requirements of context and human scale in architecture. An earlier, more modest church in the Greek style had been under construction here when Napoleon ordered it razed so that a monument to his Grand Army could be built on the site. (The modern civilian army, an invention of the era, was itself a perversion of humane values, for in it the organization was of supreme importance and the individual human beings that comprised it were disposable entities distinguished only by rank, rather like soldier ants.) In 1814, Louis XVIII declared that the Madeleine would henceforth be a church, though in 1837 it was nearly converted to the city's first railway terminal, which would have been an altogether more fitting destiny. The Arc de Triomphe was built in the same period in a similarly uninspired, slavishly derivative style, but had the benefit of a site on which it stood isolated, its impact on surrounding structures therefore minimal. It is architecture as intimidation.

"If we had more time," I said to Chris outside the Madeleine, "I'd picket this place with a sign that says, 'This is not a Roman temple.' I'd be recognized as a great surrealist and awarded the Légion d'Honneur."

"You go ahead," she said, "and we'll be down the street in Maxim's having tea and scones."

"At Minim's, next door," said Hilary. "It's cheaper."

More beautiful and endearing, for me, are the buildings that came before and after the Church of Reason had had its day. We walked on to Place Vendôme, a masterpiece of seventeenth-century architecture with its columned arcades, its wonderful symmetry and human scale, just three storeys high with dormer windows along its steeply sloping roofs. In the center of the square there had originally been an equestrian statue of Louis XIV, on a scale which suited its surroundings. This was destroyed during the Revolution, and Bonaparte replaced it with the present phallic monument made from the bronze of twelve hundred cannon captured at the Battle of Austerlitz in 1805. The column, which resembles a greatly elongated lighthouse, in no way relates to its environment in either scale or style: it is another example of the autonomous object, a status that is confirmed in its history. It was at first topped with a statue of Napoleon as Caesar. After Waterloo, this was replaced by a statue of Henry IV. When Napoleon returned for his one hundred days, Henry was removed, but there was not time to remount Bonaparte. Louis XVIII ordered the structure to be topped with a *fleur-de-lys*, but Louis-Philippe replaced this with a new version of Napoleon, now in military uniform. In 1871, the Paris Commune toppled the monument in an outburst of good taste but the Third Republic re-erected it, placing upon its domed top a replica of the original Napoleon, in a toga. Through all of this no one thought of razing the buildings of Place Vendôme, because they were not objects in the sense of idols, but structures integrated with their human occupants and environment. The famous Ritz Hotel now occupies part of one side of the square.

From Place Vendôme it is only a few blocks up rue de la Paix to the Paris Opéra, built between 1862 and 1875, in an era when reason's wretched excesses had been rejected as "blind and dehumanized," in William Blake's words, to be replaced by the romanticism of Goethe, Coleridge and Wordsworth. The twinned columns along its front façade quote the façade of the nearby Louvre, its profusion of sculpture celebrates artists and their art, and although the building has a busily overdressed look about it, it is warmly and unapologet-

ᚷ ᚷ ᚷ

ically human. History, the building seemed to be saying, is actually the story of the evolution of consciousness.

The Louvre itself, of course, is stuffed with artifacts from all over the world. The idea of the museum, an institution which displays objects for their own sake in a neutral context, is, not surprisingly, an inspiration of the Age of Reason, and the very embodiment of Ockham and Descartes' notion of the object as autonomous entity. It was in the early nineteenth century that the dominant style of museum architecture evolved; that of the temple. A museum was a temple in which to worship artifacts as icons. During the Napoleonic era, all of the great cities of Europe opened museums, most of them in buildings of the classical school.

Today's museum creators self-consciously reject the notion that they are presiding over temples to materialism: museums are nowadays touted as places which "speak the language of the real thing" as opposed to the language of the digital or analog reproduction. But, to the extent that they continue to treat as "the real thing" objects uprooted from their natural context and regarded as wholly autonomous, museums have not changed in their essentially distorted outlook, in the two hundred years in which they have been in existence. To see an object in a museum rather than in its native context is like seeing lions in an iron cage in a zoo rather than on the savanna of East Africa. There is only so much to be learned from lions in cages: to understand them requires observation in context, in the wild.

We walked back through the gardens of the Tuileries, across the Pont-Royal where the streets bordering the Seine dip underground to ease the flow of traffic, as they do a few blocks downstream at the Pont-de-l'Alma where Princess Diana and her friend Dodie Al Fayed were to die in a senseless accident on their way home from dinner at the Ritz just two weeks later. These were people as icons; worshiped, and ultimately treated as objects, as commodities. Diana, of course, has since become the focus of a theme park on her family estate.

Y Y Y

We looked in the windows of the antique shops and galleries along the quai de Conti and peeked into the magnificent rotunda of the École des Beaux Arts. By now the light was dying and it had grown chilly and on rue du Bac near the University of Paris where Aquinas and Ockham had held forth and where Schoolmen had found Joan of Arc guilty of heresy and where in our own time students regularly rise in revolt over government policies, as they have for nearly a thousand years—on rue du Bac we found a pizza parlor peopled by locals. The food was good and the wine was cheap and none of us complained that it was not "French." It was a sign for me that we had made the city our own. In the process it had lost some of its exoticism and mystery, but it had gained immeasurably in richness and texture of detail; we were beginning to be able to see beyond the imposing monuments to the real city. Paris had become part of us, we had begun to participate in its reality, and we were seeing it with new eyes. When we returned, and all of us would return, though probably Simon and Hilary would be traveling on their own, we would see yet another Paris, for the world is capable of infinite change while it remains the same. That is the nature of reality; the world is what we make it.

ɤ ɤ ɤ

Paris to Toronto

An Unpleasant Flight ❧ Thoughts on
the Dignity of Service ❧ Home at Last
❧ A Strange Encounter ❧ Breakfast with
Berkowitz ❧ Watermarks and Cathars
❧ Creating Reality ❧ Chris' Erudition
❧ Human Values

O ur flight back from Paris was an unpleasant one,
thanks to cabin crew on the aircraft who believed that
service to others was beneath them. Our purser, the
crew's straw boss, shored up his self-respect by wearing enough Cartier jewelry—a gold Panthère watch, heavy gold neck-
lace and gold and diamond bracelet—to make it plain that he did not
really need to work at this sort of job, that he was really cut out for better things. He had perfected a superficially cheery demeanor beneath
which seethed a stew of self-loathing and contempt for his clients
that expressed itself in barely-masked rudeness so outrageous it made
us laugh in astonishment. Others among the crew were merely uncar-
ing and incompetent, though always with a pasted-on smile.

The idea that service to others is demeaning is a modern one—
for most of human history it has been a noble, and ennobling, pursuit.
And very sensibly so, for what could be more worthwhile than helping

other human beings along the difficult path of life? In late twentieth-century Western civilization, service jobs are among the lowest paid and least secure in the economy. (Doctors are the exception that proves the rule, largely because a majority of them are self-employed; nurses are more typical in their meager salaries and intolerable working conditions.) Those who care for society's most needy—the abused, the handicapped and the destitute—are typically paid less than the lowest-paid mechanics or technicians, if they are paid at all; a great deal of this necessary work is done by volunteers. Teachers' aides who care for severely disturbed or handicapped students one-on-one earn far less than janitors and grounds keepers in the same schools. This seems to me a clear symptom of the low esteem in which we hold ourselves as human beings, in this positivist world of ours. It is also clear evidence that our modern society is much more troubled with social stratification than were our medieval ancestors. Medieval society well understood that we are all equal, though we hold different positions in the social structure. When a humble monk "kissed the hand" of a Church prelate, it was the ring, which symbolized the position within the body of the Church, not the hand of the man, that was kissed. When a serf or a knight pledged fealty to a lord, it was to the position within the structure of governance and not the man to which respect was accorded. What we perceive as class injustice in medieval society—the callous and arbitrary treatment of serfs at the hands of a pampered and privileged clergy and the all-powerful feudal lords—is really evidence of abuse of legal authority, a phenomenon which can hardly be said to have been exclusive to that period. Modern jurisprudence has limited such abuses, but the social gap between the rulers and the ruled, both material and psychological, is far greater today than it was in the thirteenth century. Wealth and position count for more in the late twentieth century than they ever have, because the distinction between person and position has been lost and because actual variances in standards of living in society are greater than they have ever been.

χ χ χ

At the same time the radical individualism that has come with the loss of any sense of common cause among us, the sense that we are each individually adrift in an indifferent or even hostile universe, has given us a horror of being, or being perceived as, subservient to another. We do not want to be slave-like; we want to be seen as free men and women. But our behavior often betrays us. In his *Studies in Words*, C. S. Lewis takes a close look at the word "free," which is our way of expressing a concept the Greeks named *eluthros*. To call a man *eluthros* was to identify his legal status as freeman as opposed to slave, but to call his behavior *eluthros* was to say that he displayed the qualities that a free man ought to have. In contrast to these are the qualities of servility, which we nowadays might describe as cringing, flattering submissiveness. But to the Greeks (and Romans), servile qualities were quite different, as is made clear in their drama and other writings in which: "The true servile character is cheeky, shrewd, cunning, up to every trick, always with an eye on the main chance, determined to 'look after number one'. . . . Absence of disinterestedness, lack of generosity is the hallmark of the servile," says Lewis. This pretty well describes the behavior, overt and implied, of our return-flight purser. I should add that the Greeks naturally recognized that servile status and servile character need not coincide: Menander said, "Live in slavery with the spirit of a free man and you will be no slave."

It was raining when we had retrieved our luggage and located the shuttle to take us to where our car was languishing in long-term parking. The gloomy weather no doubt contributed to our impressions, but it seemed to us that there was a marked shabbiness about the airport, its structures and furnishings, its uniformed personnel and its taxis and buses. The down-at-the-heels impression continued as we drove across the top of Toronto on the multilane Highway 401 and on eastward towards home. Where, in France, there would have been center dividers of flowers and shrubbery, here there was only drab concrete. Where there might have been park-like settings

Ɏ Ɏ Ɏ

for sculpture along the roadside, here we were lucky to find a few struggling trees. Vehicles on the road were, in general, older and more rundown than we'd been accustomed to seeing on the highways of France, and this was especially true of service vehicles like buses, taxis, utility maintenance vehicles, delivery vans and so on. Overall, we were struck by the widening gap in living standards between Europe and North America, and the even sharper realization that public amenities were relatively poorly funded on this side of the Atlantic. Coming home was discouraging, for the first time in my experience of travel.

It was well after one a.m. when we drove up our long driveway through the trees: the outdoor lights were on, but Berkowitz was in bed in the guest room. We hauled in our luggage and without unpacking turned in ourselves. In the morning I was up early for a quick trip into Toronto to pick up some proofs from my publisher. I was back at 11:30 and people were just beginning to turn up in the kitchen, rubbing sleep from their eyes, looking for breakfast. Chris was first.

"The strangest thing happened to me in town," I told her.

"What! Is the car okay?"

"No, no, nothing like that. I was walking back to the car with the proofs, moving along at a pretty good clip, and I passed an old man with a white cane. He was shuffling along, tapping the sidewalk, and he was stooped over at about a fifty-degree angle. I just kind of glimpsed him as he walked by; he looked to be about eighty and he had on a suit and an old raincoat and a cloth cap. I was already a few yards ahead of him when I realized he'd said something to me when I passed. So I went back and I said, 'Excuse me, sir, were you speaking to me?' He said, 'Yes, I was.' He was so stooped that when he talked, he was speaking to the sidewalk almost directly in front of him. I had to bend over myself to hear him."

"Poor man," Chris said.

"He said, 'I asked how far I am from Brunswick Street.'"

ʏ ʏ ʏ

"You know how I am with directions. I said, 'We're already on Brunswick . . . aren't we?' He became quite agitated and said that couldn't possibly be. He was so upset I looked around frantically for a street sign and realized we were on Harbord, and Brunswick was two blocks ahead at the next light. I laughed, you know, at my own stupidity and told him where we actually were.

"'It's no laughing matter if you're blind,' he said. And so I apologized and explained I don't get into town often. He asked me where I lived and I told him, and we started to walk along together, really at a snail's pace because he took steps of literally two inches, and I'm bent over double so I can hear him, and we're walking along having this conversation. He wanted to know what my last book was about and I told him, and he said, 'Communications technology? You should be writing about the way people treat each other these days.' And that kind of freaked me a bit, you know, and I said, 'Well, as a matter of fact my new book will be mostly about exactly that.'

"'Good,' he said, and he asked me what the title was and so on. And meanwhile we're still creeping along at this incredibly slow pace and I'm hunched over like him, and he asks me if I've ever read George Steiner, and I said yes, and he said, 'His latest book is really marvellous. It's called, I think, *Words and Silence*. You really must read it.'

"And so as soon as I get to the car I whip round to Book City which is just a few blocks away . . ."

"You left him on the street?"

"Well, yes. I mean, he knew where he was going, obviously, and it's a nice day out. I don't think he wanted a ride. Anyway I get to Book City and I ask at the cash for them to check for the title *Words and Silence* by Steiner. Well, they finally turn it up under the correct title, which is *Language and Silence*. And guess what? It hasn't been published yet. It hasn't come out. So how could he have read it?

"Maybe he read a review of it, or somebody read the review to him, I mean."

⚔ ⚔ ⚔

"Yeah, I suppose," I said, feeling a little foolish for not having thought of that myself. Still, there was more to the story.

"But that's not the freakiest part," I said to Chris. She was spooning coffee into a Melitta filter. "The guy at the cash pointed out a couple of other recent Steiner books on the display tables they have all along the main aisle and I look at them but they're too expensive and so I walk back to the discount tables and there I find . . . just a second, I left them in the car."

"God, more books . . .?"

"Wait'll you see this!"

Hilary was up now, pouring cereal into a bowl. When I got back in the house, books in hand, Berkowitz was there as well, in pyjamas and dressing gown. He seemed comfortable enough like that: I on the other hand could never be comfortable outside my immediate family unless fully dressed.

I shook his hand.

"Hilary and Simon have introduced themselves?"

"Yes, and two more charming and intelligent children I could not imagine."

"Flatterer," Hilary said.

"He's got a job," Chris announced. Berkowitz looked sheepish.

"No kidding. Congratulations! What's the job?"

"Oh, it's nothing spectacular. Just to pay the bills. It'll tide me over."

Chris gave me a look that said, don't push it.

"Well, that's good news," I said, and left it at that. "I picked up these paperbacks at Book City, volume one and two of something first published in 1912, called *The Lost Language of Symbolism*. Five bucks each," I added for Chris's benefit.

"What are they about?" Simon asked, between mouthfuls of cereal. Berkowitz took a volume and began leafing through it.

"They appear to be about the language of symbolism, and how it's been lost," he said.

⚥ ⚥ ⚥

Hilary laughed and Simon gave her a withering look.

"That's what they're about, all right," I said, "but the guy's main argument, this guy Harold Bailey, is that the Cathars hung on long after the Inquisition and the proof is in the symbols he's discovered in the watermarks in medieval documents. That's what it says on the back cover, anyway. I haven't had a chance to get into them yet, obviously."

"Well, it says here," Berkowitz offered, "it says in the introduction that symbols in watermarks first began appearing in paper in 1282 and carried on until the second half of the seventeenth century. He says they were put there by members of heretical sects such as the Voudois and Cathars, whom he says were important in the paper-making trade, which had just been imported from Asia, which is also where the sects originated."

"Sounds reasonable so far," I said.

"Let's see. . . . He says that printers' marks used the same symbols and—aah—'The awakening known as the Renaissance was the direct result of an influence deliberately and traditionally exercised by papermakers, printers, cobblers, and other artisans—'"

"Cobblers?" Chris said.

"'—Therefore the nursing mother of the Renaissance, and consequently of the Reformation, was not, as hitherto assumed, Italy, but the Provençal district of France.'"

"Wow," I said. "That's quite a stretch!" I held out my cup while Chris poured coffee.

"Let's see here," Berkowitz continued. "It says that the Huguenots were major owners of paper mills and they were also the successors to the Cathars. He says, 'The revocation of the Edict of Nantes ostensibly wiped the Huguenots—whom Pope Clement XI identified with "the execrable race of the ancient Albigenses"—completely out of France.'"

"Huh. I hadn't realized the Church made that connection. They also connected the Cathars to the Manicheans, which would mean

⚥ ⚥ ⚥

that they saw a continuing line of heretical thought all the way from Mani through to the Huguenots and presumably from there to the Protestants of the Reformation."

"But, let's see. The point he goes on to make is that in spite of the massacre of the Huguenots after the Edict of Nantes was revoked, the forces of dissent were alive and well in southern France because it was a battalion marching on Paris from Marseilles that turned the tide in the French Revolution."

"I don't get it," Hilary said. "What's that got to do with watermarks?"

"I guess the idea is that the Revolution was pretty radically anti-Church, and the watermarks are evidence that that feeling can be traced directly back to the Cathars. Interesting. If you kind of half close your eyes, you can see it all as a vast cosmic battle stretching over hundreds of centuries between two competing versions of reality. One side holds the upper hand until about the seventeenth century and then the other side wins a series of decisive battles we call the Reformation and the scientific revolution and the Enlightenment. And now it seems pretty hopeless for the opposition. I wonder what the equivalent of those Cathar watermarks is in today's world, how the other side is keeping its flame alight?"

"T-shirt slogans," Berkowitz suggested. "Aged, hunchbacked hippies printing T-shirts in dank basements." We all laughed.

"We should make a proper brunch," Chris said. "We can eat out on the deck."

And so we did just that, and talked through to late afternoon.

"So I got your e-mail, when? Yesterday? The day before. You were at the Crillon," Berkowitz said. "Could you pass the syrup?"

"And?"

"And I think I agree with most of it, but I don't see how you're going to get people back into the habit of thinking of material things in the correct way, as creations of their own minds. I mean, I can see how it would make a big difference in the world if people did

ᛉ ᛉ ᛉ

realize that they create their own reality, but I don't see how you can convince them of that."

"Yeah," Simon interjected. "People aren't that dumb."

"That's not quite what I meant," Berkowitz continued. "I mean that the propaganda of the other camp, the materialists, the positivists, is everywhere, all the time."

"Ubiquitous," Hilary said.

"Thank you. I mean, the world just isn't set up any more so that a person who believes he's going around creating his own reality can survive. For one thing, there's no time any more to be that thoughtful about things. You just have to accept what's on the label as being an accurate description of the contents and get on with doing whatever it is you have to do."

"But I don't think it's really a question of teaching people to think that way," I said. "I think we *start out* thinking that way, and a lot of time and effort goes into switching us over to the materialist view that each object is self-sufficient unto itself. Anybody who's had kids or watched them grow can see that. It's as plain as the nose on your face. Kids start out with a magical, transactional view of the world around them. That's why they are so full of amazement and creativity. The world to them is this amazing interactive game they can play whenever they like. No more amazing game could be imagined. You can see it in their faces, in the way they draw, in the way they talk about things. And we adults devote ourselves religiously to disabusing them of all of that. We drum it into them day after day that the world is really just a dull, ordinary place, a kind of museum, really, and they have no real connection with it except as observers and users. I mean, observing can be pretty sensational on its own, and being able to use things is handy, but it's nothing like creating, nothing like being part of the whole cosmic process."

Chris had raised her index finger the way she does when she wants to make a point: "I think that even as adults we're all aware at some level that we're kind of living a lie when we talk about the world in material ways. I think it takes a constant effort of propaganda to keep us from backsliding into truer perceptions. If you talk about things the way they really are, you're called childish."

"Or schizophrenic," I said.

"Or an artist," Berkowitz said.

"Right. Or an artist," Chris said. "But we think of artists as childish people, don't we? We patronize them."

"Well, anyway," I said, "it seems to me that all we need to do is turn off the contrary propaganda and the transactional view of reality will re-emerge, because I think its normal and natural."

Simon said, "That would mean that all primitive societies think like that."

"Exactly. And they do."

"They do?"

"We call it animism, or used to. We used to think they imagined gods and nymphs and whatnot everywhere in nature, but in fact they were simply expressing the idea of transactional reality, of their own personal involvement with objects outside themselves, and vice-versa. That was how they expressed it, in that poetic way. Like Homer did, in fact, in preliterate Greece."

"Hmm," Simon said.

"We always dismiss the ideas of so-called primitive peoples we come into contact with, like the Europeans did in dealing with North American Indians, but at the same time we've always had a sneaking suspicion that there was some real wisdom there, wrapped up somehow in what was obviously a very different way of perceiving the world than our own scientific model."

"That's right!" Hilary interjected. "But we think of native people as childish. I mean, we think their ideas of nature and our place in nature are beautiful and romantic and all that, but childish and not practical. Kind of like we think of art."

"It's interesting that you used the word wisdom," Berkowitz said.

ϫ ϫ ϫ

"In the Old Testament, 'wisdom' and 'salvation' are the same thing."

"Or 'enlightenment.' Wisdom, enlightenment, salvation are all synonymous. That's right," I said.

"So," he continued, "in *The Wisdom of Solomon*—which is apocryphal, I know, but still it represents the thinking of the time around the birth of Christ—in *The Wisdom of Solomon*, wisdom is a beautiful woman who . . ."

Chris interrupted: "No, no. That's *The Wedding of Wisdom*. It's from the same period, but I think it's in the Acts of Thomas."

"The acts of who?" I asked.

"Thomas. It didn't make the final cut into the Bible when they were doing the editing back in Roman times." She explained to Berkowitz, whose jaw had dropped noticeably: "I used to study this esoteric wisdom stuff back when I had time on my hands. B.C.—before children."

"I *am* impressed," Berkowitz said with a courtly nod. "And here I thought you were a mere artist and propeller-head. Please proceed."

"Well, it's a Gnostic text and the Gnostics identified wisdom with Sophia, the Virgin of Light. She was a kind of handmaiden to God, and when she descended to earth to check out the creation they'd both been working on, she somehow got trapped in the material world. When she asked for help, God sent down Christ to rescue her. It's all incredibly complicated, this esoteric, apocryphal stuff, but later on, Wisdom was identified by the Christians with the Holy Spirit, part of the Trinity. That, I suppose, is how wisdom is tied in with the idea of God."

"Nice fairy tale," said Simon.

"Oh, God." Hilary rolled her eyes. "Don't you have *any* poetry in you?"

"Of course I do, but you shouldn't mix up poetry and facts and that's what you're all doing right now!"

Berkowitz began singing like a rabbi: "'For God loveth none but him that dwelleth in wisdom. For she is more beautiful than the sun and above all the orders of stars. Being compared with light, she is found before it.' Psalm something-something."

We all applauded.

"Simon, another white wine and orange juice for Rabbi Berkowitz, if you don't mind," I said.

"Certainly," he replied, and stepped into the kitchen, sliding the screen closed behind himself.

"Nice chap," Berkowitz said.

"He can be a real prince," Chris said. "When he's not trying to convince us that nuclear energy is the way to go or that sociobiology got a bad rap."

Berkowitz laughed. "He'll grow out of that. He's bound to think exactly the opposite of the way you do at this age."

"Maybe so," I said, "but it makes being a parent pretty tough, if you think it's important to teach your kids values. There is no place for values in a strictly scientific, materialist worldview. Some of the things he comes out with drive me crazy. Hilary does too, though she tends to go more on her instincts and as a result doesn't get so many perverse ideas in her head."

"Boy, are you out of touch and old-fashioned," Berkowitz laughed. "Didn't you know that you're supposed to leave the teaching of values to the school system?"

"Sure thing," I said.

Simon returned and placed Berkowitz's orange juice on the table.

"*Muchas gracias*," said Berkowitz, with a flawless Castillian lisp.

"Schools don't teach values any more," I said, "for the very good reason that they teach tolerance instead."

"Tolerance is a value," Simon said.

"Yeah—isn't it?" Hilary asked.

"Not really. It's a value-substitute. It is a *lite* value, to go with lite beer and lite everything else. The way you kids have been taught tolerance is that everybody's values are to be given equal weight and

x x x

equal respect. That way nobody gets offended, nobody is excluded, nobody's discriminated against."

"That's right," said Hilary. "What can possibly be wrong with that? What else can you do when people in your school come from all over the world and have a dozen different religions?"

"Being of Spanish extraction," Berkowitz said, "I am very sensitive to this. If you would pass me the strawberries, Christine."

"The mistake," I continued, "is not in having respect for others' values. It is in thinking and acting as though all values are equally weighty and equally important. If all values are the same, then choosing among them becomes just a matter of taste, or fashion. They are not values anymore, they're preferences. But the very idea of values implies a prioritizing, in which some goals are more worthy than others. And that, naturally, implies some ultimate value or other, because if you have a hierarchy, something has to be at the top. Assigning equal importance to all values simply means making them all equally unimportant. So, for instance, survival becomes as worthy as heroism. Or self-fulfillment becomes as worthy as self-sacrifice. The good life, the worthy life, is whatever you want it to be. The irony is that if all values are of equal weight, then the value of tolerance itself is of no particular merit. It deserves no higher priority than any other value."

"I don't think people can live their lives that way," Chris said. "I think people need some sort of value structure so that they can make sense of their lives. Otherwise everything that happens is random and pointless."

"So you want to force everybody to believe in some fairy tale about sets of rules being handed down from some . . . some divine authority . . ."

"Simon," I said, "Jesus, Buddha and Mohammed were all historical people, not fairy tale characters. For that matter, so were Socrates and Plato and Plotinus and Zoroaster and Mani and Confucius and any number of other moral teachers."

"Yes, but they all claimed to be talking on behalf of God."

ﻉ ﻉ ﻉ

"Okay, but it's not that simple. There is a fundamental dilemma in all of this that was resolved once and for all by Socrates: he said that the good is not good because the gods approve it, but the gods approve it because it is good. At a human level you could take that to mean that ethical behavior is not about obeying rules, it's about understanding the good."

"Hold it a minute." Simon was pondering. "'The good is not good because the gods approve . . .'"

"Look it up. It's in Plato's *Euthyphro*. The point is we're not talking about forcing anyone to do anything. We're talking about simply recognizing that there is some hierarchy of values, some ultimate good, that is not necessarily accessible to instrumental reason, the kind of reason that merely calculates the most efficient means to an end. In other words, we're talking about human values, which are bound to seem irrational at least some of the time if you believe only in instrumental reason, because humans have needs and aspirations that are not measurable in terms of efficiency or productivity. Otherwise we'd be automatons. Or ants."

"Hah! Your famous *oc*-speaking ants. I enjoyed that card. In fact, I have it here, somewhere about my person." Berkowitz pulled a post-card from his dressing gown pocket and held it up for us to see.

"So then," Hilary asked me, "how do you get people from different religions and different values to get along together?"

"That's a whole other question. But I certainly do *not* think you achieve it by doing away with everybody's value structures. In other words, the answer to conflicting moral values is not amorality. Not in my humble opinion, anyway."

"I'll put on some more coffee," Chris said.

CHAPTER 21

Home Alone

BERKOWITZ'S NEWS ☙ FACTS AND VALUES

☙ A CRUDE ANALOGY ☙ FAITH AND SCIENCE

☙ SIMON'S FRUSTRATION ☙ A FINAL SERVICE

Berkowitz rose from his chair, stretched his rather short legs and straightened his dressing gown. "I think I shall stroll up to the mailbox and collect the *Mop and Pail*," he said, "before some amoral person purloins it."

He meant the *Globe and Mail*, Canada's national newspaper, which is also sometimes called the *Gloom and Pall*.

As we watched him walk across the lawn to the driveway, the maroon of his slippers and dressing gown standing out against the multihued greens of the grass and the trees beyond, Chris leaned towards me and said: "The job he's got is with the Hospital Restructuring Commission. He said it was the only thing he could get. He had to take it."

"My God, how awful. So now he's in the business of firing nurses and shutting down hospitals."

"Only 'inefficient' ones."

"Whatever that means in newspeak. Shit. The poor guy."

I poured us both some more coffee and we sat in silence for a while. Hilary and Simon were clearly enjoying being back home. You could see it on their faces as they looked around at the house and the yard.

☙ ☙ ☙

"Schools should stick to teaching facts," said Simon.

"Pardon?"

"I said schools should stick to teaching facts, and not values."

"I don't see how that would be possible, even if it were a good idea, Simon. And the reason is that every fact has value attached to it. It can't be any other way, because people decide what is a fact and what is not, and they decide it in the context of some system or other. That's just unavoidable. You could even say that there are no actual facts, only fact-fragments, pieces of the larger 'fact' that is the whole system of which they are each a part.

"You could also say that when you collect facts and put them together in a pattern the way science does, and philosophy and religion do as well, then what you are doing is building within a larger system, and incorporating its values, whether you realize it or not."

"Wait a minute," Simon objected. "Only science collects and deals in real facts. Philosophy and religion don't deal with verifiable things, things that are measurable."

"In other words," I asked, "you're saying the 'facts' of a religion are based on faith rather than quantifiable proof?"

"Exactly. More or less. I think." He grinned.

"Well, then, the question is, what is faith? What if I say that faith is very similar in meaning to trust, trust that some event or entity or belief is 'true.' Would you agree with that?"

"I suppose . . ."

"Okay, then let's take a scientific concept like gravity. You have trust that when you jump up in the air you're not going to shoot off into the stratosphere and on into outer space."

"I don't have trust. I know it. It's a fact."

"Come on, Simon. You know that science can only predict. Gödel proved that."

"Oh, all right, but the prediction that I won't fly off into outer space has such a high degree of probability that it might as well be a fact. I mean, get serious."

"Thank you very much. You've just made my point."

"And that is . . .?"

"And that is that all intellectual research and all moral activity rests on the assumption that the universe we are trying to figure out is indeed figure-outable, in other words, is an intelligible system. Otherwise, why bother making the effort? Would you agree with that?"

"I suppose so . . ."

"I think you'd also agree that you can't know the whole of anything by examining a small part of it, or even any number of small parts. It's like the old story of the blind people examining an elephant by feeling its tail and its trunk and so on. They have no clue what the larger object is, though they all think they do."

"So?"

"So the point is that since science works by selecting and examining small, individual pieces of it in isolation from everything else, our assumption that the universe is intelligible is really based on faith, or if you prefer, trust. So, Simon, science operates on faith just as religion does."

"But . . ."

"I mean, you have to admit that science has done a pretty dismal job in terms of the so-called soft sciences or social sciences, where it's dealing with everybody's everyday experience. There's been remarkably little of real value to come out of those areas despite enormous effort. I'm thinking of psychology in particular."

"Are you kidding? What about all the new psychoactive drugs. What about Prozac and the drugs they use to control schizophrenia? Are you going to tell me they don't work?"

"I can tell you a story that describes *how* they work. A researcher is conducting experiments on a dog. On the first day, he teaches it to fetch a stick he has thrown across the laboratory floor, which it does, with great joy. The next day, the researcher surgically removes one of the dog's legs and again tells it to fetch the stick. The dog hobbles across the lab and brings back the stick. On the third day, the researcher cuts off another leg and again tells the dog to go fetch. The animal drags itself across the room and returns with the stick. On the fourth day, the researcher removes a third leg. Somehow the dog still manages, with enormous pain and effort, to cross the room with its one leg and return the stick. On the fifth day, the researcher cuts off the remaining leg and tells the dog to go fetch the stick. It doesn't move. He tells it again and again. And still it does not move. And the researcher writes in his note book, 'Day five. Removed final leg. Result: dog has become deaf.'"

"Dad, that's sickening," Hilary said.

"It is, but it also contains some truth. Treating spiritual problems with drugs that alter your personality seems to me wrong-headed and even obscene in the same way. It's an idea Comte might have come up with. Granted, sometimes you can treat symptoms so that they will go away and that gives you a chance to work on the deeper problem. But if you've created a materialist society that causes people to live under conditions of enormous insecurity and anxiety and guilt and angst and then go about 'fixing' it by feeding people mind-altering drugs, then there's something very seriously wrong, isn't there? It's not that drugs aren't sometimes appropriate and necessary. But that is the *only* 'fix' science can offer, because science conceives of people as machines, or, in the social sciences, as human resources. If a machine squeaks, you simply oil it. For that matter, now that I think of it, most of the so-called management theory I used to study was really just approaches to the same kind of behavior modification only without the use of drugs."

"Yeah, b . . ."

I held up my hand.

"One more point. The scientist has faith that the universe is intelligible to the extent that if water boils at a certain temperature at sea level one day, it will behave pretty much the same the next day, and he won't need a pressure cooker or ice cubes to do the job. He trusts his methods and formulae to get the job done. Well, then, how about religion? Religion asks that people have trust in certain events, people and structures or mechanisms. If you follow certain procedures, certain outcomes will occur. You will find peace. Or joy. Or fulfillment in life. Or salvation. Or you will get to know the godhead."

"There! That's where you go wrong. In science the outcomes actually do occur. They don't in religion." Simon sat back in his chair with a satisfied smile.

"But they do! How else can you account for the fact that so many people subscribe to religions? And have for I don't know how many millennia. How do you account for Joan of Arc?"

"Well, they certainly don't for me!"

"But that's because you don't have faith. You don't have trust in the system. And so you don't try to make it work for you. Admit it—you've never even tried. Science wouldn't work for you, either, if you didn't have faith in it."

"Of course it would! Faith has nothing to do with it! I can have grown up in a chicken coop raised by hens and when I drop a brick it will still hit the ground."

Hilary giggled: "He's got a point there, Dad."

"Yes, but Simon, the issue is not whether the brick hits the ground but what causes it to hit the ground. In other words, we're not talking about whether the world works, because obviously it does, but whether science works as an explanation of what's going on. You might believe, as I understand chickens do, that the great hen goddess who dwells at the center of the earth devotes all of her time and psychokinetic energies to keeping objects from flying off into space."

"You'd be wrong. Gravity is what makes the brick fall. Gravity is a physical force. It can be measured. There are particles called gravitons . . ."

"Which nobody has ever seen, except by inference, in instruments, and in mathematical formulae. So, you can measure, but not

ɣ ɣ ɣ

observe it. And it's not gravity that is measurable, but its effect on things. As far as you know, all of that could be just another way of describing what is actually the work of the great hen goddess. Or take Galileo's other big idea, inertia. It says that an object in motion will continue on the same path at the same speed so long as it isn't interfered with by some force like friction or gravity. Before that, people thought that the natural state of all objects was to be at rest. But the thing is, there is no way to observe pure inertial motion, because any observer within a finite distance will always exert some degree of attraction on the object and disturb its motion. You can make a mathematical model of pure inertia, but you can't observe it. You have to take its existence on faith.

"When you think about it, most, if not all, scientific laws have this feature of the limiting case being unverifiable by direct observation. The way you establish a law in science is to take a phenomenon like motion, isolate it from its context, and set up an ideal experiment, in other words, a thought experiment, to examine the relationships among variables. Then you try to confirm your findings in the real world. All of these ideal experiments are alike in that they have limiting cases, in which the variables are each, in turn, reduced to nothing to see what happens. It seemed to the medieval thinkers, who were worried about this modern new approach to figuring out how the world worked, that the limiting case—for instance, perfect inertial motion, or when you reduce friction to 'zero' in considering rolling bodies and so on—the limiting case was *incommensurable* with conditions in the real world. In other words, the limiting case could *only* exist in another world, and not in this one. And they were right about that, weren't they? You just can't *have* perfect inertial motion, or a frictionless surface. In strict scientific terms, those limiting cases, even though they define the law, are pure fiction. They were not simply extensions of the argument to a logical and reasonable conclusion, they were a leap from this world to another, perhaps impossible, one. In that sense, all of these 'laws' of nature have a very strong metaphysical or supernatural odor about them.

"Face it, Simon, we have no more idea of what gravity is than Newton did, and he at least had the grace to admit he hadn't a clue. All we have is a set of beliefs about it. Facts are not what you think they are."

A memory made me pause, and smile: "In fact, somebody's pointed out that 'fact' is actually just the past tense of 'fiction': both words come from the same root, 'to make or to fabricate.'"

"Hah!" Hilary exclaimed. "That's cool! Who said that?"

"A feminist writer named Donna Haraway. I hope you'll read her one day. She's famous for having said, 'I'd rather be a cyborg than a goddess.'"

"What's that supposed to mean?" Simon asked, irritably.

"I think she was arguing that there is not so much difference between technology and nature as we generally think, because they're both the products of human imagination. We can make women goddesses, or cyborgs, as we choose."

Simon's patience had expired: "This is ridiculous!"

"The point I'm trying to make, Simon, is that we manufacture the world we live in. In the past we used philosophical and religious 'facts' as our building blocks and today we use scientific 'facts.' But there is no reason to say that one is innately superior to the other, since they're all equally creations of our own imaginations. The only way to judge between them is our experience of which works better for us, in terms of what our goals are. We can manufacture worlds that are either pleasant to inhabit or hellish. It's up to us. And if we find that we've created a world that is unpleasant, or destructive, we ought to change it. And the way to change it is to start with our perceptions, because that's where the creative act begins. That's where we determine what's a so-called fact, and what isn't."

Simon leaped to his feet in frustration. "This is crazy. Facts are facts." He banged the table, rattling the breakfast dishes. "This table is a table. It's not some figment of my imagination."

ꭓ ꭓ ꭓ

Berkowitz had returned, the fat paper under his arm, slippers flapping on the cedar decking. He smiled benignly at us as he sat down at his place and began flipping through the sections. He extracted the book review section and began to read.

"But it is *exactly* that," I said to Simon. "Not just a figment of *your* imagination, though, but all of our imaginations. Look. What if I were to tell you I can make our friend Berkowitz here, disappear."

Berkowitz looked up from the paper. "Wha . . .?"

Simon snorted.

"Okay, let's see you do it," Hilary laughed.

Chris looked uncomfortable.

"Now hold on a minute," Berkowitz objected.

"Don't worry," I said. "It'll be a completely painless process since you never existed in the first place."

He smiled wanly and shot a nervous glance at Chris.

I asked Simon, "Had you ever seen him before today?"

"No, but we've talked about him."

"And I've seen you write him postcards from France," Hilary added. "Of course he's real. Aren't you, Mr. Berkowitz?"

"Well, I certainly thought so. I *was* in your class, you know," he said to me.

"Actually," I said, "someone a lot like you was in my class. You, on the other hand, are mostly a figment of my imagination."

He put down the paper: "Really, now . . ."

"How's your Castillian?"

"Non-existent, actually, but that certainly doesn't prove . . ."

"I created you in order to help me make some points I wanted to stress. Now that the book is almost complete, I really have no further use for you. Perhaps we'll get together again in another book sometime. But for the moment, that's it. You can help me make one final point by disappearing."

And he was gone. So was the newspaper. We cannot get delivery of the *Globe* on the rural route where we live. We do not match the approved demographic profiles established by its marketing people, so, for the *Globe*, we do not exist. Berkowitz's place setting at the table remained, although there was no evidence anyone had eaten there.

"Wicked!" said Hilary. "Dad, that was amazing!"

"So," said Simon, who was surprisingly cool about it, "how much of the trip to France was real and how much was a figment?"

"It was all real!" Hilary insisted. "Wasn't it?"

"It was mostly real, but I must confess, I invented bits and pieces here and there to help the narrative along, or sometimes to help make a philosophical point. Of course I didn't tamper with the history or geography in any way."

"And those delicious meals . . .?" Chris asked.

"As real as can be."

"The wonderful hotel rooms?"

"Real, all real. Although, I did take some liberties with the furnishings."

"Oh, great," Hilary said, a despairing note in her voice. "How are we supposed to know what we actually did and what we didn't do? How are we supposed to know what's true?"

"The points where I've done some inventing are, I think, the truest parts of the book," I replied.

Chris was making anxious gestures. "You're not going to do anything with the children. . .?"

"Of course not. I couldn't if I wanted to. They're too firmly established in reality. They have histories, relationships, they've impinged on the world; I could never get a consensus on their non-existence the way I can with Berkowitz. Remember, reality is mostly a matter of consensus."

I turned to Simon, who was looking pensive. "Well, Voltaire, have I changed your mind?"

"I'm thinking," he said.

"Good," I said. "That's mainly what I hoped to accomplish."

⊻ ⊻ ⊻

Notes

Chapter 1

1. Wallace Shawn and André Gregory, *My Dinner With André*, a screenplay for the film by Louis Malle (Grove Press, 1981).
2. Erich Fromm, *Psychoanalysis and Religion*, Bantam Books (1950), 76.
3. François Perroux, *La Coexistence pacifique* vol. 3 (Presses Universitaires, 1958), 600, as translated in Herbert Marcuse, *One Dimensional Man* (Beacon Press, 1964), 33.
4. In connection with the writing of *Spirit of the Web: The Age of Information from Telegraph to Internet* (Somerville House, 1997).

Chapter 5

1. Lucien Lévy-Bruhl, *How Natives Think* (Princeton University Press, 1985), 116.

Chapter 6

1. Will Durant, *The Age of Faith* (Simon and Schuster, 1950), 77.
2. Jules Quichart, *Procés de condamnation et de réhabilitation de Jeanne d'Arc*, 5 vols. (Paris, 1841–9), vol. 4, 496–97: quoted in Edward Lucie-Smith, *Joan of Arc* (Penguin Books, 1976), 126.
3. See Edward Lucie-Smith's *Joan of Arc* (Penguin Books, 1976).

Chapter 8

1. Henry James, *A Little Tour of France* (Farrar, Straus and Giroux, 1983), 144.

Chapter 9

1. Richard Halliburton, *The Royal Road to Romance* (Bobbs Merrill, 1925), 40.

Chapter 10

1. Eric Havelock, *Preface to Plato* (Basil Blackwell, 1963), 200.
2. Marshall McLuhan, *Understanding Media: The Extensions of Man* (Signet 1954), 85.

3. Regine Pernoud, *Blanche of Castille*, translated by Henry Noel (Coward, McCann and Geoghegan, 1972), 176.

C H A P T E R 1 1

1. Emmanuel LeRoy Ladurie, *Montaillou: The Promised Land of Error* (Vintage Books, 1979), 141.
2. James B. Givens, *Inquisition and Medieval Society: Power, Discipline and Resistance in Languedoc* (Cornell University Press, 1997).
3. Viktor Frankl, *Man's Search for Meaning* (Washington Square Press, 1963), 106–7.
4. Ibid., 122
5. Ibid.
6. Ladurie, op. cit., 123.
7. Ibid., 132.
8. Frankl, op. cit., 154.

C H A P T E R 1 3

1. Josef Pieper, *Guide to Thomas Aquinas* (Mentor-Omega, 1964), 115.

C H A P T E R 1 5

1. Erich Fromm, *Psychoanalysis and Religion* (Bantam Books, 1950), 86.
2. Bert Hölldobler and Edward O. Wilson, *Journey to the Ants* (Belknap Press of the Harvard University Press, 1994), 59.

C H A P T E R 1 6

1. Bertrand Russell, *History of Western Philosophy* (George Allen and Unwin Ltd., 1946), 234.
2. Herbert Spencer, *Social Statics* (D. Appleton and Co., 1865), 413.
3. W. G. de Burgh, *The Legacy of the Ancient World* (Penguin Books, revised 1947), 501.
4. See Ernest Gellner, *Thought and Change* (Weidenfeld and Nicolson, 1962).

C H A P T E R 1 7

1. André Maurois, *A History of France* (Farrar, Straus and Cudahy, 1948).
2. Susanne K. Langer, *Philosophy in a New Key* (Mentor, 1942), 138.

Ɣ Ɣ Ɣ

3. Lewis Mumford, *The Conduct of Life* (Harcourt, Brace and Co., 1951), 126–7.

4. Jean-Anthelme Brillat-Savarin, *The Philosopher in the Kitchen* (first published 1825) (Penguin Books, 1970), 264.

5. Jean-François Revel, *Culture and Cuisine* (Da Capo Press, 1982), 1.

6. Rowland, *Spirit of the Web*, 351–2.

7. Brillat-Savarin, op. cit., 74.

8. Ibid., 12.

9. Revel, op. cit., 149.

10. Brillat-Savarin, op. cit., 132.

C H A P T E R   1 8

1. E. A. Burtt, *The Metaphysical Foundations of Modern Science* (Humanistic Press, 1952), 117.

C H A P T E R   1 9

1. Langer, *Philosophy in a New Key*, 232.

ӿ ӿ ӿ